A Lady and Her Magic

TAMMY FALKNER

sourcebooks
casablanca

Published by Sourcebooks Casablanca, an imprint of
Sourcebooks, Inc.
P.O. Box 4410, Naperville, Illinois 60567-4410
(630) 961-3900
FAX: (630) 961-2168
www.sourcebooks.com

Printed and bound in the United States of America
VP 10 9 8 7 6 5 4 3 2 1

*For Thomas and my boys—because
they make me believe in magic.*

Unpardonable Errors

1. Never let a human adult see you in faerie form.
2. Never let your dust fall into the hands of the untrained.
3. Never share the existence of the fae.
4. Never use your magic to cause harm.
5. Never, ever fall in love with a human.

One

August 1817

IF THE DUKE OF ROBINSWORTH HAD KNOWN IT WOULD be so difficult to raise a daughter alone, he never would have killed his wife. He would have coddled her, wrapped her in lace and taffeta, and put her on a shelf so the whole world could view her beauty.

Even though he'd never admitted it, everyone knew he'd killed her. And though he refused to share the details, they were all correct.

His daughter broke him from his reverie when she stomped her foot and demanded that he purchase not one, but two, sweets from the vendor.

Ashley was quite used to the antics of his daughter, and although they were annoying, they never bothered him overmuch. When she became too unruly, he simply left her with a nurse. If it happened at home, he left the manor. He'd even left the country once. But she was always there when he returned, always just as petulant as she had been the day he left. He'd resigned himself to the fact that she would never change.

Anne was a perfect re-creation of his late wife. Her long blond curls danced around her face. Her porcelain skin and blue eyes reminded him of a doll he'd seen once in a shop window. The only difference: the doll didn't have a temper like Anne. Yes, she had inherited that from her mother, too.

When Anne was younger, she would drop to the ground and kick and scream when she didn't get her way, flopping about like a fish out of water. Now she simply scrunched up her pert little nose and screeched.

Ashley winced as she shrieked out the words, "I want it!"

He took a step toward the child, fully prepared to throw her over his shoulder and drag her back to her nurse, who waited on a park bench nearby, when a woman stepped forward. His breath caught in his throat as she entered his line of sight. She was the opposite of his late wife, who'd been blond and thin and fragile.

His gaze traveled over the woman's rounded hips to her ample breasts, nearly hidden among the frills and folds of her light-blue gown. He lingered there, imagining how she would look in a gown that didn't have quite so many trimmings hiding her curves. When his eyes finally rose to meet hers, her flashing hazel orbs held censure. Ashley coughed into his hand in a horrible attempt to hide the smile that wanted to erupt. It had been years since he'd been so well scolded. And she'd yet to even speak to him.

Before he could say a word to her, the auburn-haired nymph looked down her nose at his daughter and said, "Ladies do not shriek."

His own little termagant rolled her eyes in a horrid display of social ineptitude.

The woman raised her eyebrows at Anne and said, her voice a bit crisper, "Ladies do not roll their eyes."

"But I want another," Anne snarled, stomping her foot.

The beautiful woman smiled at his daughter, a dimple appearing in her left cheek. People very rarely smiled at Anne because she was so obnoxious that most gentlewomen turned from her in disgust.

"May I tell you a secret?" she asked of Anne. Then she looked at Ashley, who nearly fell over trying to avoid leaning toward her so he could hear her soft voice as she spoke to Anne. "Do you mind?" she asked, smiling as she asked him for permission to speak to the girl.

"No," Ashley said, waving his hand negligently. "You may disclose all the secrets you wish." He wanted to add that she could whisper a few in his ear as well, but he assumed she'd take that as an insult.

She knelt down to Anne's level and whispered in her ear. Anne's nose turned down slightly until she suddenly smiled. She covered her mouth with her fingertips and giggled.

"Go on." She nudged Anne forward. "Try it." She shot Ashley a quick look that encouraged him to play along.

Anne tugged gently on his sleeve. "Yes, Anne?" he said quickly, finding it painful to tear his gaze away from the stranger long enough to look down at his own daughter. But when he did, he was surprised to see the pleasant smile that curled her lips.

"Papa, may I please have another treat? I regret to inform you that they are pitifully small."

Ashley glanced up at the lady, who smiled at what must have been his perplexed look. He stared at her for a moment, unable to draw his eyes away, until Anne tugged at his sleeve and whispered, "I should like to grow up to be as sweet as the lady someday."

Ashley turned to the street vendor and asked for two more treats. He promptly gave one to his daughter, who was delighted by her newfound ability to win her father's favor. Then he looked over at the lady who'd transformed his daughter and winked.

∽✦∾

Sophia felt certain she turned ten shades of red when the man turned and winked at her. It was such a masculine gesture, and not one that was commonly tossed in her direction. Of course, considering that he was the Duke of Robinsworth, Ashley Trimble, to be more exact, it was completely fitting.

It did gratify Sophia a bit to see that the child took her advice and approached her father in a gracious and respectful way. She smiled softly when he placed the treat in the girl's hands and bent to kiss her forehead.

Sophia turned to walk away but heard quick footsteps behind her. "Miss?" The child called for her. Sophia looked down at her smiling face. She held up a second treat and said, "My papa said this one is for you."

Sophia hesitated for a moment before she took the wrapped square from the child. "Thank you very much."

"Wait." When the girl's father's voice reached her, it hit her like a runaway horse, making the hair on her neck stand up and her belly drop toward her toes. His quick footsteps hurried across the cobblestone walk toward her. He stopped, his blue eyes darting to and fro in the nearly empty park. "If your chaperone sees me speak to you, I fear she'll steal you away almost as quickly as you appeared." He let the last trail off as he waited for her to fill the empty space.

Quite the opposite. Her grandmother had contrived the scheme so they could meet in the first place. "I appreciate the flattery, but I have not required a chaperone for a number of years. We do things differently where I'm from, you see."

"And where might that be?" His blue eyes danced at her.

Unpardonable Error Number Three: Never share the existence of the fae. "I'm certain you've never heard of it."

His eyes narrowed almost imperceptibly. Should she extend her hand to him? Try as she might, she was unable to remember all the social proprieties this world was based upon. Her grandmother had repeatedly tried to drill them into her throughout the years. And failed. "My name is Sophia Thorne, Your Grace," she finally provided.

His gaze grew shuttered at the words "Your Grace," almost as though a heavy curtain dropped between them that was difficult to see through. She wished she could bite the words back as soon as they left her lips.

"My reputation must precede me," he said as he looked away. Sadness suddenly overwhelmed his features. "I'll let you be on your way." He bowed slightly and turned from her.

"Your Grace?" Sophia called. He stopped and looked back over his shoulder, no hint of the playfulness she'd seen earlier present in his gaze.

"I've never rested much faith upon the opinions of others, Your Grace," she said slowly. "I prefer to draw my own conclusions."

A sardonic smile broke across his face. "You could very well ruin *your* reputation by being seen in my company, Miss Thorne."

She shrugged. "One must have a reputation in order to ruin it, Your Grace. And to be more succinct, one must care."

A smile that might be genuine slowly lifted the corners of his lips. "I thank you for the help with my daughter. How did you do it?"

She shrugged again. She'd simply treated the child with respect and firmness, both of which the girl was surely lacking. But that was neither here nor there. "Most women learn to manage men at an early age," she laughed. "It appears as though your daughter has not."

"Not until today."

"I was happy to help." Sophia held up the wrapped square of candy. "And these are my favorite," she admitted, unable to keep from smiling at him.

The little girl tugged at her father's sleeve. "Can we go home now, Papa?"

The duke pulled his watch fob from his pocket and flipped it open. "Actually, I do have some things to attend to," he said apologetically as he touched the top of his daughter's head. "Tell Miss Thorne good-bye and thank you," he instructed her.

Instead of dropping into a curtsy, the girl locked her arms around Sophia's waist and squeezed. Sophia was almost too surprised to return the embrace.

"Perhaps I'll see you again another day," she said to the little blonde.

"I can only hope," the duke said quietly, his gaze meeting hers only briefly before he turned away, took his daughter's hand, and started down the lane that led to the entrance of the park.

Sophia took a moment to catch her breath. It wouldn't do for her to swoon in the middle of the park. Not at a mere suggestion from the dangerous Duke of Robinsworth. The man was a walking scandal. A walking scandal that made her pulse pound so loudly she could hear it.

"Well, that went better than I expected, dear," her grandmother said as she stepped into her line of sight.

"Better than I thought," Sophia lamented.

"I wasn't sure if you'd be able to feign the mannerisms of the British *ton*. But you did fairly well."

She certainly still had a lot to learn about this world. The land of the fae might look similar, but none of its magic was present in this world. Here, people wore full clothing, and not a single one of them had wings or pointy ears the way she did. Just willing her own wings away was difficult and not something she usually had to concentrate so hard to do.

"He seemed discontent about my lack of a chaperone," Sophia said. "Do you think I need one, to look like one of them?"

"Perhaps we should have Margaret shadow you a little more," her grandmother suggested.

Sophia moaned. The idea of Margaret watching everything she did made her nervous. The house faerie didn't like this world or anything about it, including its people. The maid wouldn't say why, but she had a feeling it had something to do with Sophia's mother. "I need to learn to walk like them."

"Stiffly and unyielding?" her grandmother said with a laugh. In their world, comfort reigned. Clothing was serviceable. There were no layers worn simply for show. In order to fit through keyholes and slide under doors, one must be appropriately attired.

"Maybe I should have saved this mission for Claire after all." Indecision rose within her. No. She could do this. She could help the Duke of Robinsworth's daughter.

"You must learn to use your senses, your mind, and your heart more than your magic. You can do it, Sophia. I wouldn't have allowed you to come if I didn't believe it."

"Oh, come now," Sophia cajoled. "You wanted an opportunity to come through the portal, to see the fish."

"I'd love to know their crimes. Knowing they were once fae scares me a little." Her grandmother shivered lightly.

"They seemed amiable enough."

"Only because you had something they wanted to trade for passage. Otherwise, we'd still be at home waiting for the night of the full moon."

The fish that guarded the portal were granted a reprieve on the night of the moonful, the night the midnight wind swirled, carrying passengers from the fae world to this one. Any other night, wary travelers must trade something of value to get past the fish and away from the land of the fae.

"This mission is very unlike my others," Sophia said, more to herself than to her grandmother.

"Most missions don't include a handsome duke." She grinned. "A duke who makes one's heart go pitter-patter." For some reason, her grandmother's mild, cherubic smile sent fear skittering up Sophia's spine, making her wonder what devious plot was hiding behind her grandmother's innocent facade.

Two

ASHLEY STEPPED THROUGH THE FRONT DOOR OF HIS home to find his butler, Wilkins, standing at attention in the entryway. The regal, spry old servant rushed forward to take his hat and coat.

"Any news for me, Wilkins?" Ashley asked absently as he shrugged out of his jacket, took the correspondence the butler placed in his hands, and sorted through the stack of notes quickly.

"Your brother awaits you in your study," the butler said.

A smile broke across Ashley's face. "I imagine he's sampling my best whiskey?"

Wilkins smiled, then added glibly, "Not since I removed all the decanters upon his arrival, Your Grace. You should be aware that he partook of more than his share of spirits before he arrived."

His brother had never been one for taking spirits in moderation. Ashley chuckled. "That bad, is he?"

"Worse, Your Grace," Wilkins said, nodding his head slightly.

"Oh," Ashley said as he turned and held up a finger.

"Did you have any luck finding a suitable governess for Anne?"

The man sighed. "Unfortunately, no. The agency refuses to send another of their applicants. Not after what happened the last time."

Ashley tried to remember. "Remind me of what happened last time."

"Lady Anne set the governess's hair on fire. On purpose."

"Oh, yes. I remember. There was a stench for days." Wilkins's lip curled as he obviously remembered the same smell. "Are there other agencies you can try?"

"I'll keep looking."

"Thank you." Ashley smiled as he walked down the corridor and turned the corner to enter his study. There, seated in a deep leather chair, was his younger brother, Lord Phineas, or Finn, as his friends called him. "I heard a rumor that you were in my study and that evasive maneuvers had to be taken to keep you out of my stock," Ashley said, extending his hand.

Finn rose to his feet unsteadily, grasping for the arm of his chair as he lost his balance. The man looked positively miserable, his eyes rimmed with red, his face blotchy and pale. "Ah, yes. But he forgot the bottle you keep in your private stash," Finn said as he held up a glass, lisping a little on the last word.

Of course, his brother would feel free to invade his private space at will. Never one to mince words, Ashley said, "You look like hell."

"I feel like hell," Finn grumbled back.

"Dare I ask what the matter is? It's a bit early in the day to be so deep in your cups." He urged his brother to sit before he toppled over. He was nearly as big as Ashley, so it would take at least two footmen to bring him back upright.

"Oh, I had a bit more enjoyment than I'd planned," Finn groaned as he adjusted himself in the chair.

Ashley sat behind his desk and steepled his hands in front of him, waiting for the man to tell him what the matter was. It didn't take as long as he thought for his brother to unburden himself.

"Do you remember the chit I set up in Mayfair?"

"Vaguely." If Ashley remembered correctly, there was nothing truly remarkable about the girl.

"She's up and left me."

"And?" Certainly, worse things could happen to a man. Like being shunned for killing one's wife.

"And she started a bit of a rumor."

"About?"

"My lack of physical attributes and attention to her needs," Finn mumbled.

Ashley tried to hide his chuckle behind a cough into his closed fist.

"It's not amusing," Finn pointed out.

"Certainly, it is," Ashley said, laughing a bit louder.

"How do you deal with it? The whispers behind your back? The constant judgment from your peers?"

Ashley shrugged. "One becomes accustomed to it with time." He'd had seven years to learn to accept his lot in life. The only time it rankled was when he met a lady like Miss Thorne. Then he wished he was anyone but himself.

Finn reached for the whiskey bottle again. Ashley intercepted it and moved it out of his brother's reach.

"Drinking any more will be a waste, because you'll not remember the taste of it when you wake up."

Ashley stood and called for Wilkins. The man appeared within moments. "Let's find a room for Lord Phineas and help him to it, shall we?" he asked of the butler.

Wilkins nodded his head and called for footmen to assist. "If I may be so bold, Your Grace, the rest of London should know what a good man you can be," Wilkins said.

"I prefer to let them think the worst." Ashley sighed. "They've no expectations of me that way."

Ashley returned to his study and began to open his correspondence. Despite his sordid past, he was a bit too well connected to be ousted completely from society. For the first two or three years following his wife's death, he'd been avoided as though he had a communicable disease, as though the propensity to murder was contagious.

Then the few friends he had, namely his brother Finn, Matthew Lanford, and Jonathon Roberts, whom he'd met at Eton many years before, had rallied around him and forced him to resume his place in the House of Lords and step back into society. They all believed him innocent of any wrongdoing. It was unfortunate that they were all incorrect.

The clip of quickly moving slippers in the corridor made him groan and hang his head. Within seconds, the Duchess of Robinsworth flung open his door and burst inside his sanctuary, without even the good graces to knock.

"Mother," was his only response as he looked

down at the note before him. "What brings you to my home?"

"You really should replace that butler," she scolded.

"And why should I do that?" he asked as he closed his ledger. She obviously had a purpose for visiting. And would most likely get to it as soon as she got over whatever slight Wilkins had given her. He would curse the man, but the butler seemed to be one of the only people who could keep his mother in line.

"He's impertinent. And rude."

Said the pot about the kettle.

"He blocked my entrance to the old library. The one in the west wing. He stood right there in the doorway and refused to let me pass. Of all the nerve." She harrumphed and dropped into a chair.

That wing of the old house had been closed for longer than Ashley could remember. Since before his father had died when he was a boy. "And what purpose did you have for visiting the west wing, Mother?" he asked as he poured himself a liberal dose of the whiskey Finn had left behind.

"It's awfully early to be drinking, dear," she scolded.

"It's awfully early for you to be visiting, Mother," he returned. His mother never rose from bed before the luncheon hour. "Shouldn't you be sleeping off the excesses of the night's activities?"

"I wouldn't call them excesses," she mumbled.

He fished a note from the pile of correspondence Wilkins had given him. "You do not find one thousand pounds to be an excess?" he questioned.

"Give me that." She held out her hand and leveled him with a stare that would have made him quake in his boots when he was younger. With her icy glare and pinched brows, she could freeze him in his tracks when he was a boy, but no longer.

"I think not," he returned. Then he took a deep breath and dove directly into the issue at hand. "I believe it's time for you to move back to the Hall, Mother." He would hate having her underfoot, but he couldn't keep an eye on her if she wasn't at hand.

She pulled back and turned up her nose. "I'll do no such thing. My town house is perfectly acceptable."

"You mean *my* town house," he clarified.

"It's mine in theory," she huffed as she sank primly onto a chair across from him.

"The amount of money you're losing at the gaming tables is tremendous," he said as he withdrew more notes from his drawer. They arrived nearly every day. From people his mother had gambled with and lost. They all knew she wasn't good for the debts. Yet they played with her anyway because the Duke of Robinsworth never left a debt unpaid. His presence in their drawing rooms might not be valued. But his purse certainly was.

"I'll take those," she said again.

"Why, Mother? You cannot begin to pay them."

Her face fell. "I do not know why you feel you have to be so cruel," she said as her eyes welled up with tears.

"I do not understand why you gamble with money you don't have." He tapped the cards on the table. Then he made a clucking sound with his tongue. "But I'm prepared to pay them in full."

"As you must, Robin," she said quietly, using his childhood nickname.

"On one condition," he amended.

Her face contorted slightly. "Which is?" she said from between gritted teeth.

"I'm closing the town house effective immediately. You'll be moving back to the Hall."

She jumped to her feet. "I will do no such thing," she gasped.

He continued as though she hadn't spoken. "I will reconcile your debts. Every last one of them. Then you will cease gambling with money you do not have. You may use your pin money any way you see fit."

"But there's not enough," she protested.

Still, he continued. "You will spend nothing more than your pin money. You will move back to the Hall. You will assist me with my daughter."

"Anne hates me."

Anne hated everyone. "You will assist me with your granddaughter. She could use a feminine presence. You will behave respectably and set a good example for her."

"You need a wife," she snapped. "It's unfortunate that no one of respectable breeding will have you."

Oh, his mother knew how to throw the barbs that would hurt the most. "Then I am free from the wife search, it seems, since no respectable woman would pay me her favors." He leveled her with a glare. Though Miss Thorne had graced him with a smile and no fear in her eyes.

"It took years for me to get over your past deeds. To find my way back into society. You have no idea how arduous the task was." He couldn't gather sympathy for her, despite the look of anguish in her eyes. "If I move back to the Hall, I will once again be cast beneath your dark cloud of suspicion."

"Do you think I killed my wife, Mother?" he clipped out.

"Of course not," she rushed on.

"Then I would assume a mother who finds no fault with her son will be quite content to return to the family estate."

"My friends won't know what to think."

"Quite frankly, Mother, I don't give a damn what they think," he drawled. "I'll have Wilkins begin the preparations to move your household."

"And just when do you think this will take place?"

"As soon as I bellow down the hallway," Ashley replied. Wilkins would take great pride in ruffling the duchess's feathers.

"That man hates me," she grunted. "When I'm in residence, I'll expect him to treat me as befits my station."

"He'll treat you as well as you treat him, Mother."

"I'd prefer being dropped into a vat of hot oil over being nice to that man." She jumped to her feet and headed for the door.

"I'm certain that can be arranged," Ashley called to her retreating back.

Three

THE DUCHESS ARRIVED THE FOLLOWING AFTERNOON IN a flurry of activity. Ashley leaned against the newel post and surveyed the staff who scurried up and down the corridors of his home.

"How did you do it so quickly?" Ashley asked, shaking his head in wonder.

"Sheer strength of will, Your Grace," Wilkins replied with a haughty smirk.

"One would think you'd be hesitant to take on such a task, since doing so means you'll have to see Mother on a daily basis." Then Ashley caught the direction of Wilkins's gaze as he stared at his mother's housekeeper, whose bottom was in the air as she rummaged through an open trunk. "The effort could come with a boon, it would seem?" Ashley tossed in casually.

The man's face flushed for a moment. But only for a moment. "I certainly hope it will be worth it," he finally said with a grin.

"At least one of us might get to enjoy the favors of a benevolent lass," Ashley lamented.

This caught his butler's attention. "I can send a message to—"

Ashley held up a hand to stop his offer. The last time Wilkins had arranged for an assignation, Ashley had found himself with a beguiling lady, one who quaked in her slippers at the very sight of him. It simply wasn't worth the effort. They were all the same, be they barmaids, wenches, whores, or members of the gentry. They all saw him as tarnished. As fearsome. As the dangerous Duke of Robinsworth.

Ashley clapped Wilkins on the back with a smile. "Good luck with that little piece of baggage," he said with a good-natured chuckle as his very staid and very proper butler picked up a valise and followed the housekeeper down the corridor. Wilkins never carried baggage. It was well beneath his station. Yet, it was quite apparent that performing below his station might yield some results beneath the housekeeper's skirts.

The very thought brought Ashley's mind back to the comely little lass he'd met in the park that afternoon. Little wasn't a good description at all. She was tiny compared to him. Tall by most standards, she came up to his chin. He could probably tuck her beneath his chin and hold her close.

"Robin," interrupted a voice from the doorway. He turned and found his mother, her face red with what he assumed must be anger. "Why is that Wilkins insists on interrupting my beauty rest?"

He raised one brow. "Because he enjoys torturing you?"

"He could at least have waited until after luncheon."

"Where would the humor be in that?"

"I hope you don't regret your decision to bring me here," she said.

"Regret having my mother under my roof?" He already regretted it. But he continued smoothly. "Never."

His mother's smile suddenly brightened. "I had the most wonderful idea last night when I was discussing my new accommodations with some friends."

"Crying over" would probably be a more apt description of this discussion. Or "hysterically wailing." "I assume you plan to tell me of your idea?" he prompted.

"I plan to have a house party," she answered, the smile on her face evidence that she was immensely pleased with herself.

"Absolutely not," he bit out. Of course she would want a house party. His mother had always lived to entertain.

"You could allow me to tell you why, Robin," she sniffed, "before you say no."

He took a deep breath. A room full of nosy gentlemen and ladies, all of whom would attend if for no other reason than to get a glimpse of the dangerous Duke of Robinsworth. "*Why* do you want to have a house party at my home, Mother?" he acquiesced.

"So that my friends can see what a dear boy you are, of course," she explained. "They see so little of you that naturally everyone is curious."

Now he was a carnival attraction. Fabulous. "No," he clipped out.

"My friends have been led to believe by many who are in Town for the season that you are more than just a recluse. That you're a murderer. That you killed your wife. That you have two heads. That you have a curved backbone that twists your body into absurd proportions." She stopped and took a deep breath. "Yes, all of those things have been whispered about. I want to show them that you're none of those things."

More likely, she wanted to show off the Hall. Show off her position in society. Show off her wealth. Or his wealth, actually. But, to her, it wouldn't matter. "And just who do you plan to invite to this gathering?" That would make all the difference in the world.

His mother began to tick off names of prominent members of society, many of whom had marriage-able daughters.

"Absolutely not, Mother!" he said, throwing his hands in the air. "I will not allow you to play match-maker." Truth be told, none of those women would have him. They'd quiver and stare and stammer when he came into a room. They'd pretend to be interested in him, but only long enough to gather fodder for the scandal sheets.

"Don't you think a house party sounds like a grand idea?" She beamed with pride as she glanced around the marble entryway of their ancestral home. "The estate has been much too quiet of late. It's like a great sleeping beast and only needs someone to breathe some life into it."

"No more than ten guests, Mother," he sighed. "And I will not be attending. So, do not think you will find a wife for me." He turned on his heel, trying to avoid his mother's frantic clapping and shrill shriek, but she reached for his sleeve.

She patted his arm. "I could find a mistress for you, if you prefer. It would help your temper greatly."

A mistress? Good Lord. "I have no need of a mistress, Mother," he ground out.

"How long has it been, Son?" she whispered dramatically. "Years? Months?" She nodded to herself, a silly smile playing about her lips. "A paid woman would accept you."

"Mother," he snarled.

"Oh, never mind," she said with a wave of her hand. "I promise not to even try to make a match for you."

"No courtesans. No widows." If he kept going, the party would cancel itself simply by lack of participants.

She mulled it over, tipping her head from side to side. "I accept," she finally said.

He turned to walk back to his study. "No match-making, Mother," he called back to her.

"You won't regret this, Robin," she called to him.

He already did.

❧

Sophia cringed as her grandmother placed a vial of shimmery pink dust in her hand. "This one is for truth. Use it sparingly, Sophia," she said with a frown.

"I am not certain I'm ready for this one."

"I completely agree, but you've been taxed with unlocking the secrets in a little girl's mind. They're secrets she's not even aware she's carrying." Her grandmother took Sophia's hands in hers and squeezed. "Use it with great caution. Because if you use it for the wrong reason, the results can be disastrous."

"Disastrous? In what way?"

"In a way that will affect your life forever," her grandmother warned.

Sophia tucked the dust vial into her reticule and stood. She glanced quickly around the rooms her grandmother had let upon their arrival in London. The accommodations weren't too different from the land she came from. But the clothing certainly was. Sophia tugged at her bodice. She wasn't used to wearing so many layers of clothing. She turned to face the family matriarch. "What type of dust did you use to coerce the dowager duchess into inviting us to her house party?"

"None at all, my dear." Her grandmother smiled benevolently at her. "I simply paid her a visit. She was deep in her cups at the time, but she still remembered me."

"You've walked between the two worlds enough that you have old friends?" How odd that her grandmother had never told her of her escapades.

"Indeed, I have," she said cryptically.

"How long has it been since you've been on a mission? I don't remember you traveling when we were younger." In fact, she remembered her grandmother as always being a solid presence in her life. Much more solid than the parents she'd never met.

"My own travels were before you were a light in your mother's eye," her grandmother said softly.

"Do you plan to see her while we're here?" Sophia asked, instantly hating the way her voice quivered.

Grandmother's face softened. "Do you?" she returned.

Tears pricked at the back of Sophia's lashes. She tried to blink them away. She had no memory of her mother. Perhaps it was best that way.

"It's all right if you want to go and see her," Grandmother advised. "I can help you find her."

"I'd rather not." Sophia swiped a hand across her nose. Her mother probably wouldn't even recognize her.

Her grandmother closed and locked the last trunk and turned to face Sophia. "That's enough lamenting about the past."

No one had ever told Sophia or her two siblings why their mother had to leave the land of the fae, never to return. Why she wasn't a part of their lives. But in the quiet times at night, she'd heard whispers of her mother's misdeeds from the other beings who occupied the land where she came from. Those fireflies were a blasted nuisance. And, despite their beauty, they liked to tell tall tales. Tall tales full of doom and gloom. And remorse.

Sophia shook the thoughts away. She'd long since given up her search for answers about her mother. This was certainly not the time to rekindle them. This was the time to work her fae magic for a little girl. And she might even get to help the dangerous Duke of Robinsworth in the process.

The man looked haunted behind those sky-blue eyes, and pain rolled from him in waves when she was in his company. She'd very nearly swooned from the power of it when he'd realized she knew about the stigma attached to his name. It wouldn't do for her to go reeling into the bushes at the mere presence of the man. She'd have to work on her response to him. To his pain. To his daughter. To his past.

Unpardonable Error Number Two: Never let your dust

fall into the hands of the untrained. She opened her reticule and glanced inside, wondering about the vials of dust she had stored in the small space. Each had a different purpose, most of which were benign. Yet the dust for truth, the newest one, made the hair stand up on the back of her neck. What if the truth was too burdensome to bear?

Four

ASHLEY STOOD IN THE SHADOWS ON THE UPPER LEVEL and glanced down into the foyer from behind heavy drapes. His mother was in her glory, greeting her guests and introducing those who didn't know one another. He watched closely as people filtered into the entryway, each one stopping to stare at the glamour that was the Hall.

He had to admit that the Hall was fairly stunning. It was his home after all, his refuge. It was his shelter from the storm that had been his life for so long. He'd rarely left it in the days following his wife's death. It was much easier to hide.

He'd pampered his home with endless attention, mainly because it had never said terrible things to him. It had never accused him of misdeeds and had never once mentioned the word "murder."

The only place he didn't go was the west wing. No one was allowed to go there. Not after that fateful night.

Anne dragged him from his reverie when she tugged his sleeve. "That's the lady from the park, Papa," she said softly, her face glowing with happiness as she leaned over the railing to look down into the entryway. He jerked her back so quickly that she jumped and rubbed absently at her arm. "Ow," she murmured, looking at him from below lowered lashes. She looked just like her mother when she did that.

"Apologies, Anne. You know how I feel about the railing. Please stay back."

"Sorry, Papa." Anne had no idea why he was so cautious when it came to high places. Hopefully, she never would. "But that's the lady from the park."

Ashley narrowed his eyes and looked down into the foyer. It was difficult to make out faces from that height, particularly when he really wanted to linger in the drapes and have no one notice he was there. But then she looked up at him and his heart lurched. Miss Sophia Thorne, the lady from the park, stood at the bottom of the stairway looking up at him like the innocent she was.

A grin tugged at his lips, despite the fact that it was a foreign feeling. She inclined her head at him in silent acknowledgment, and he raised a finger to his lips. He didn't want the rest of the party to see him skulking in the drapes. They'd assume he was hiding. And, although he was, there was no need to draw attention to it.

She smiled broadly when he raised his finger to his lips, but she obviously understood his desire to have his presence remain a secret, because she turned to the older woman with her and devoted her attention to his mother.

"I want to be like her," Anne whispered from her spot beside him where she clutched his hand. There were worse ladies she could emulate, like her mother.

He tipped her chin up so she'd look at him. "You be like you, and it'll all turn out just fine," he said. She grinned her toothless little grin at him. He leaned toward his daughter's face. "When did you lose your front tooth?" he asked.

She poked a finger at the empty space. "It came out this morning."

"Perhaps the tooth faerie will come tonight," Ashley said.

Anne's smile faltered. "She didn't come the last time," she said with a sigh.

"Why on earth not?" Certainly Wilkins hadn't let the opportunity to coddle his daughter pass him by? Then Ashley shook his head. When had her care fallen to Wilkins? Ashley would have to do better.

"Wilkins said she must have been busy." She shrugged.

Ashley drew his daughter against his side and hugged her. He needed to find a governess for his daughter. Someone who could be solely devoted to her care and well-being. Wilkins was a good substitute, and he made certain the staff took care of her, but she wasn't his charge. She wasn't his priority.

He would have to do better.

❧

Sophia watched him from the foyer as he stood there in the shadows. The duke was a regal presence, totally at home with the opulence of his estate. She'd noticed him lurking there long before he'd seen her. He looked like he'd rather be drawn and quartered than forced to host a house party. He raised a finger to his lips, as though they shared an unspoken secret. A shiver crept up her spine.

"Are you all right, dear?" the duchess asked of her. "You're not taking on a cold, are you?" She snapped her fingers at the butler, who stood sentry over the servants who hurried about with the arriving guests. He glared at the duchess, raised his nose in the air, and very promptly dismissed her without saying a word. "I detest that man," the duchess mumbled. "He'll learn his place if it's the last thing I ever do."

Sophia smothered a laugh.

Sophia's grandmother smoothed a hand down the duchess's arm. "Good help is so hard to find." The duke's daughter skipped down the steps toward them. Sophia couldn't keep from smiling at her, particularly since her father still lurked behind the drapes. She tried not to look directly at him and draw attention to his position behind the drapes, but it was incredibly difficult not to. Knowing he was there made her want to study him, to watch him as closely as he was watching his guests. Despite his unsociability, he was obviously interested in the proceedings.

"It looks as though you have someone's attention," her grandmother murmured at her.

"It would appear so," Sophia whispered back. That was part of her task, wasn't it? "But he's frowning a bit. You don't think that's on my account, do you?"

"He smiled when you looked up at him, Soph," her grandmother chided with a soft smile. "I'd say that's a good sign."

"Good morning, Miss Thorne," the little girl chimed as she finally reached the bottom of the stairs.

Sophia put her hands on her hips and pretended to look affronted. "Well, look who's here," she said playfully. "Do they know you've sneaked into the party? I say, the duke is going to be none too happy if he finds out there are party-crashers about." She shook her skirts out. "Perhaps you should hide in my skirts so they won't toss you out into the street. I hear the duke doesn't like urchins."

The little girl's eyes grew as big as saucers. . ."I am not an urchin. I am Lady Anne."

Sophia rubbed at her chin between her finger and thumb and pretended to contemplate the situation. "You'll never pass for Lady Anne. I'm sorry, it simply cannot be done. I hear Lady Anne is the most regal of creatures and that she always has a smile for everyone. When I saw you in the park, you certainly were not smiling. You were being quite a termagant."

"But my papa is the duke," the child said, and Sophia feared she would stomp her foot and fling herself into a tantrum any moment.

Sophia knelt down with a conspiratorial whisper. "The man in the park with you was the duke? The Duke of Robinsworth?"

The girl looked supremely satisfied with herself as she nodded. She pointed toward the drapes, but no one lurked in the shadows. "He was there a moment ago." Her face fell. Then she shrugged. "It's of no importance. He bade me to give you a message."

"Is it written in blood on secret paper?" Sophia asked.

Lady Anne covered her mouth and giggled. "No, it's in my head."

Sophia straightened back up to her full height. "That's

the best kind of secret, then. Let's hear it. If such a thing exists." She looked down her nose at the girl.

Lady Anne giggled again. "He'd like to welcome you to the Hall."

Sophia leaned toward the girl's ear, and cupped her hand around her voice. "He might just have to come out of the drapery to do so, won't he?"

"He doesn't do that," the little girl said. "But he's waiting for you in the garden."

Sophia's heart skipped a beat. "Which way?" she asked.

The little girl slid her hand into Sophia's. "I'll show you." Then she gave a gentle tug and started down the corridor.

Sophia shot a look at her grandmother, who responded with an ever-so-tiny nod. She became immediately thankful of Anne's guidance as they traversed the maze of corridors that was the Hall. It seemed almost as though one turn led to another. And another. And another, until Sophia found herself lost.

Then suddenly, they arrived at a door that was manned by a servant who immediately stepped out to open it. "Do the guards get changed at midnight?" she asked of Anne.

"The one on this door does," Anne informed her, as though it was the most normal of occurrences. "This is my father's favorite place. And no one but he is allowed to visit it." She grinned sheepishly. "Except for me, of course. But only if I behave."

"Of course," Sophia replied. "I'm honored to be invited into the inner circle."

"It's just a garden. Not a circle."

"It can be whatever the lady desires," the duke said

as he stepped into their path. He looked astonishingly at ease. He glanced down at Anne and said, "Why don't you go and check on the duchess. I assume she would like your assistance greeting guests."

"But Grandmother doesn't like me," Anne protested.

"Grandmother loves you," he began, but he didn't have one single thing to say about how or why she loved her. He clamped his lips together instead.

"*My* grandmother will love you." Sophia leaned down to whisper dramatically at Anne, "And she has confections in her pocket." She placed her finger over her lips and made a shushing sound. "But she doesn't want anyone to know. She likes to give them out to really well-behaved children."

"I'm really well-behaved," Anne chirped.

"I'm certain you are," Sophia agreed. She addressed the duke. "She's a fantastic guide," Sophia informed him, and the little girl beamed under her praise.

"May I go?" she said, dancing in place as she asked.

"Run along," the duke said to his daughter. He looked almost relieved as she scurried away. He faced Sophia with chagrin. "It's not often I make arrangements to meet young ladies in the garden," he began to explain. "But it appears as though the rest of my house has been overtaken. It's difficult to find a refuge." He looked behind her, as though an interloper lingered. "Do you have a maid with you?"

She'd brought a house faerie who served as her lady's maid, but she couldn't take Margaret everywhere with her. Particularly not when she was on a mission. "No, it's just me," she informed him.

"Is that safe?" he asked, arching one dark brow at her.

"You tell me," she said, unable to keep a laugh from escaping.

"You are a breath of fresh air, Miss Thorne," he tossed out.

"Because I am not afraid of you?" She wished she hadn't said it as soon as the words left her mouth. "I'm not afraid of you," she rushed on to say. "In case you were curious."

"I was quite curious," he admitted. He turned to pick some dead leaves from a nearby bush that had obviously seen happier days. He didn't continue for several moments. Then he speared her with a glance. "Why is it that you're not afraid of me? Grown women quake at the very thought of me."

"I'm a grown woman," Sophia protested.

His gaze traveled slowly down her body and back up to her face. "How old are you?"

It was probably the fact that she wasn't part of the *ton* that allowed her to answer truthfully. "Six-and-twenty," she said.

"Firmly set upon the shelf?" he asked, the corners of his lips tipping up. He seemed relieved to hear of her age.

"I imagine it would depend on whether you're referring to a cupboard shelf or a ballroom shelf." She stepped closer to him.

"What's the difference?" He tilted his head when he looked at her, reminding her of an inquisitive puppy.

"Perspective." One flitted onto a cupboard shelf when one needed privacy. She'd never sat on a ballroom shelf. That would just be odd.

He chuckled. "True." He continued to fuss with the

plant he'd been pruning with his bare hands. The poor thing would be bald before they were done talking.

"Did you call me to your private sanctuary for a reason?" she finally asked.

"I wanted to welcome you personally." He bowed slowly. "Welcome, Miss Thorne."

"Thank you, Your Grace," she said with a tiny curtsy. His face hardened almost imperceptibly at her choice of using his title. "It's quite gratifying to find that you do not have a hunched back. Or a horn growing out of your forehead."

"Oh, so they're comparing me to the great mythical unicorn, are they?"

"They're cantankerous animals. You'd think they'd be more complacent, since their only magic rests in that knobby, unattractive horn."

His eyes narrowed as he appeared to mull over her statement. "Beg your pardon?" he finally asked.

"You were speaking of unicorns, were you not?"

"I was."

What an odd conversation. "They're nearly untrainable. And very high in the instep, the lot of them."

He tossed his head back and laughed. "I believe I'm going to like you, Miss Thorne," he said.

She certainly hoped he did. Her mission rested upon it.

The clatter of warring voices arose from the other side of the door she'd entered through to get to the garden. His eyebrows shot together. "Will you excuse me for a moment?" he had the courtesy to ask.

"Of course," she replied. She watched his rigid carriage as he strode toward the door. His Hessians were perfectly polished, his clothing immaculate. Only his hair looked disorderly, as though he'd run his hands through it over and over. His shoulders were broad, his hips narrow.

"You should not be looking at the duke's backside," a voice full of censure called out from behind a nearby bush.

"I beg your pardon?" she asked as she strode toward the noise. She shoved some foliage aside and looked down. "Oh, you!" she groaned. "You should not be here," she scolded.

The garden gnome glared up at her. Ronald was only as tall as Sophia's knees, but he could have easily been glaring down at her with the way he made her feel. "I still think it was a bad idea for your grandmother to bring *you* here. I can only see bad things in your future." He began to pace back and forth, wringing his hands in front of him. "Only bad things. No good things at all. This is all wrong. All bad."

Sophia put her hands on her hips. "Has fortune-telling become a new power of yours? The last I heard, your kind was good for no more than gossip and an occasional errand." She was being purposefully obtuse, of course. Everyone knew gnomes were speakers of the truth and were revered for their wise counsel. Only this time, he could shove his counsel up his...

"This is not good for you. You should not be here." He shook his head and sighed heavily. "The duke is dangerous."

"So his nickname might suggest," Sophia said with a nod. "But he has been very nice so far."

"He lusts for you already," the gnome mumbled.

"And you would know this how?" She hadn't seen a single solitary sign of any such intent on the duke's part.

"You are too much of an innocent to see it. And you had better stay that way." He shook a finger at her. The fae were held to the same societal rules as the *ton*. And if Sophia wanted to keep her wing color pure, she'd stay chaste. Everyone knew when a fae crossed from innocence to… not innocent. She had no intention of allowing her wings to change colors. It was like wearing a badge of dishonor on one's back. "Do not allow that man any liberties with your person. Do you understand?"

Sophia bent down until they were nose to nose. "Or what?" she questioned. "He'll devour me like the great beast that he is?"

A voice from behind her jerked her from her conversation. "As much as I'm enjoying the view, I feel like I've missed half of the conversation. Do you often talk to yourself?"

The dangerous Duke of Robinsworth enjoyed the view of her backside in the air?

"Told you so," the gnome sneered before he disappeared.

Sophia stood and turned to face the duke. "You caught me," she said with her hands upheld as though in surrender.

He shook his head slowly, a glint in those steely blue eyes. "I haven't caught you yet, but I'd certainly enjoy a good try."

Sophia's heart skipped a beat within her chest.

Five

"AND I DON'T TYPICALLY CONSUME INNOCENTS IN ONE big bite," he informed her. Her mouth opened, but nothing came out. She looked a bit like a salmon there gasping for words. "I save the big bites for those who are not quite so innocent." Her mouth snapped shut and he silently rejoiced, so he continued. "I like to take my time with innocents," Ashley explained as he crossed his arms and gave her his most imperious glare. He'd heard her comment about him devouring her *like the great beast he is*. And it had pricked at him for just a moment. But he was quite used to the hostile stares and comments under people's breaths.

She tilted her head a little to the left and smiled slowly. "What makes you think I'm innocent?" Her hazel eyes were hooded by heavy lashes that batted at him like those of the best coquette.

He forced himself to close his own mouth, for fear of doing her fish impersonation. But he was afraid it was too late. He needed more than a minute to recover from the shock of her question. "Are you trying to tell me something, Miss Thorne?" he asked.

She shook her head, making those auburn curls bounce around her shoulders. Her eyes flashed with mirth. It was quite obvious the chit was an innocent. She may as well wear it like a badge of honor on her gown. "I am untouched" oozed from her very person. And it made him want to touch her even more, particularly when she looked at him like that. God, it had been too long since he'd had a woman. He swiped a hand down his mouth.

"So, how many bites would it take for me?" she asked with a giggle. Then she held up her hands as though to fend him off. "Just for personal knowledge. It's not often I meet a dangerous duke. I can't let the opportunity pass me by. A lady needs to know these things."

He could have her disrobed in ten seconds and could be devouring her within…

"Your Grace." She jerked him from his reverie with her soft voice.

"Yes?" he responded, as soon as he was able to draw his gaze back up to her face.

"While I can understand your reticence, please permit me an opportunity to offend you before you presume I have."

"So, what great beast were you referring to, in your touching soliloquy?" He found it difficult to draw his gaze away from those lashes. She closed her eyes for a moment, inhaling deeply. Her lashes lay against her cheeks like dark fans.

"I certainly wouldn't call my speech to myself 'touching,'" she prevaricated.

"What would you call it?" He went back to

working on the poor bush he'd nearly pruned into submission a few moments before. It was much safer than looking at her.

"I would call it weighing my options," she said, her voice a bit uncertain.

He didn't even look up at her. "And what options would those be?"

"I look forward to getting to know you better while we're here," she replied. She stepped closer to him and the scent of bluebells reached him. He looked around his private garden. Not a bluebell in sight. It must be her. He continued to pick at the plant until her hand landed on top of his own. He drew in a heavy breath as she squeezed it gently.

"You'll kill the poor plant if you don't stop that." She drew her hand back. "I promise I don't bite." She grinned wildly at what must have been a stricken look on his face. "And, although I have it on good authority that you do…" She laughed deeply, a rich sound that made him want to smile with her. She dropped her voice down to a whisper. "Although I have it on good authority that you *do* bite, I feel fairly safe in your presence." She eyed the plant. "The foliage, on the other hand…" She let her voice trail off.

"Tell me why you're here, Miss Thorne," he said. It meant a lot to him to have a true answer, but the odds of getting that were slim to none.

"I'm on a mission," she said, a grin tugging at the corners of her lips.

"A mission?" He wanted to kiss her. He hadn't wanted to kiss anyone in a very long time. It made him feel slightly off balance.

"Yes, a mission. But I can't tell you more than that." She twirled around in his garden, gazing at the sun. If he didn't know better, he'd say she glimmered there in the sunlight. It had been too long since he'd been in the proximity of a beautiful lass.

"So, I'll have to remain ignorant and hopeful. A typical state for a man," he murmured.

"What was your interruption?" she asked with a tilt of her head.

"I wouldn't call my wife's death an interruption," he said before thinking. But she covered those rosebud lips with the tips of her fingers and withheld her laughter. "You weren't referring to that, were you?" he asked with a chuckle and a self-deprecating grin.

"I was referring to the noise at the door a moment ago," she laughed. It was a melodic sound, one that made him feel happy. How long had it been since he'd felt truly happy? A very long time.

"That was my brother, Phineas, who wanted entrance to my garden," he explained. "So, he could complain about our mother, no doubt. My footmen kept him out."

"So, this truly is your sanctuary, as your daughter explained."

"It is."

"Why is it special to you?"

"My problems are not admitted into my garden," he explained as cryptically as he could. And as he searched for appropriate words to explain it, the need to do so was robbed from him.

"What's that beautiful sound?" she gasped as she turned and rounded the corner of his garden.

He didn't hear a thing. But he followed her as she disappeared from sight.

❧

Sophia didn't know what the sound was or where it came from, but she knew it was one of the most beautiful sounds she'd ever heard. It was better than raindrops on a tin roof. Better than the songs the crickets chirped at dusk, better than anything in that moment.

"Can you hear that?" she asked of no one in particular as she turned a corner in the garden and stepped into an open area, with a fish pond directly in the center. She stepped away from the fish. Fish were not a faerie's friend. Of course, these fish appeared to be small. They probably weren't a threat at all.

The wind picked up the hair on her forehead and the tinkling sound began again. It took her attention, so much of it that she didn't even notice that the duke stood beside her until she heard him breathing harshly beside her.

"The next time you'd like for me to give chase, Miss Thorne, you need to warn me so I can commit to a full breath."

The wind stopped and so did the sound. "Where did it go?" she cried, glancing left and right, trying to find the source.

"Where did what go?"

"The music," she tried to explain. But he, a mere human, would never understand.

"I heard no music, Miss Thorne," he said, looking at her skeptically.

"It was there. I promise." She placed a hand over

her heart and regarded him stoically. Then the wind lifted the hem of her gown and the leaves rustled gently. The tinkling began anew. Sophia closed her eyes and hummed with the music. When it stopped, her eyes flew open, only to find the Duke of Robinsworth looking at her with skepticism. "Didn't you hear it?"

"Do you mean the chimes blowing in the wind?" he asked, his voice incredulous. He pointed to a nearby post, from which dangled several strings full of tiny, hollow, silver balls. When the wind moved just right, the balls struck one another lightly, each producing a different note that sounded like a sweet symphony to her ears.

"Wind chimes…" she breathed, closing her eyes as the tinkling sound enveloped her. She listened until the wind shifted and the sound stopped. Then she opened her eyes, only to find the duke leaning against the fountain, regarding her with more than curiosity. She wasn't certain what else it was, but she sensed something there.

"Are you quite all right, Miss Thorne?" he asked. He'd caught his breath, and now he looked like he just needed to catch his wits.

"I should probably explain," she began with hesitance.

"That would be nice," he said rather drolly. She liked the duke more than she'd expected.

"But first I'll have to get to know you better."

"Beg your pardon?" His jaw dropped.

"I cannot reveal all of my secrets until I know you better. And even then, I'd never be able to reveal much."

He pointed to the silver balls. "But the wind chimes?"

"My name is Sophia," she tossed out, prevaricating as she looked for a way to explain.

He looked at her as though she'd grown two heads.

"Do you have a name?" she asked casually, still trying to figure out how to tell him about her love of music.

"Doesn't everyone have a name, Miss Thorne?" He sighed heavily when she frowned at him, then continued. "My friends and family call me Robin."

"No, your real name," she tried.

"No one has called me by my given name since I was a boy, Miss Thorne."

"Sophia," she corrected. "I give you leave to use it." He had a look on his face that made her doubt anyone had given the duke leave to do anything in a very long time. What his rank didn't afford him, his past did. People feared him because of his rank, and they feared him because of his past. So, by either standard, he was allowed to behave as he pleased. And most people stayed at least ten paces from him, much less getting close enough to afford him leave.

Then the wind shifted again and she couldn't keep from twirling as the music in her head began to form shapes. It was odd. She could usually push the music out of her mind, no matter how much she wanted to let it settle inside her. But this music was different. The wind stopped. "And you?" she asked as she stopped twirling.

"My name is Ashley," he finally said, very quietly, as though speaking with any force would put a stop to their conversation, no matter how absurd.

She stepped forward and laid a hand on his chest. "And do you give me leave to use it?"

"I would probably give you leave to do anything," he muttered, as he swiped a hand down his face. "Have you enchanted me in some way, Sophia?"

"Oh, no, I can't do that," she began. Then she drew her bottom lip between her teeth and worried it. He didn't draw his gaze from her mouth. "I love your wind chimes."

"I can tell as much." He studied her. Hard.

"Do you give me leave to call you Ashley?"

"If anyone heard you call me by that name, they'd think there's something untoward going on between us."

"But there is," she said. He had no idea yet of the depth of her involvement in the days to come. But she'd be more involved in his life than he'd ever dream.

He turned his head and coughed into his closed fist. Probably a stall tactic. Like her own inane ramblings.

"Ashley, I must go," she said softly as he took a step toward her.

But he reached out and hooked his finger beneath her chin to gently tilt her head up. He looked into her eyes. "Did someone pay you to do this?"

"To do what?"

"This," he said sharply, gesturing to what she assumed was the here and now.

"You'll have to define this," she coaxed. Mission faeries didn't receive payment for their work. It was their lot in life.

"Did someone pay you to get into my bed, Miss Thorne?" he asked sharply.

"Oh, no. Absolutely not. Why would anyone have to pay me to do such a thing?"

She reached out to smooth the lapels of his coat, taking in the sandalwood scent of him that she couldn't smell until she got really close. She breathed deeply.

"If someone is guiding your hand in our interactions—" he started.

But she shushed him with a gentle sound as she laid a hand over his heart. It was beating like mad. "No one has to pay me to like you, Ashley," she said.

He inhaled deeply. "You had better go, Sophia. Your family will be worried. And people will talk."

"You worry very much about things people say, don't you, Ashley?"

"When you've lived a life like mine…" He didn't even finish the thought.

"When one has lived a life like yours, I bet one has many interesting stories to tell. I hope I get to hear them while I'm here," she said, then she bobbed up on her tiptoes and kissed his cheek quickly.

"Until later," she called over her shoulder. She thought she heard him grunt in response.

As Sophia dashed through the corridors, trying to find her way back to her grandmother, she cursed the fates for putting that wind chime in her path. Ashley probably thought she was a complete ninny at this point.

She was a ninny. A very big one. A very big and most ridiculous one. Because she liked the duke even more than she'd thought she would. This was good, but she had a feeling it wasn't good in a good way. Dash it, she wasn't even making sense to herself.

Sophia spent half the hour wandering the corridors

of the duke's home, until she found a footman who informed her that her grandmother had been shown to her room for a rest after their arrival. She tiptoed into her own chambers.

"How was your meeting with the duke?" her grandmother asked anxiously from a chair beside the fireplace. Of course, her grandmother would be waiting for her. She was much too nosy to nap like a normal old lady. She'd obviously been knitting in Sophia's room while she waited. Their house faerie, Margaret, was busy unpacking the meager trunks they'd brought with them.

"I don't know," Sophia said. And truly she didn't. She would have to sit and formulate a plan.

A knock sounded on the door. Margaret moved to open it and stepped aside to admit a footman. Sophia clamped a hand over her mouth to stifle a gasp.

The footman looked particularly ill at ease, with the long strands of metal balls dangling from his fingertips. "His Grace ordered that these be brought to Miss Thorne and installed outside her window."

"Oh, my," her grandmother said, with a stern look in her direction. Everyone knew music would entrance Sophia. But it didn't typically overload her senses and make her feel light-headed. Not like these chimes had. For some reason, they had a strong effect on her. She'd be worthless every time there was the slightest breeze.

"You'll have to take them back," Sophia began.

"One does not send a gift back to His Grace, miss," the servant informed her, his nose rising in the air.

Very well. Sophia raised a breezy hand at the footman. "Do what you must."

The man set to work installing the chimes, and Sophia dropped heavily onto the settee. She'd have to tie them together to stop their tinkling. But how thoughtful of Ashley to send them.

"I believe we need to talk," her grandmother said, her eyes dancing with mischief. If anything, Sophia had expected censure.

"I suppose we do," Sophia said as she settled deeper into the settee.

Six

THE DUKE OF ROBINSWORTH TAPPED THE TABLE between him and his brother, signaling that he'd take another card.

Finn looked at him and raised a golden eyebrow. "Perhaps you should join the others below stairs. With luck like yours, you could take all their money before Mother gives hers up to them." He slid a card across the table to Ashley, and then he cursed when he saw a two and that Ashley had a total of twenty-one. "Damn you, Robin. You may not be lucky in life, but you certainly are in games of chance."

"Life is a game of chance, my dear Finn," he said, recognizing the grim sound of his own voice. "We play the cards we're dealt."

"Unless we stack the deck."

Ashley chuckled. "Obviously not the case in my situation," he said. He'd played the cards he'd been dealt since the day he was born. He'd been raised for greatness. Raised to be a duke. Raised to be respectable. It was unfortunate that his deck had been stacked against him.

"Yet still you play," Finn lamented.

"I sent a gift to Miss Thorne this afternoon," Ashley suddenly blurted out.

"Am I familiar with the lady in question?" Finn appeared to search his mind and came up empty-handed.

"I doubt it. I met her in the park a few days ago."

Finn sat back, his eyes opening wide. "Pray tell," he encouraged.

"There's nothing to tell." Ashley shrugged. "We met very quickly when she took Anne to task over something."

Finn laid his cards on the table. "Someone took Anne to task?"

"Quite effectively," Ashley continued. "She appeared as though from nowhere and told Anne how a lady behaves."

"And…?"

"And Anne listened. It was quite profound."

"And all of this provoked a gift from you?"

Ashley never should have opened his big mouth. He should have kept his secret to himself. But whiskey did have a way of loosening the tongue. And he'd had more than his share. And Finn's tongue had been loosened as well. He set his cards to the side. Obviously, Finn wanted to gossip more than he wanted to win his money back.

"It was nothing, really."

Finn shook his head. "Robin, I haven't heard you speak of a lady in quite some time. It must have been some meeting."

"She's in residence," Ashley admitted.

"In London?"

"Here, at the Hall."

Finn sat back and glared at Ashley. "Here? Have I met her?"

Ashley shrugged. "About as tall as my chin. Dark hair." He took a deep swallow of his whiskey. When he noticed how quiet Finn was, he looked up to find his brother with his mouth agape. He threw a card at him. "Stop looking at me like I'm bound for Bedlam."

Finn chuckled as he gathered the cards into a neat pile. "Someone is interested in a lady," he sang out loudly. Then he ducked as a whole deck of cards sailed past his head. "And touchy about it, too," he laughed. "What's her name?"

"Miss Sophia Thorne," Ashley groused good-naturedly.

"Thorne... Thorne..." Finn repeated as he searched his mind. "It doesn't ring any bells for me. Is her father a peer?"

Ashley wasn't certain. He knew nothing about her. "No idea. She's traveling with her grandmother."

"But you'd like to learn more about her." It wasn't a question. It was a statement.

Ashley sighed and pushed back from the table. "She doesn't quake in fear at the sight of me, if that's what you're wondering. In fact, she has told me on more than one occasion that she's not afraid of me at all."

"Well, there's a fortunate turn of events. Mother was ready to find a comely, blind, deaf widow with whom you could while away your days."

"Mother should mind her own matters."

"But she has such a good time minding yours."

Finn cleared his throat loudly. "What are your intentions with Miss Thorne?"

"I intend to launch a full investigation into her character," Ashley said without even cracking a grin. "If I'm to marry the chit, I'll have to find out how many skeletons are in her closet. If she has more than one murder in her past, then she outdoes me, and I simply cannot have that."

"You can be such an arse," Finn said.

"I do try," Ashley drawled. He hit the table gently with his open palm. "Deal the cards."

Finn regarded him stoically. "Would you like for me to investigate her?"

"It's not necessary," Ashley began. The lady would probably never speak to him again once she spent some time at the Hall and heard all the stories about him from his mother's guests. It would be no great loss either way. At that very moment, dinner was going on below stairs. He'd refused to attend. But Miss Thorne was probably there. And she was certainly being informed about his past.

"What kind of gift did you send her? Flowers?"

"A wind chime," Ashley replied without even thinking. "The one from my garden." At Finn's perplexed look, he kept going. "She admired it greatly."

"You allowed her into your garden, did you?" Finn said as he began to deal. "You don't even let me into your garden."

"I don't allow problems in my private space. And you carry a lot of baggage." He laughed. "Like Mother." He pretended to mull over his cards, but he wouldn't know twenty-one if it bit him on the arse, not now that the subject of Sophia Thorne had arisen. "She's charming," he said quickly. Then he waited for Finn's response.

Nothing. Absolutely no response at all.

"Don't you have a comment? An unsolicited suggestion? An unwanted barb?"

"An uncommon quiet. Take it for what it's worth."

"And what might that be?" Ashley hated it when people were cryptic about their feelings.

Finn laid his cards on the table. Literally. "I think you like the lady. And I, for one, am damned happy to see it. So, don't go scaring her off with your scowls and dark looks."

"I do not scowl."

"You look as though you've sucked a lemon most days, Robin," Finn said good-naturedly. "Or two."

"You don't know what it's like…" Ashley began.

"No, I don't. And I probably never will. But I know what it's like to be lonely. And I think you've been lonely long enough."

Ashley snorted. "Lovely. Now you've become some great philosopher."

"You could think of a better name to call me."

"They're all rolling around in my head, waiting for an opportunity to bruise your pride."

Finn said, "Pride… hide… As long as something is bruised, I know I'm alive."

"One must hurt to be alive, is that it?" Ashley watched Finn's face.

"Then you have been alive for a very long time, have you not?"

Ouch. Perhaps his brother would do him the honor of pulling the knife from his chest after that one.

"Apologies, Robin," Finn said with a heavy sigh. "It's nice to see you interested in someone. Something not involving your land, tenants, or business interests. Something recreational."

"Bedchamber activities are not for recreation. They're for procreation."

"Ha!" Finn exploded. "I knew we'd get to the meat of the matter. You want the chit in your bed."

It was better to let Finn think his interest was entirely carnal. That couldn't be further from the truth. "Bed, corridor, against the wall," he said as drolly as he could, pretending to ponder his hand. "It matters not where."

Finn shook his head slowly. "You're a terrible liar."

"Am I?" Ashley asked innocently. Let Finn figure it out for himself. His imagination was much more entertaining than Ashley's life. "Let's finish up this hand," he directed. "I have to go and deliver a gift to Anne."

"Isn't she asleep?"

"She should be. But that German governess we had a few months ago told her tales of a faerie that comes and takes a tooth from beneath a child's pillow and leaves a gift in return." Finn looked at him like he had two heads. "Some fluttery little being."

"The German governess? Wasn't that the one who found frogs in her bed?"

"I don't recall." Ashley scratched his head. Anne had done so many terrible things to the people charged with her care that they began to run together after a time.

Finn threw his cards down when he saw that he'd been beaten. Then he rose, took one long swallow of whiskey, draining his glass, and said, "I'll see you tomorrow. Mother has threatened my life, not to mention my stones, if I should dare to desert her during the party. I think it's ballocks, since it's your house and I am the one being made to suffer."

"Better you than me," Ashley said as he watched Finn slip out the door. It was much better that his mother call upon Finn to entertain her guests. Anyone would be better than Ashley himself.

✌

Sophia sighed heavily as she closed the door to her bedchamber and discarded her wrap. Margaret gave her a scolding glance. "How many times do I have to ask you not to throw your things on the floor?" the house faerie said with a disgusted shake of her head.

"I thought dinner would never end," Sophia groaned as she sat down on the edge of the bed and began to unlace her shoes. "You'll have to help me get out of this gown," she warned, just in case Margaret had decided to leave. "I don't know why they make their clothes with so many hooks and loops and layers."

"Perhaps they like all the layers to warm their icy hearts," Margaret said as she spun Sophia around none too gently and began to work at the fastenings on the back of the gown. Sophia was well aware that Margaret held a severe dislike for the human world and those who occupied it. But she had no idea why.

"Are you going to tell me what has you tied up in knots? Or will you force me to suffer along with you?" Sophia shoved the gown down over her hips and stepped out of it. Margaret made a move to pick it up. "What is it about this world that has you up in arms?"

"It's not that I dislike it here," Margaret began with a sniff. "But Ronald says—"

Sophia held up a hand to cut her off. "You've been talking to Ronald?"

"He came to see you a little while ago, but you weren't back from dinner yet."

Sophia shook her head. That gnome would be the bane of her existence.

"He means well," Margaret said. "And I think he may be right."

Well, even if he was, Sophia would never admit it.

"He says the duke wants you in his bed."

He wanted no such thing. They'd barely spoken more than a few words to one another. Sophia scoffed. "He doesn't even know me."

Margaret sent her a pointed glance. "A man does not have to know you to want you in his bed, miss," she informed Sophia.

"How did Ronald get up here?"

"He climbed the trellis. He was in the foulest of moods." Margaret covered a giggle. "I did hit him with a fireplace poker when he tried to lean his body out the window and take down those chimes."

"I'm very proud of you. What made you do it? I know you hate the chimes as much as he does." Everyone worried about Sophia and chimes. Or music of any kind.

"I assumed the duke would be none too happy to see his silver balls smashed to bits on the garden floor."

"Good point," Sophia encouraged.

"Ronald's legs are too short to reach them, anyway. You should have seen the look on his face when the poker hit his backside." This time, the house faerie chuckled loudly.

"Shh," Sophia reminded her gently. "Or Grandmother will feel the need to come and interject herself into the conversation."

"What if Ronald's right, miss?" Margaret asked gently.

"A rest in the duke's bed is not on my agenda for this mission."

"I doubt he'd want you to do much resting." Margaret held out Sophia's nightrail, but she waved it away.

"I need to go out. Can you get my blue dress?" The webbed dress was her favorite, made from the softest strands of a spider's web, laced together to form cloth. Then it was conditioned by the same spiders to be formfitting, which allowed Sophia to slide through keyholes with ease, and the trailing bits of fabric that covered her legs were made in such a way that they would simply fall off the overskirt of the dress, should she snag it during one of her escapades.

"If you damage this dress, I'll not be the one to go back to the spiders and barter for a new one," Margaret said. She hadn't even gone the last time. Sophia had gone herself. And barely come out of it with a new dress.

Sophia fluffed the tendrils of fabric that fell, making it tickle around her knees where it stopped. "Do I look all right?" she asked as she regarded herself in the looking glass.

Margaret reached up and began to pull the pins from Sophia's hair, letting it fall down around her shoulders. "Good idea," Sophia said as she massaged her scalp. She certainly didn't want to leave hairpins behind if she had to make a mad dash for safety.

"Be careful," Margaret warned as Sophia willed her wings into existence. Then she shrank to the size of a child's toy.

"Can you get the window?" Sophia asked, as she fluttered in the air. She could get the window herself, but it would take time that she didn't want to waste.

Margaret opened the window and Sophia glanced at the chimes. No breeze broke the stillness of the night, and the chimes were uncommonly silent. It was almost as if they were a great sleeping beast just waiting to wake and steal her concentration. She shook herself from her reverie. "I can let myself back in, if you want to go to bed. Just leave the window cracked."

"Your grandmother would never forgive me if I left while you're on a mission. I'll wait."

"Well, take a nap. Your disposition could certainly use it." Margaret was often cross, but never cross and obnoxious, not unless she was tired.

Margaret harrumphed. "I can plan my own night's activities, thank you very much."

Sophia flittered out the window and into the damp night air. Sophia loved the night air and everything that came with it. She circled the house quickly, fairly certain she'd be able to find Lady Anne's chambers from the exterior of the house. Then she'd just have to find a way inside, once she had her bearings, so she could go through a keyhole or slide beneath a door.

But as she went from window to window looking inside, she finally came upon a window that was

partially open. She landed gently on the windowsill
and bent to slide beneath the crack. She very nearly
got stuck. If her bottom wasn't so big, she wouldn't
have any trouble at all. But such was her cross to bear.

Sophia stood on the inner sill and dusted herself off.
Someone really should tell Wilkins that the sills were
dirty. He'd probably get the housekeeper right on it.
A voice broke the stillness of the night.

"I knew I smelled a mission faerie," the voice said.
"I'd know that stench anywhere." Mission faeries and
gift faeries had been enemies for centuries. Their very
natures warred with one another.

"What are you doing here?"

"There's a tooth to be had," the faerie said. He
tapped his foot impatiently where he stood on the
bedside table. "Do not think to stand in my way."

"Shh, or you'll wake her," Sophia warned as she
glanced at Lady Anne, who slept soundly, her little
hand curled beneath her cheek. Her nurse probably
slept in the adjoining room and would be as likely as
Anne to hear them if they made any sort of disturbance.

"When did you begin servicing England?"

"We service anyone who believes," he said with
very little emotion.

"I hope you brought a gift for her." If a gift faerie
could get away with stealing the tooth and leaving
nothing in its place, he could sell the tooth, which had
a modest amount of value, depending on its size, and
not have anything invested in the exchange at all. Pure
profit. Purely ridiculous. Wholly forbidden.

"Why should I? Gift faeries are a myth, even in the
minds of the believers. They speak of us, and then they

do our work for us," he groused, growing more and more impatient.

He was right. The few people who did tell their children stories of gift faeries had grown disillusioned by the many faeries who were thieves. He glanced toward the window. "The night grows shorter. I have many, many gifts to give before the sun rises."

He yawned loudly and tapped his open mouth as he did so. He shook his magic bag at her, which clanked loudly in the stillness of the room. Anne's hand stretched open beneath her cheek as if she was startled from the noise, and then she settled deeper into her pillow, her mouth open as she breathed softly.

Sophia could just imagine the gift faerie's next move. He'd take the tooth, leave nothing in its place, and be holed up with a fallen faerie as soon as his pocket jingled with coins from the sale of the teeth.

Soft footsteps from outside the door reached her ears, just before the door handle began to turn slowly. Sophia dashed behind a lamp as quickly as she could, as the gift faerie dove beneath the skirts of one of Lady Anne's dolls. Sophia rolled her eyes. Of course, he would choose there.

Sophia peeked out from behind the lamp and watched as the duke himself slipped into the room. He wore his shirtsleeves, and his throat was bare. A very light sprinkling of dark hair dusted his chest. His hair was messy, like he'd run his hands through it over and over. Shadows darkened the skin beneath his eyes. He looked tired. And that tugged at Sophia's heart a little.

Ashley sat down very gently on the edge of the bed and sneaked his fingers beneath the pillow. He retrieved Anne's tooth from beneath her feather pillow and dropped it into his pocket, as he pulled out a length of pink silk. He wound the ribbon around his finger and held it for a moment, sliding the pad of his thumb across the silky surface. Then he tucked it beneath Anne's pillow and kissed her gently on the forehead. The little girl didn't even move. He left as quietly as he'd arrived.

"You owe me for that," the gift faerie groused.

"You should have been quicker," Sophia tossed back. True, if Sophia hadn't interrupted him, he'd probably have had that tooth and would have been long since gone.

"And you wonder why we dislike you so," the other faerie muttered.

She'd never wondered any such thing. She knew exactly why they didn't like one another. They had very different goals and lived by different covenants. Gift faeries weren't bound by the same Unpardonable Errors; theirs were not nearly as stringent, nor were the consequences as harsh if one erred.

"You hate us because we're beautiful," she said instead. "That's the tooth, the whole tooth, and nothing but the tooth. Admit it."

"You mission faeries should be swimming with the fish," he grumbled as he moved toward the cracked window. Only the really, really bad faeries were turned into fish to live out their days.

Sophia cast one long look toward Lady Anne. She wanted to stay and see if she could learn anything about the little girl by looking through her personal belongings. But that might have to wait until the next day, because the girl's nurse could already be heard moving about the adjoining chamber.

Sophia flitted back to the window and slipped beneath it. She really needed to lay off the sweets so she could fit more easily in small spaces. The webbed clothing could only do so much.

The gift faerie shot her a dirty look. "See you around," he said as he put his wings in motion.

"Not if I see you first," Sophia called back.

Sophia made her way back to her own window, surprised to find Margaret wide awake and waiting for her. Margaret helped her out of her webbed dress and into her nightrail. Then she turned down the bed and moved toward the door to go to the servants' quarters.

"Will you wake me bright and early? I'd like to get an early start and wander about a while tomorrow before anyone else wakes."

Margaret huffed. "Certainly, miss. You can keep me up until all hours of the night and then expect me to rise from my warm bed to wake you at the crack of dawn. Certainly. Not a problem."

"Margaret," Sophia sighed.

Margaret held up a hand to stop her. "I know, I know. Your mission rests upon it." She moved toward the door. "I believe you'd tell me your mission rested upon it if you wanted a cup of chocolate, too, for what it's worth."

"Good night, Margaret," Sophia said to her retreating back. The house faerie was still muttering as she went out the door.

Sophia slid beneath the counterpane and had just laid her head upon her pillow when she heard the sound. She bolted upright. What was that noise?

Seven

ASHLEY CLEANED UP THE MESS HE'D MADE WITH THE cards and then waited for Simmons, his valet, who would arrive to make certain the duke didn't need anything before retiring. The man was as predictable as the clock striking the hour. Ashley rubbed at his eyes. Sleep was often elusive for him, and he felt remorseful for keeping his servants up so late to take care of his needs. But, try as he might, the ones who had been with him the longest seemed to take great pride in being available despite his odd schedule.

Just as he'd expected, there was a scratch at the door. "Enter," he called absently.

His valet of twelve years entered the room and nodded politely. "I trust you had a good evening, Your Grace."

He'd had worse. "I suppose," Ashley said as he rose and moved toward the wardrobe.

"Allow me, Your Grace," Andrew said as he stepped in Ashley's path and reached for his night robe.

"Go to bed, Simmons," Ashley growled as he stumbled over a footstool. Simmons stuck one foot out and slid the stool out of the duke's path with a hard shove. "Thank you," Ashley muttered.

"Would you care for a tonic, Your Grace?" He said it with such dignity. What he should have said was, "Would you care for a drink that might make you feel a little better when you wake up, despite the fact that you're foxed out of your skull?"

"That special concoction you make will do nicely in the morning," Ashley muttered as he tugged his shirt from his waistband. He'd discarded his neckcloth and waistcoat hours before. But Simmons knew Ashley slept naked. So, he simply laid the duke's robe across the bed and bustled about the room, tidying up behind him. Ashley could take care of his own clothing when he was ready for bed. He fully believed that a man, unless he was a complete fop, could disrobe on his own. Such a simple task.

"Would you like for me to look after your brother while he's in residence, Your Grace? I noticed he didn't bring along his valet." The servant watched him closely.

"If Lord Phineas wants a valet, he can bloody well acquire one himself," Ashley complained as he dropped onto his piano bench and turned to face the pianoforte. He laid a hand on the keys and plunked at them lightly, sending a gentle tune floating into the air. Having such a piece of musical equipment in his suite of rooms was a huge luxury, but he was a duke, after all. He could be as eccentric as he chose, and the censure from his peers could not be any worse than what he already dealt with. "You may go, Simmons," Ashley directed.

The man bowed quickly. "As you wish," he said as he disappeared as quietly as he'd come. Ashley had the best staff in England. They were loyal. They were discreet. Though it was well below his station to admit it, they were his friends. They were the people he talked to when no one else was about. And while Ashley did like to maintain a certain degree of propriety, he valued each of them, and each for a different reason.

Ashley laid his fingers on the keys and thought about the house party going on below stairs. By now, everyone would be heading for their rooms, probably with his mother's money lining their pockets. He had no doubt there would gambling going on below stairs. It was his mother's favorite recreational activity, after all.

He began a quick Beethoven tune, enjoying the way the sound of his pianoforte broke the quiet of the night. Perhaps he chose to play so often in the waning hours of the evening because it kept him from his melancholy musings. It kept him from absolute silence. He let his fingers tickle the keys as he played, in very much the way he would a woman's body, gentle and soft, and then solid and strong.

The click of his door handle from behind him caught his attention, but only for a moment. "Did you forget something?" he asked Simmons.

A flutter of white lace entered the corner of his vision and caught him off guard. He looked up, startled, as the flutter settled beside him on the piano bench.

"What the devil?" he breathed softly, his fingers stilling over the keys. "Miss Thorne?" he asked hesitantly.

"Ashley," she breathed softly, her voice like a whisper

in the quiet of the night, one that threatened to shatter his very being.

"What are you doing?" He glanced toward the door, which she'd closed behind her.

"I heard music," she said, a smile unlike any he'd seen before on her face. She gazed at his pianoforte as though it was a most wondrous object. She reached out a delicate little hand and stroked across its front. What he wouldn't give to be a piano in that moment. Her wrist was encircled by a white lace cuff, which led to a billowy white sleeve. He let his gaze wander to her throat, which was enclosed in the same billowy lace. The lady had arrived at his suite of rooms in nothing more than a nightrail? And looking as though she was entranced. Perhaps she'd had as much to drink as he had.

"Are you foxed, Miss Thorne?" he asked, removing his hands completely from the keys. Her smile fell into a frown.

"Beg your pardon?" she asked quickly, as though shaking herself from a haze. "Why did you stop?"

"It's not every day one is accosted by a strange lady in one's bedchamber, Miss Thorne," he said. "It's a little disconcerting."

"I did not accost you."

"A man can hope," he replied. And pray. And beg. And plead.

"I should not be here," she said quickly, finally looking into his face. Her hazel eyes flashed with something he didn't understand. She scooted to the edge of the seat as though she planned to retreat. He wasn't quite ready for her to do that yet. He reached out a hand to still her.

"Stay," he said softly. "For a moment." He took a deep breath. "If you want." He must sound like an inept adolescent. But he'd had enough liquor not to care. He still couldn't believe that she wore nothing but her nightrail. Her toe hit the side of his stockinged foot. Even her feet were bare. It made him wonder what else was bare beneath that thin piece of virginal cloth.

"I should not be here," she said again, as though trying to convince herself. "But I couldn't resist when I heard the music. I had no idea you could play."

Was he the one playing, or was she? "You came here because you heard me play?"

"Yes," she breathed. "And it was beautiful." She laid a hand on his leg and squeezed it gently. The touch shot straight to his heart. And other areas. "Will you play more? Just for a moment? Please?" She reminded him of an overly anxious child at Christmas.

"Miss Thorne…" he began. He should send her immediately from his chambers.

"My name is Sophia," she said with a tiny laugh. "I gave you leave to use it, Ashley."

His name on her lips hit him like a stab in the gut. "Say it again," he prompted.

"Please?" she said. He'd been referring to his name. But he really just wanted to hear her talk. "Please," she said again, her voice a little softer as she gazed at him with those beautiful eyes. He could deny her nothing.

Her hand still rested on his thigh as he turned back to the piano. It seared through his trousers like a brand. But she didn't move it, even when he lifted his leg to adjust his seat. Only a little to the left, dearest, he couldn't help but think. But then he laid his hands on the keys and picked up the tune where he'd left off.

He watched her face as he began to play. Her mouth fell open slightly, a harsh breath escaping her lips as the music began to fill the room. Her eyes closed, and her hand upon his thigh began to contract with the beat of the music. Dear God, she'd undo him with a simple touch.

"So lovely," she breathed in one big rush of air.

"Yes, you are," he agreed quietly. She appeared not to hear him. The piano filled the silence left by her wicked little breaths as she grew more and more comfortable against him. She leaned into his shoulder, the ruffles of her nightrail squished against his body. The side of her breast touched his arm, but she appeared not to notice.

No one could be such a practiced flirt, not even the most jaded of courtesans. He'd met plenty of women and bedded more than his share, and he'd never seen such an intriguing combination of innocence and beguiling beauty. She moved so that her breast brushed him, and he could no longer concentrate. His hands refused to play. They warred with his mind, which wanted to do nothing more than touch her.

He jerked, sliding the stool back only slightly. She startled and jumped at the movement, shaking her head quickly, as he did when he was properly foxed and couldn't get his bearings. But before she could rise to her feet, he scooped her into his lap, turning her toward him so that her legs dangled over his thighs and she faced him. He wrapped one hand around her hip to hold her in place. Her warm breath touched his forehead as he ran his fingers into the thick of her hair at the nape of her neck, and he forced her to look into his face.

"Don't stop," she cried.

He didn't intend to.

❧

Sophia pulled back, fighting the gentle pressure of the duke's hand at the nape of her neck, but he wasn't holding her tightly enough to scare her. What did scare her was that she had little recollection of how she came to be in his lap. She wasn't entirely uncomfortable being there, but one moment she'd been fully engrossed in a Beethoven tune and the next she was sitting across the duke's thighs with his whiskey-laden breath tickling her lips.

Ashley's thumb stroked across the ridge of her hip as he held her gently within his arms. "What are you trying to do to me?" he whispered against her mouth.

"The music," she started, but before she could continue, his lips touched the corner of her mouth ever so softly. His hand was strong at the back of her head, but gentle as his fingers loosened and his clasp turned into an exploration. Playful fingers tickled across the back of her neck, making the hair on her arms stand up.

"What music?" he murmured as he very gently touched his lips to the opposite corner of her mouth.

There had been music only moments before. But now the only sound she heard was the pounding of her own heartbeat in her ears. "Do you plan to kiss me, Your Grace?" she asked, wanting nothing more than to chase his lips with her own as he did everything *but* kiss her fully on the mouth.

His eyes were the color of the sky on a stormy day, ominous and foreboding, as his lips lingered there beside her cheek. "Do you want me to kiss you, Miss Thorne?" he breathed back. He adjusted her in his lap and groaned as though in pain when she wiggled her bottom against his thighs.

"I'm sorry," she said, startling from her reverie at his torturous noise. "Did I hurt you?"

He chuckled lightly, his chest rumbling beneath her hand as it lay over his heart. "Not in the way you think," he said quietly, his eyes flashing. Then he sighed heavily and removed his hand from the back of her neck.

His palm cascaded down the fall of her hair like water over the rocks at the edge of a brook, softly and slowly. He toyed with the ends of hair that fell over her shoulder and down the front of her nightrail. He picked up a lock of hair and brought it to his nose, inhaling deeply.

"Why are you in my bedchamber, Miss Thorne?" he asked, his voice raspy and quiet.

How could she explain? She couldn't. Not without sounding like a complete ninny. *Well, you see, Your Grace… I was in my own bedchamber and I heard music. And like some great beast had clunked me over the head, I lost all sense of propriety and dashed from my room in my bare feet to come and find it.* That would never do. "I'm too heavy for you to hold me in your lap," she said instead, as she moved to rise. But the hand that was clutching her hip just tightened.

"You're perfect for sitting in my lap, Miss Thorne,"

he said. "Stay." It didn't sound like an order. It sounded like pleading.

She raised her elbow to rest on his shoulder and let her fingertips play in the hair over his forehead. His eyes closed tightly and she saw a muscle tick in his jaw just before he inhaled deeply and relaxed, turning his cheek into the crook of her arm. His thumb began a slow slide across her waist. When her own hand slowed in his hair, he pressed the side of his head into her hand. It made her think of the caterpillars and the way they liked to have their backs scratched. They would do anything for a good tickle.

"You like a good tickle, too," she said quietly.

He smiled a self-deprecating smile. "It appears as though I do," he said quietly, almost as though he was speaking more to himself than to her.

"Have you been drinking?" she asked, trying to distract herself from the feel of his silky locks running through her fingers. She moved closer to him, her right breast pressed fully against his chest. If she could, she would straddle him and press every inch of her body against his. But somehow, she feared Grandmother would not approve. Not approve at all.

"I have had a little to drink, I'm afraid," he said, tensing below her. She immediately castigated herself for mentioning it. He was on guard now, where he hadn't been before.

"Does this feel good?" she asked, letting her fingertips move from his forehead to the nape of his neck and back again, abrading very gently as she did so.

He inhaled deeply and closed his eyes. "It feels wonderful," he said. But then he sighed heavily, a sigh of resignation, and caught her hand in his tight grip. He brought it to his lips and pressed a long kiss against her knuckles. "Why are you here, Miss Thorne?" he asked, his eyes boring into hers.

"To get you to kiss me, Your Grace. Why else?" She tried to keep from smiling but was unable. She pointed to the left corner of her mouth and tapped it gently. "You kissed me here." Then she tapped the other side of her mouth. "And here." She leaned closer to his lips. "And you keep calling me Miss Thorne," she whispered heartily.

He looked at her from beneath heavy-lidded lashes. Then he leaned forward, as though to kiss her soundly. He was fully intent upon the task and smashed into her cheek when she turned her head at the last moment. A laugh rose from deep within her belly.

"Think you're clever, do you?" he growled as he squeezed her tightly. There was playfulness beneath that gruff exterior. And she fully wanted to explore it.

"Not nearly as clever as you."

"I'm not clever enough, unfortunately. Because I cannot figure out how to kiss a lady who has slipped into my bedchamber in the dead of night." He swore lightly beneath his breath. She thought she heard him mention being a dolt, but she wasn't certain.

"Don't be too hard on yourself. I can't determine a way to get you to continue playing." She laughed despite herself. She couldn't determine whether she wanted him to kiss her more or to play. Neither was conducive to her mission. *Unpardonable Error Number Five: Never, ever fall in love with a human.* She snorted. Like that would ever happen.

"Is something amusing?" he asked, his head tilting to the side as he regarded her.

"Not in the least."

"I distinctly heard you snort, Miss Thorne."

"Sophia, Your Grace," she corrected. She'd get him to say it if it was the last thing she ever did.

"Ashley, Sophia," he whispered with a large grin. She'd never had such an odd conversation in her life.

"Ashley," she breathed, drawing his name out, enjoying the sound of it on her lips for as long as she could. "No one has called you that in a long time?"

"A very long time," he said with a quick nod.

Sophia leaned her forehead against his and stayed there until he began to tickle her waist. "Stop!" she cried over her laughter.

"Stop... don't stop..." he teased. "You really should make up your mind."

She stilled within his grasp. She might be at his home to help his daughter, but to do so, she might have to help him as well. What would be the harm in allowing the duke to kiss her? Not nearly as much harm as having him play for her, obviously. She caught both his hands in hers and squeezed gently. "I wish I could tell you why I'm here," she said softly. Then almost wished she could bite the words back. She could easily erase his memory with her dust. But that would be a travesty.

"I should escort you back to your room," he said with resignation.

She'd offended him by being candid about her desire to reveal herself to him. But he had no way of knowing that's what she meant, did he? Now he probably thought she purposefully kept secrets from him. And to tell him more would serve no purpose, aside from easing her own conscience. It would allow her to grow even closer to him. That would not be a good thing. "I imagine I can't linger here on your lap all night."

"That would be an impossibility." He sighed deeply. "You're not safe in here."

"Oh, posh." She chastised him with a gentle slap on his shoulder. "I'm perfectly safe with you."

"You're in my lap, dearest, and have been for more than a few minutes."

It felt like a lifetime. Like it could be a lifetime. "And you haven't harmed me. You make it sound like you're some great beast with no self-control."

"Self-control can only take one so far," he said with a grunt.

She took a deep breath and then asked the question she knew she shouldn't ask. "Will you play for me? For just a moment?" Perhaps she would be able to figure out why the music drew her to him, like a moth to a flame. It was absurd that it affected her so much more than other music did. But it was so beautiful. So compelling. So... perfect.

He removed his hand from her hip and laid it upon the keys. She held her breath. Then he hit a key, and the sweetest of music reached her ears. His fingers moved over the keys in the same motion he'd used to tickle her. He stiffened a little beneath her as he leaned forward and played a quick tune. She turned toward the piano, and his free hand caressed the outside of her thigh. His fingernails very gently ruched the fabric of her nightrail. She couldn't determine which was more powerful, his fingertips playing across her skin or his playing of the piano. One warred with the other.

"I should escort you to your bedchamber," he said again with a sigh as his fingers slowed and then stopped.

She supposed that he should. His hand fell from her thigh, and he gave her bottom a bump to eject her from his lap. She rose quickly and circled around the bench. "I can find my own way back," she said. But could she? Not very likely. She didn't even remember how she'd gotten to his chamber in the first place. Sophia glanced down at her nightrail and immediately felt much too exposed. "Oh, dear," she muttered.

Ashley crossed to his bed and picked up his robe, then draped it over her shoulders. "You can't walk back looking like that." He smiled broadly at her. "If my footmen saw you in your nightrail, I'd never be able to get them back on task."

How ridiculous. "I highly doubt they'd notice."

"I can't do anything but notice," the duke muttered. She closed the robe around her body. It hung all the way to the floor. Only a complete ninny would journey out without appropriate clothing. She flexed her toes in the rug.

"Would you like for me to carry you?"

Her heart leapt at the very idea.

"That won't be necessary. But thank you." It was almost as though she was turning down tea, rather than his actual proposal that he wrap her up in his strong arms and carry her all the way back to her chamber. How scandalous.

He walked to his door and turned the handle

slowly. "Shall we?" he asked, as he held out his crooked elbow.

Shall we walk back to your bedchamber and pretend like I'm not in my nightrail, wearing your robe? Why, certainly! She took his arm, relishing the way his muscles contracted as soon as her fingers wrapped around him.

She felt the need to apologize for interrupting his quiet time. "I'm sorry," she said, as they started down the corridor.

"Sorry for?" A lock of hair tumbled across his forehead as he looked down at her.

"For being a bother," she began. But she couldn't find appropriate words. She stumbled over her own tongue.

"You weren't a bother." He held up a hand to stop her when she would have protested. "You are a delightful breath of fresh air."

"Why do I sense a 'but' coming at any moment?" she murmured.

"But," he finally said. "I care for your reputation even if you don't."

"I don't give a good damn about my reputation," she said. But ladies didn't speak in such a way, did they? Not true ladies. She groaned beneath her breath.

He chuckled. "I give a good enough damn about your reputation for both of us."

They were quickly approaching the door to her bedchamber. She'd tried to remember the path through the maze of corridors that was the Hall. Hopefully, she would remember adequately. They stopped in front of her door.

"Good night, Your Grace," she said softly. But she gasped when she looked up at his face. His eyes intently peered into hers, as though his gaze alone could divulge what was in his soul.

"I need to warn you of something, Sophie." Not Sophia. Sophie. She liked that.

"All doom and gloom again, are you?"

"Take me seriously," he said, his voice crisp as clean bed linens. But not nearly as cold. In fact, his voice was as hot as a fire on a cold winter's night. He cupped the side of her face in his hand. "The next time you come to my room, Sophie, be prepared for me to kiss you."

He wanted to kiss her? She wanted nothing more. But that was not part of her mission. She couldn't mess this mission up. "Yes, Ashley," she whispered.

He inclined his head swiftly and left her standing there in her doorway. She watched him as he strode away, his steps swift and full of self-assurance. It was only when he was gone that she realized she still wore his robe. She brought it to her nose and inhaled deeply. Yes, she'd be fully prepared for him to kiss her. That's why she must stay out of his room and out of his path entirely. It was necessary. *Stay away from the duke.* He was dangerous in more ways than one.

❦

Ashley turned a corner and cursed himself for being raised a gentleman. Any other man would have tossed Sophia Thorne onto his bed and not let her come up for air until the next morning. Damn his sense of decorum. Damn his desire to do the right thing. Damn his moral hide. He had a raging manhood, a desire for Sophie that wouldn't be easily appeased, and now he couldn't get the little minx off his mind. He stopped and started to go back to her. But then a door opened to his left and his brother stepped directly into his path.

"What the devil?" Finn muttered as Ashley nearly bowled him over.

Ashley regarded Finn's state of dress, which mirrored his own. Their valets would skewer them if they knew they'd been seen in public in such a state. But it was the middle of the night, after all. Finn's neck was bare, his shirt hanging open. Ashley glanced down at himself. His shirt was untucked. Thank God, it was untucked, or he could be forced to explain the state of his manhood. Fortunately, the very sight of his brother was taking care of that for him.

"Where have you been?" Finn asked.

"You first," Ashley grunted. He glanced toward the door Finn had just exited and raised an eyebrow.

"Must you know everything?" Finn murmured with disgust as he turned to walk toward his own room. A mere day ago, his brother had been lamenting the loss of his mistress. Not to mention his prowess when the woman had complained about his lack of "attention to her needs."

"That mistress is off your mind, I assume?" Ashley asked casually.

"What mistress?" Finn asked with a grin. Then he raised a brow of his own and looked down his nose at Ashley. Not an easy feat when his brother was an inch shorter than he was. "Who were you with? Anne's room is at the end of the opposite end of the house."

"I was escorting a lost lady back to her chamber,"

Ashley admitted. No need to tell him who the lady was, was there?

"And you just happened to stumble upon her in the corridor?" Finn scoffed. "Try that on someone who doesn't know what a recluse you are. You rarely leave your chambers."

"Perhaps I'm changing," Ashley tried.

"Perhaps you're a poor liar," Finn laughed. "How *is* Miss Thorne?" he asked casually.

"Perplexing," Ashley admitted.

"Perplexing can be good," Finn tried.

"It can?"

"On occasion," Finn said with a shrug. He stopped and regarded Ashley with seriousness. "You like this chit?"

"She's not a chit," Ashley began. But Finn just smiled. Damn his brother for knowing him so well. Ashley didn't know how to continue. But his brother would certainly understand his reticence.

"What do you know of her?"

Finn was a bit of a sleuth. "She's quite unique," Ashley said. Give Finn an inch and he'd take a mile. He'd know more about Sophie than Ashley did within days. He clamped his lips shut.

"I don't want her shoe size, Robin," he said.

Tiny. Her feet were tiny.

"Specifics, Robin," Finn snapped.

"One grandmother, with whom she's traveling. That's all I know." Aside from the fact that she had flashing hazel eyes that reminded him of a golden meadow, then a forest at dusk. Damn, it had been too long since he'd had a woman.

"I'll get right on it."

"I don't want her to know," Ashley started, resigning himself to the fact that Finn would put his nose in where it didn't belong. And that he would do so with glee.

"You don't want her to know you like her? I'm afraid it's too late for that. Because you'd not leave the safety of your chambers to visit some lady you've no interest in."

"I really dislike you at times," Ashley said.

Finn clapped him on the back. "I know. I feel the same way about you."

Eight

SOPHIA WOKE EARLY THE NEXT DAY, DESPITE MARGARET'S
grumblings about having been kept up all night and
then being expected to rise at the crack of dawn.

"And I returned His Grace's clothing to his valet,"
Margaret said, her voice full of censure. "Though I've
no idea why you ended up in his clothing at all." She
sniffed with disdain.

Sophia rolled her eyes. "I didn't end up in his clothing."

"Then it was my imagination that you were
wrapped up in his dressing gown this morning?"
Margaret snorted. "I thought Simmons was going to
kiss me when I returned it, he was that excited. It was
all I could do to evade the man's grasp. He has an
affinity for the duke's clothing."

"Perhaps he takes *his* job seriously?" Sophia taunted.
Margaret had been with Sophia's family since long
before Sophia was born. She had been her mother's
maid at one time, though Margaret never spoke of her.
Servants in their land were different from servants in
England. They took much more liberty and weren't
held to societal standards.

"He certainly takes the duke's clothing seriously. You'd think the man had spun the threads himself."

"I don't think men here do that sort of thing," Sophia said absently, as she appraised the upsweep Margaret was making of her hair. She'd left just enough trailing to tickle Sophia's neck. But the rest was piled atop her head in an artful arrangement. One Sophia would surely ruin as soon as she left the room.

"Are you certain I can't wear it down?" Sophia pressed lightly on the tips of her pointy ears to ensure they were hidden in the mass of hair. The duke would get quite a surprise if he noticed that particular trait. It was one of the only pieces of evidence that marked her as fae.

Margaret batted at her hands. "No one can see them. So, stop your fussing. I know you'd rather wear it down, but you can't go out looking like a gypsy, no matter how much you'd like to," Margaret warned. "The duke wouldn't like having another hoyden under his roof."

"Another?" Sophia turned to face Margaret. "Who's the other?"

"His daughter, from what I hear below stairs. She's quite a bit untamable." Margaret poked at Sophia's curls and grimaced. "A lot like your hair."

"I sincerely doubt anyone will be up at this hour," Sophia said with a toss of her head, which threatened to dislodge her coiffure. She patted at the tightly restrained curls. They'd be down around her shoulders within an hour. At least then she wouldn't have to worry about her ears.

"His Grace has breakfast every morning with his

daughter around this time, before he goes riding," Margaret said cryptically.

Sophia had planned to spend the morning snooping. But if Lady Anne was up and about, and the duke would be going out, she might be able to spend some time with the girl instead. "Thank you for the information." She pulled on her gloves and started for the door. "You haven't seen Ronald lurking about, have you?"

Margaret just shook her head. But then she sobered and looked at Sophia with all seriousness. "Be careful, miss," she said.

Sophia started down the corridor toward the common rooms downstairs. Her grandmother would still be in bed, since she'd spent most of the evening gambling with the dowager duchess. But if she hurried, Sophia might be able to catch Lady Anne once her father left. She felt a bit like a thief lingering in the shadows as she waited for some sign that the duke had left the area.

The clearing of a throat caught her attention. "If you'd like lessons on how to lurk about without being seen, I'll see if my brother is available," the voice said. Sophia spun to face it, only to find a tall man with sandy hair, who looked remarkably like the duke but much lighter complexioned. His brother, if she had to wager.

Sophia patted the hair over her ears, ensuring the tips were still hidden. This man would notice, otherwise. "I won an award once for lurking. I'm just a little out of practice."

His amber gaze walked lazily up and down her body, which made her feel decidedly uncomfortable.

She shifted her stance. "You look like you might be good at subterfuge," he acknowledged, his voice full of skepticism. People usually liked her. From the start. They never doubted her motives.

"Perhaps there's a future for me in professional lurking. It seems to be working for you." She arched a playful brow at him. It probably would be best if the duke's brother liked her, at least a little.

"I took you for a professional. But a professional *what* is the question." He let his voice trail off.

Sophia squared her shoulders, fully prepared to give him a piece of her mind. Things happened when she got angry. And they weren't always good things. In fact, they rarely were.

"You don't like me, do you?" he asked as he leaned casually against a doorjamb.

"I wouldn't say that." She could easily loathe him, particularly if he stood between her and completing her mission.

"Shall I go ahead and point out the elephant in the room? Or shall we continue to dance around him and pretend he's not here?"

"You needn't compare me to an elephant, my lord. An ode to my beauty would please me so much more." She smiled broadly at his taken-aback expression.

"Score one for Miss Thorne," he said with a low whistle.

She made a big circle with her thumb and fore-finger. "Score zero for the duke's... brother?" she hesitated and then asked. She held out her hand to him. Perhaps she should make more of an effort. "Sophia Thorne, my lord."

He didn't bother to give her his name as he took her hand and bowed over it.

"I would say it has been nice to meet you," Sophia began. And she couldn't stop herself. "But I'd be lying." Goodness, that was probably the wrong thing to say.

"Practice makes perfect, Miss Thorne?" he asked.

"Practice makes proficient," she corrected. "Yet I didn't carry that one off very well, did I?"

"No, you quite adequately let me know how you feel about me."

"As did you," she replied. "Though I've no idea why you disliked me at first sight."

"It's not that I don't like you. It's that I don't trust you."

"Are you so distrustful of everyone you meet? Or just ladies?"

"Is that what you are, Miss Thorne? A lady?"

"I do try," she replied drily.

He leaned toward her as though to tell her a conspirator's secret. "I do not allow anyone to hurt him, Miss Thorne. So, if your intentions with my brother are not honorable, I'd suggest you stop them now."

Sophia whispered dramatically back at him. "And what if he likes my dishonorable intentions? Shall we have him tell me that he doesn't appreciate them?" She pointed toward the breakfast room where she knew he was behind the closed door. "We can ask him if he likes my attention or your protectiveness more." She took a step toward the door. "Are you coming?" She turned back to look at him. "Or are you afraid of what he'll say?"

When he didn't answer, she continued, fully irate and worried that her face was flushed scarlet. But she didn't truly care. Real ladies didn't get angry, did they? Good grief, she was messing this all up. She rubbed at her forehead.

"I will find out all about you, Miss Thorne. I'm very good at it."

He would only find out her past if he could find the land of the fae, and that was blasted near impossible. Even she couldn't find the portal without her dust. Much less get past the fish.

"Good luck with that, my lord," she said and she inserted herself directly into the room where the duke dined alone with his daughter. His footmen moved to block her path, but she paid them no heed.

Ashley jumped to his feet, wiping his mouth quickly with his napkin. "Miss Thorne," he choked. He looked over her shoulder toward his brother, who she knew stood scowling from the doorway. "What's going on?" he asked.

Sophia picked up a biscuit from the sideboard and took a healthy bite. She chewed for a moment and then said, "Your brother distrusts me."

"He told you that?" the duke barked as he shot his brother a look. The duke's brother just shrugged as though he didn't care. Ashley cleared his throat. "I'm very sorry if he offered you any slight."

"Oh, he didn't offend me. I find him to be quite amusing."

Now it was the offending brother's face that turned red.

"Amusing, Miss Thorne?" Ashley asked.

She laid a hand on his sleeve. "Could you ask him to go away so I can join you for breakfast? I'd rather not eat with him breathing down my neck like a bloodhound."

"Well, that's not very nice," his brother protested.

"True," Sophia sighed. "It's a terrible comparison for the hounds." She looked up into Ashley's still-startled face. "May I join you for breakfast?"

At Ashley's nod, a servant rushed forward and pulled out chair for her. She perched delicately on it. "Good morning, Lady Anne," she said to the grinning girl.

"Yes, it is," the duke murmured.

❧

Ashley filled a plate for her himself, trying to still his racing heart. He waved a servant away when he moved to take over the chore; Ashley needed a moment to compose himself before he faced her. At least he hoped he would be able to rid his face of the shock he felt all the way to his toes. He couldn't immediately discern whether he was more surprised by the sight of her or the look on his brother's face as she took him to task. First his daughter, now his meddlesome brother. She was a formidable creature, even if she was tiny. He let his gaze roam up and down her body as he placed a plate in front of her.

"One might think you have plans for something other than breakfast, Your Grace, with the way you're appraising my person," she murmured quietly to him. Good God. Did the woman ever have a thought that didn't rush out of her mouth like a team of runaway horses? He was starting to doubt it.

"My father doesn't gobble ladies up in one bite," Lady Anne said primly.

Sophia smiled a most cheeky grin at his daughter. One that made Ashley want to smile along with her. "So, I've heard," the lady remarked as she spread jam on a piece of toast. Then she glanced back over her shoulder at his brother, who still gawked from the doorway. "Do you think he'll stand sentinel over you all day? Or only until I leave?"

Probably the entire day. "Do you need something, Finn?" Ashley asked him.

"I need to speak with you," his brother said, his tone crisp enough to make the air in the room crackle.

"Can it wait until after breakfast?"

"That depends on how long you linger over breakfast," Finn said, glancing at his watch fob as though he had somewhere to be.

Ashley pointed toward a vacant chair with the tines of his fork. "Either take a seat or vacate the room. You make me nervous standing there."

"It wasn't you I'd hoped to make nervous," Finn said sarcastically. Sarcasm wasn't nearly as pretty on a man as it was on a sprightly young lady.

"Well, it appears as though you've failed with her, too," Ashley lamented.

"Quite," Sophia said between bites. She relished her food almost as much as she relished the verbal sparring with his brother, apparently. He could sit and watch her eat all day. He wondered if she did everything with such passion. Such thoughts would only get him in trouble.

"Come and see me later, Finn?" Ashley suggested.

"Will she be with you later?" Finn grumbled.

"Only if I'm lucky," Ashley muttered to himself. And she apparently heard him, because she smiled. It was a smile that could knock a grown man to his knees. Blast and damn. She knew how much she affected him.

Finn bowed quickly and backed out of the room.

"Care to tell me what that was about?"

"Lurking," she said around a mouthful of baked eggs.

"He was lurking?" Ashley asked.

"No. I was."

She was lurking? Why did Ashley feel as though he was missing something? "And was there a reason for your lurking?"

She shrugged her little shoulders. "I wanted to see you," she said with no apparent premeditation.

Ashley's heart lurched.

"I'm sorry I interrupted your quiet breakfast," she said, wincing a little, as though she expected him to chastise her.

"I'm not," he said with no thought at all. The grin he got in response was worth the discomfort his pride suffered. Damn, but he was a novice at flirting. It had been much too long.

Her gloved hand landed on top of his, the warmth seeping into him like the rays of the sun in his garden. "Thank you for playing for me last night," she said quietly.

Ashley glanced at his daughter. But she was staring out the window at a butterfly that had landed on the bush just outside. She paid them no attention at all. "You're welcome." He wanted to slap his own forehead. *You're welcome* was about the most inane comment he could have come up with. He wanted to beg her to visit him again in the darkest hours of the night. To plead with her to show him her favor.

He turned his hand over so that his cupped hers. She didn't draw back. She didn't shrink from him. She didn't recoil. She smiled and gave him a gentle squeeze. Damn, he loved that smile. He would do just about anything to provoke it. Yet he had to do nothing, which made it even sweeter.

Anne turned away from the window and looked at them both. Sophia very gently tugged her hand from his grasp and laid it on the table beside his. "Did it fly away?" she asked absently of Anne.

His heart? It certainly felt like it.

"No, it's still there," Anne said with a heavy sigh.

Sophia's forehead scrunched up as she appraised his daughter. "Is something wrong, Lady Anne?"

"Not really," Anne said with another sigh. "I'm supposed to attend Grandmother today while she embroiders."

"Well, that sounds like it will be entertaining," Ashley began. At least his mother was making an attempt to interact with his daughter.

"Sounds like drudgery to me," Sophia interjected.

His daughter smiled. And it was a genuine smile, one that looked like it suppressed laughter. She covered her mouth. "You're amusing, Miss Thorne," Anne said as she wiggled her feet so quickly she bounced in her chair. His mother would be mortified. Ashley was delighted. His daughter was giddy, and that was a good thing. And all because the little slip of a lady called Miss Sophia Thorne made her laugh.

"You don't like embroidery, Miss Thorne?" Ashley asked of her.

She opened her mouth to speak, but then closed it quickly. So, she did have some filters. "I'm certain your grandmother has a good reason for teaching you to embroider." She cast Ashley a smile that made his heart do that little fluttery thing again. Damn her. "And I do like to look at beautiful embroidery. I've seen artistry in some pieces my grandmother's friends have made." She shrugged.

"I've just never had enough patience to sit and do it myself. Pushing and pulling a piece of string through a piece of cloth and forming designs? It's not for me. But I have a great deal of respect for people who can do it. Perhaps you'll be someone who excels at it, Lady Anne." She laughed. "Or perhaps you'll find it as tedious as I do. We shall see." She raised her eyebrows playfully at Anne. Her gaze roamed over his daughter's face. "That's a lovely pink ribbon you have in your hair. Did the tooth faerie leave it?"

Anne preened under her appraisal. "Yes."

"How did you know about the tooth faerie?" Ashley couldn't help but ask. It wasn't a legend in England, and very few people he knew had heard of such a myth.

Sophia pointed at his daughter's mouth. "The missing tooth gave it away," she said with a grin. His daughter sorted through her hair until she could run the silky ribbon through her fingertips. "You're a fortunate girl," Sophia went on to say.

There was nothing fortunate about his daughter's life thus far. But Ashley would love to change that.

"I wish I had a ribbon like that," Sophia said with a tiny sigh.

He'd buy her a boatload of ribbons if it would make her smile. "How unfortunate that you've lost all your baby teeth," Ashley said to her. "Or perhaps the tooth faerie would leave one for you."

"Oh, I sincerely doubt that. They hate my kind." Then she bit her lip as though she'd just said something she'd intended to keep to herself.

"Your kind?" he asked.

Sophia smiled at his daughter. "What do you plan to do today, Lady Anne? Aside from learning to embroider?"

Anne looked toward him with a questioning glance.

"The reason I ask is that I considered walking to the village today," Sophia rushed on to say. "I was going to ask if you'd like to join me." She glanced quickly at Ashley. "If it's all right with your father, of course."

"If you need something from the village, we can send a servant," Ashley interjected. There was no reason for her to walk all that way.

"I like to walk," Sophia said with a smile.

"People are not always kind," Ashley said quietly. In fact, they could be downright mean. To both him and to his daughter. Ashley did all he could to spare her from that. When they took walks to the park, people were respectful, if reserved. But even then children said cruel things behind their hands.

"Then we shall have to teach them a thing or two about kindness," Sophia said with a grin. Then she waggled her eyebrows playfully. "Or else we can invade your father's garden and race around in the sunshine."

"The sun is bad for the skin," Anne said as she patted her porcelain face.

"Oh, posh," Sophia said with a breezy wave of her hand. "Nothing feels better than the sun on your skin." She laid her head back and gazed up at the ceiling, as though the sun's rays already danced across her face.

"I'll get freckles," Anne complained.

"One can certainly hope so," Sophia said, lifting her head to look at Anne. "But if you'd rather embroider," she said slowly, watching Anne's face.

"I'd rather take in the sun," Anne declared.

"You'll need to ask for your grandmother's leave," Sophia said. She looked at Ashley with a questioning glance. "Do you think she'll mind?"

Something told him she wouldn't. She would probably be glad to be rid of Anne for the day. "We can certainly ask." He laid his napkin beside his plate and said, "A morning frolicking in the garden. I can't think of anything I'd enjoy more." Aside from undressing Sophia piece by piece. But he doubted that would come to pass.

"Did we invite your father?" Sophia whispered loudly to Anne.

Anne giggled. "I don't recall inviting him."

"Regrettably, Your Grace, you will be unable to attend unless you can secure a formal invitation to our party."

"A formal invitation, you say?" Why did that sound like a challenge?

"I heard the hostess accepts bribes," she said with a grin.

Which hostess? His daughter or Sophia? For some reason, he relished the idea of finding a bribe that would favor Sophia. She may as well have waved a red flag before a bull as to offer such a challenge to him. He never backed down from a challenge. And he certainly wouldn't start now.

Nine

SOPHIA BRUSHED HER HAND ACROSS THE SMALL tabletop and then instructed the servant to leave the tray in the sunshine. Perfect. It was perfect. She glanced around the garden. His Grace's sanctuary truly was beautiful, and she could understand why he valued it the way he did. It overflowed with peace and harmony. It reminded her of home, only there was no magic at play. Or at least none that she could see.

"You should not be here," a voice called out from the nearby shrubbery. Sophia groaned to herself. Ronald. Of course, Ronald would show up, right when Lady Anne was supposed to arrive. Sophia only wanted a few moments alone with her. Why was it so blasted difficult to get some time with the child? She'd never unlock her secrets if she couldn't talk with the girl, would she?

Ronald shoved some shrubbery to the side and stuck his bald little head through the opening. Well, not completely bald. He had a tiny tuft of red hair on the top of his head that stood at an odd angle. It always made Sophia want to brush it flat with the palm of her hand. But heaven forbid she should touch him. He would never allow that. He liked to judge from afar and not be judged back.

"Gorgeous day, isn't it?" she chimed at him as she settled onto a bench. The servant had already exited the garden, and Anne wasn't due to arrive for a few more minutes.

Ronald climbed through the hole in the shrubbery until he was fully on her side, out in the open. Then he began to pace and wring his hands. "Given a lot of thought to your situation," he began. Then he repeated himself. "Given a lot of thought to it. Yes, I did." He paced back and forth, shaking his head as he did so. "Lots and lots of thought."

Sophia crossed her arms over her chest and glared at him. But he just continued to pace. Then he turned and shook his forefinger at her. "Wings. Wings. You need pure-colored wings, I tell you," he said.

Sophia sighed heavily. "My wings are still the color of my skin, Ronald. I promise." She made an X over her heart. "Cross my heart."

"They won't be for long. Mark my words. He lusts for you."

"Why are you here, Ronald?" Sophia leaned forward so she could look into his face.

Ronald held his hands out to his sides as though the answer was all around them. "Who else would take care of you? You left without a word to anyone. Without even waiting for the full moon." He narrowed his eyes at her. "What did it take for you to bribe the fish?"

That was neither here nor there. She'd gotten

through the portal. That was what mattered. "That's not your concern."

He narrowed his eyes at her. "Not my concern? *Not my concern?*" His voice got louder and louder.

She hushed him by placing a finger over her lips. "Someone will hear you."

"Not my concern?" he mouthed at her.

"I didn't ask you to follow me." In fact, she'd left with her grandmother in the dead of night just to prevent him from following.

"I can't believe your grandmother allowed this." He continued to shake his head.

Encouraged it, was more like it.

"She has always been tied to this world in a way she shouldn't be," he said.

"What does that mean?" Sophia gasped. But then she heard the door to the garden open behind her. She glanced over her shoulder and saw Lady Anne headed her way. And she towed her father by the hand. So much for speaking to the girl alone. "Go," Sophia whispered to Ronald.

He slipped back into the foliage as though he'd never been there. But not before shooting her a look that said how displeased he was with her. And how much more he'd love to say. She'd ask him to explain his comments about her grandmother the next time he came to berate her for the duke's lustiness, which she'd seen not a hint of. Not yet.

"Good morning, Miss Thorne," Lady Anne said with a quick curtsy.

"I see you brought your father." The duke took Sophia's hand and raised it to his lips, which made her heart flip over in her chest. His eyes twinkled at her, as though he knew how he made her feel. Did he?

His lips were soft and firm against her skin. His breath brushed across her knuckles like a warm wind that made her want to shiver. Then he lifted his head and said, "Brilliant deduction, Miss Thorne."

She inclined her head at him. "I suppose you were able to secure an invitation." She glanced quickly at Anne, who danced in place.

"I invited him," the girl chirped.

"What did he do to deserve the invitation?" Sophia asked.

"He asked me very nicely," the girl said. Then she turned and dashed down the garden path out of sight.

❧

Miss Thorne turned to him with her eyebrows raised, and Ashley couldn't help but think about how much he wanted to kiss her. "Where is she going?" she asked.

"I sent her on a treasure hunt," he said as he shrugged his shoulders. *I wanted to be alone with you more than I wanted my next breath.*

"A treasure hunt?" She looked up at him with the most beautiful smile he'd ever seen. "Do I get to play?"

"Do you want to play?" He hadn't hidden anything for her. Should he have? "I came out earlier and hid some things for her to find."

Sophia's face fell. "Oh," she said.

"I'm sorry. I had no idea you'd be interested in hunting for treasure." He'd never make that mistake again.

"Doesn't everyone love looking for treasure?" She looked perplexed.

He motioned toward a nearby bench. "Sit with me for a moment?" he asked.

Sophia reached for the strings of her bonnet and gave them a tug. The silk made a slow whisper as she tugged, soft as the wind. She stopped. "Do you mind if I get comfortable?" she asked.

She could disrobe if she wanted. "Allow me to help?" he asked as he brushed her hands to the side and ran his fingertip beneath her chin, then tugged the strings free. He lifted the bonnet from atop her head and laid it on the table nearby.

"Much better," she sighed as she shook her curls slightly and turned her face up toward the sun.

"Lovely," he murmured.

"It is a beautiful day, isn't it?" she asked as she sat down on the bench. He settled beside her. He wasn't referring to the pretty day. Not at all.

"You're not concerned about the sun?"

She suddenly looked startled. "Should I be?" She pointed to her nose. "You don't like my freckles?" Then she grinned. A grin that nearly split his heart in two.

Impulsively, he learned forward and placed a quick kiss to the tip of her nose. "I think your freckles are lovely."

"They're not normal in your society, are they?" she said with a grimace.

"Neither are you, Miss Thorne," he replied gently. Thank God she wasn't the stereotypical society lady.

"I regret that I can't be more socially acceptable."

He thought she was perfect just the way she was. "I'm a bit of a pariah, myself. So, I certainly can't judge your acceptability." He took a deep breath for fortification. Then rushed on. "In fact, your reputation could be torn to shreds just by being in my company."

Her face softened and she reached for his hand. She couldn't have surprised him more if she'd grown two heads. He turned his hand over and gripped hers. Probably too tightly. But she didn't draw back. "I'll take my chances," she said. She looked up toward the sun and inhaled deeply. Then she faced him. "Tell me your story, Ashley," she said.

He tried to draw his hand back, but she squeezed it tightly. He looked deeply into her eyes. Was she real? Was she a figment of his imagination? His dreams? His wants? Was she an apparition? Would she disappear just as soon as he got used to having her around? Probably.

"I don't want to know the rumors. I want to know about you," she said. "You're known for being a recluse."

"I appreciate my privacy."

"Your daughter is delightful."

"You're the only one who thinks so," he said with a laugh. "Aside from me, that is."

"You were never formally accused of killing your wife." She looked up at him from beneath her heavy lashes.

"No, I wasn't." This time he did draw his hand back. He used it to smooth his trousers.

"But you may as well have been."

"Probably," he said cryptically. He narrowed his eyes at her. "Don't you want to ask if I did it?"

"No." That's all she said. Just no? He didn't expound upon it.

She jumped to her feet and started down the

garden path. "Where are you going?" he called to her retreating back.

She spun to face him and spun back all in one big breath. "To see how Anne fares on her treasure hunt," she said mid-spin.

She brought up the subject of his dead wife and wanted to know nothing about it? Everyone wanted to know about it. It was all people talked about. Ashley jumped to his feet and rushed after her. He caught her hand. "Will you come and visit me tonight?" he asked anxiously as he drew her hand up to his mouth. He probably looked like an overeager puppy. But he didn't care.

"Will you be playing?" she asked, her mouth lifting in a grin that was absolutely adorable.

A smile tugged at his own lips. He'd done without a smile for so many years; it seemed foreign to feel so lighthearted all of a sudden. "Does it matter?" he asked. How did his playing of the pianoforte figure into her decision?

"If you're playing, I'll have little choice in the matter," she said. Then she darted in the direction Anne had gone, and he had to run to keep up with her.

He'd be playing. For damn certain, he'd be playing.

Ten

SOPHIA DARTED IN THE DIRECTION ANNE HAD GONE, hoping the duke wouldn't follow. But she could hear his footsteps pounding behind her. She'd never get time alone with the child if he didn't allow it. But she had to admit that she enjoyed spending time with him. In fact, she more than enjoyed it; she relished it.

She'd never met a man who'd made her forget her mission. Who made her want to conform to his world. Who made her want to be more to him than a faerie who would heal them all and then disappear. She shook the thoughts away. They would get her nowhere. She couldn't live in this world. She simply could not. *Unpardonable Error Number Five: Never, ever fall in love with a human.*

When she rounded the corner, she found Anne in a fit of tears on a bench. Her list was torn into small pieces that littered the ground. Sophia turned to Ashley and raised a brow. He mouthed "temper tantrum" at her and started toward his daughter. But Sophia held up a hand to stop him. He paused, imitated her brow raise, and motioned with his hand for them to continue. But something told Sophia he wouldn't wait too long to take the situation in hand. His hand probably involved tossing Anne over his shoulder and delivering her to her chambers. To her nurse. That was the last thing the girl needed.

"It's regrettable that the treasure hunt has ended so abruptly. I had so looked forward to it," Sophia said absently. Then she turned to walk back down the path the way she'd come. She motioned for Ashley to follow.

"Where are you going?" Anne sobbed out.

Sophia turned back only briefly to say, "I had anticipated a treasure hunt. But all I see is a beastly little girl who's throwing a fit. I can find better entertainment elsewhere."

Anne jumped to her feet and screamed at the top of her lungs, her face turning redder than anyone Sophia had ever seen in a temper-fit before. "I can't find anything on the list!" She stamped her foot so hard it made Sophia want to wince for her.

Sophia looked down at the scattered remains of the list Ashley had given her. He watched, his expression slightly amused while Anne wasn't looking. Did he think she would be taken down by a little girl? A faerie? Taken down by a mere slip of a human? She'd faced spiders, for God's sake. Not very likely. "No one can find anything on the list once it has been torn to pieces." Sophia reached for Ashley's elbow and slid her arm inside. "Will you escort me back to the house, Your Grace? It appears as though your daughter is bound for embroidery."

"Absolutely," he murmured as he turned to walk back toward the house.

"But what about me?" Anne said from behind them.

"Messes are not allowed in my garden. A fact of which you are well aware of, Anne." He nodded toward the remains. "Clean it up and go find your grandmother." Then he walked back toward the garden door with Sophia in tow.

"Did I do all right?" he murmured at her, dipping his head only slightly.

"You did beautifully," she whispered back, afraid she was probably much too happy about the current state of events. "You place too much importance on her attitude. And not enough on the detriment she causes to herself with her tantrums."

"You speak as though you've experience with children, Sophie." *Sophie, not Sophia.*

She had plenty of experience with children. She couldn't explain it to him. But he was the first person who'd ever made her want to. That was saying something, wasn't it? "Some," she said with a shrug. "Now she doesn't get to hunt for treasure at all." She nudged him by leaning into him. "What would you have done if I hadn't been there? Delivered her back to her nurse?"

He thought about it a moment. "Probably. But then she would have gotten my attention, no matter whether it was good or bad. And that was probably her goal all along?"

"Precisely," Sophia said. "In fact, I bet she's so awed by your lack of concern over her actions that she's planning to fix it."

Just then, Anne raced around them, clutching the pieces in her hand. "I can put it back together," she said breathlessly, looking more than a little uncertain about her approach.

"Put back together the party?" Ashley asked. "After your tantrum, I highly doubt you can rekindle the spirit with which the party was intended."

Sophia squeezed his arm. He looked down at her briefly. Then he took a deep breath and said, "But I suppose you can try."

Lady Anne crossed to the table and began to restore the torn parchment. She pressed it flat with her fingertips. But as she began to put the pieces together, her brow furrowed.

"Should I go and help her?" Ashley murmured.

"No. She should clean up her own messes," Sophia stated clearly. She firmly believed it. And hoped he saw the value of it. The value of her.

When Anne had them assembled appropriately, she called to her father. "Can you help me find the treasures?"

Since she hadn't called to Sophia, she didn't respond. But she nudged Ashley. He approached and peered over his daughter's shoulder. "Read what it says," he prompted.

She began hesitantly, whispering the words to herself very quietly. She turned the paper slightly, peering across a torn section. She looked toward the duke. "My eyes are blue."

"They are," he affirmed. "Just like mine." He tweaked her nose. "You look a lot like your mother. But some things you got from me."

She grinned broadly at him before she dashed off into the garden.

"I wrote a riddle about her eyes," Ashley explained,

before he took a deep breath and faced Sophia. "Thank you," he said. His blue eyes danced everywhere but on her face. Then his eyes met hers. "For handling my daughter. I don't know how you did it."

"I didn't," she said. "You did."

His eyes did that little dance again, looking everywhere but at her. He was adorable when he was feeling unsure.

"What can I do to repay you?"

Sophia tapped her chin and wondered aloud, "What can you do to repay me?" she crooned. "Anything?"

He smiled broadly. "Within reason."

"Join the party for dinner tonight," she blurted without even thinking.

He did that eyebrow raise again. "Me?" His hand flattened on his chest. "I do not partake of house-party festivities."

"Why ever not?"

❧

Because doing so would make his mother much too happy. "I just don't," he said instead. "No one really expects me to." He glanced toward where Anne had disappeared. She would return soon; hopefully with a tiny skein of blue embroidery thread in her hand. Her treasure.

Sophia sat down on a bench and smoothed her skirts with her hand. "Then I shall expect you to."

"Permit me to be blunt, Sophia?" he asked as he sat down beside her. He stretched his long legs out in front of him and rested one arm behind her along the back of the bench. He wanted more than anything for her to lean in to him, to nestle herself in that little spot where his arm met his shoulder. He shook the thoughts away. They would get him nowhere.

"I'd ask no less of you."

"When hell freezes over, I'll attend my mother's house party. And I sincerely doubt that will happen before the week is out." He reached out a hand to adjust the collar of her dress at her shoulder. Then pulled it back with a grimace. "Apologies," he murmured.

"For?" she asked, her delicate little brows drawing together.

"I find myself feeling much too familiar toward you at times. I take liberties I shouldn't." He lowered his arm from behind her and clutched his hands together in his lap. All the better to keep from touching her.

"One might think the lady would get some say over what liberties you can and cannot take. Did you hear me complain?" She laughed lightly.

"I could get used to having you around, Sophie," he finally admitted on a heavy sigh.

"That is not a good thing," she said, finally looking a little chagrined. "For we all know I cannot stay in your life. Here for a moment," she said, looking around the garden. "Gone the next."

Something told him it wouldn't be that easy. She was making a mark in his life. One that wasn't entirely comfortable. But a mark, none the less. And he liked it. "What if I told you that I want you to stay?" he asked. He wanted to bite the words back as soon as he said them. But he left them hanging there in the air, instead. Like a palpable living, breathing thing.

She reached out her delicate little hand to touch

his cheek. "I would have to say no," she said softly. "Don't ask me why."

He leapt to his feet. "I know why," he said as he began to pace. It was difficult to keep the words from flowing. From pouring out his heart and soul. He hadn't met a single person that he'd wanted to spill his soul to. Not until her. Not until now.

"No, you don't," she said. "You think you know. But you have no idea about my own reservations."

"You don't want to live with my past in your face any more than I do," he spit out.

"Your past does not frighten me," she said, her voice rising.

Anne dashed around the corner, her face lit with joy, holding her prize in the air. Sophia looked as composed as she ever did as she motioned Anne near her to see her treasure. "Can you hold it for me?" he heard Anne ask. "I think I know where the rest of it is." His daughter dashed back into the garden.

"Ashley," Sophia began hesitantly.

He held up a hand to stop her. "I'm wishing for things I can't have." He hated feeling like this. It was so... foreign. He hadn't wanted anything in a very long time.

"So am I," she said quietly.

What the devil did that mean? She could have him. She could have him begging at her feet with a toss of her hair. With a glint of her eye. With absolutely nothing at all, aside from that smile. That beautiful, beautiful smile that made him want to kiss her.

"There are things about me that you don't know," she said softly.

He harrumphed. That was the story of his life. No one knew the real him. They knew the dangerous duke. But no one knew what was in his heart. Or that he even had a heart. That he wanted. Good God, he wanted. He wanted her. "I want to learn all about you," he said.

"That's just it, Ashley. I'm here on a mission. And when it's complete, I have to go."

Again with the mission?

"My kind cannot mix with your kind. Not the way you'd like—the way I'd like as well."

Was this about wealth? "Are you poor?"

"No." The truth was there in her eyes. He believed her.

"Illegitimate?"

"Not that I'm aware of."

"Is there some scandal in your past?"

"Yes, but that's neither here nor there."

Neither here nor there? "What does that mean?"

"It means that you and I would never suit," she stated bluntly. "But I want to help you."

"I'll not be your charity case," he said, realizing immediately that his voice was too sharp when her face fell.

"You're not charity. You're my mission. My meaning in life. Don't you see?"

No. He didn't see anything.

Just then, Anne ran back into the clearing. "I found it," she cried. She held out a silver hand mirror. It had been her mother's at one point and he'd thought she might like to have it. She looked overjoyed.

Sophia bent to look at her treasure, cooing over it as

though it was the most bountiful of prizes. He could see their faces close together in the reflection of the mirror. The two of them there with their heads together. They were the prize. They were what he wanted. He realized right then and there. Despite her protests. Despite her affirmation that they would not suit. There was no doubt in his mind that they would suit. He was certain of it. They would suit in all the right ways. And if they didn't, at least he could say he tried.

He pulled out his watch fob and glanced at it. He had a lot to do.

"Do you have somewhere to be?" Sophia asked with an impish grin.

"I do, actually," he said as he sat down on the bench. He couldn't keep the grin off his face. She was in his life for a reason. Now he just had to find the stones to take advantage of it.

Eleven

"It simply wouldn't do to be late to dinner," Margaret had warned. But had she listened? No. She'd lingered much too long in the garden with Ashley and Anne. But she'd had such a great time that she couldn't leave until Anne had found all of her treasures. There were only three, one of which was the mirror. Sophia would bet it held some significance aside from the benefit one received by looking into it.

Anne had also found the blue thread, which matched her father's eyes perfectly. And she'd also found a small pincushion with sewing needles. She hadn't been overjoyed with the last, but Sophia had a feeling that would change with her father's attention.

"Are you enjoying the house party, my dear?" a big booming voice said from beside her. Sophia glanced to her left, only to find a hunchbacked old woman who held an ear trumpet up to her left ear. She leaned closer to Sophia as she waited for her to speak. "Speak up, child," she said, her eyebrows drawing together when Sophia's tongue refused to work.

Should she yell back at her? Should she speak

quietly and hope she could hear? Sophia glanced toward her grandmother, but she was at the opposite end of the dinner table.

A voice boomed from the other side of the table. "Cat's got her tongue, Grandmother," the man said loudly. "First time I've ever seen you speechless, Miss Thorne," Lord Phineas said, raising his glass in a mocking toast. "I find I quite like it," he said more quietly. But not quietly enough that everyone at the table couldn't hear him. Snickers bounced from one side of the table to the other.

"Don't get used to it, my lord," she said sweetly as she raised her glass to him and took a sip. Then she turned to the woman who'd originally spoken and said, "I'm enjoying the party very much. Thank you for asking."

"Eh?" the old lady grunted, leaning toward Sophia.

But Lord Phineas leaned toward his grandmother and said, "She said thanks for asking, Grandmother."

The lady held out her glass. "You've a flask, young man? Why didn't you say so?" She shook her empty glass at him. "I could use a nip."

Lord Phineas reached into his coat pocket, pulled out a small silver flask, glanced down the table toward where his mother sat, and poured some amber liquid into his grandmother's glass. "Bottoms up, Grams," he said with a chuckle.

Sophia leaned toward him. "Should she be drinking?" she hissed.

He shrugged. "The more she drinks, the better she hears," he said beneath his breath. "She swears a little more, too, but people are used to that. It's better than the yelling."

Sophia bit back a snort. He motioned toward his pocket and arched a brow. "Would you like a nip?"

She definitely needed her wits about her. "No, thank you. I believe I'll pass this time."

"Afraid you'll lose your inhibitions?" he taunted.

"You're assuming I have some?" she retorted.

"I try not to assume anything where you're concerned, Miss Thorne," he said.

"Much safer that way," she tossed back. This verbal sparring was jarring to the soul. She stiffened her spine and narrowed her eyes at him. "I do wish you'd tell me how you feel about me, my lord. All this fawning you do when you're in my presence could give me the false impression that you like me."

He grinned. Then he raised that big booming voice again and addressed his grandmother. "Have you met Miss Thorne, Grams?"

She raised the trumpet back up to her ear. "What are you mourning, dear boy?" she asked of Lord Phineas. "Not that mistress again?" She said the last very loudly, and a low hum began around the table. "She had horse teeth and a big nose. And couldn't keep her legs closed if you paid her."

"Mother," the dowager duchess hissed from the end of the table.

"I knew her mother, if you must know. And her skirt was just as light." She took a sip of the drink he'd sneaked to her. Something told Sophia he would regret that. "Find another one to flip on her back and you'll be over her in no time."

"Grams," Lord Phineas said. "Must you be so loud?" His face was a bit flushed and he looked as though he'd had a nip too many, even though Sophia hadn't seen him take a single drink.

"You're the one who was talking about being in mourning. If you don't want your dirty laundry to be aired, don't hang it on the line." She leaned toward Sophia. "What's your name, dear?"

"Sophia," she croaked. She was about to add her surname, but Sophia was afraid it would spark more conversations about the lightskirt.

The dowager duchess motioned toward Sophia with her thumb. "Why can't you find a lady of quality like this one? Settle down and have a family. Between you and Robin, you'd think we'd have a house full of great-grandchildren by now." She narrowed her eyes at Lord Phineas. "The illegitimate ones don't count."

Lord Phineas wiggled uncomfortably in his seat. "I don't have any children, Grams. I promise."

"You should get to work on that. I'd like to see at least one boy child before I gasp my last breath. Girls are fine, but I prefer the ones with dangly parts."

Sophia choked. She couldn't help it. And Lord Phineas looked pleased by her reaction. "Something wrong, Miss Thorne?" he asked, his voice as sweet as syrup and just as smooth.

"Nothing," she gasped as she reached for her water glass.

"Mother, would you please temper your comments?" the dowager duchess barked from her seat.

The old lady waved her fork wildly in the air. "You act like you don't want to hear about dangly parts. Everyone's got them. Or at least a receptacle for them." She cackled loudly on the last.

Lady Hammersmith jumped to her feet, her lips pursed like she'd been sucking on a sour grape. She tossed her napkin onto her plate. "I don't have to listen to such poor conversation." She tapped her husband's arm. "Come along, Harold," she said. "Receptacles, indeed. I've never heard of such a vulgar thing."

"She's never heard of it?" the old lady cackled. "That must be why her husband always looks so irritated." She laughed so loudly that it made Sophia want to laugh with her. She covered her mouth, instead. The dowager duchess buried her face in her hands and groaned.

"I'm certain you're right," Lord Phineas said with a smirk.

"Eh?" the woman asked, raising her trumpet again.

"Never mind," the duke's brother said loudly. "We can discuss it later, Grams."

"I count on you to tell me all the details," she said with a wink toward his lordship.

"No problem, Grams." Lord Phineas winked back at her. If Sophia didn't know better, she might even like him.

Ashley's grandmother looked toward the head of the table where Ashley's seat sat open. "Where is that other grandson of mine?" she asked absently.

Lord Phineas arched a brow at Sophia. Damn his hide. "He's absent from the festivities, Grams. Like usual."

"That boy needs to get his head out of his arse and get back to business."

"His business acumen is not in question." Thank goodness Lord Phineas took up for him, because Sophia felt the need to do so.

His grandmother smacked the table. "The business of marriage and raising an heir."

Just then, a large voice boomed over all the others. Sophia nearly jumped from her skin when she heard it. "Do you normally speak of dangly parts and my need to breed over dinner?" the voice called from the doorway.

Sophia spun to face Ashley, who leaned casually in the door frame, his arms folded across his chest. He looked amazing. He was splendidly turned out in his evening clothes. An emerald winked from the center of his cravat. He gave a tug to his jacket and started across the room.

"Robin, what are you doing here?" his mother asked as everyone jumped to their feet. Sophia rose along with them, although she was finding it difficult to draw in a deep breath. A lock of hair fell across his forehead when his eyebrows drew together, and she wanted to brush it back for him. What a ridiculous thought.

"I'm having dinner," he said absently. Ashley snapped his fingers and held out his hand. It was almost immediately populated with a goblet of wine. He raised it high in the air. He cleared his throat, inhaled deeply, and said, "I'd like to make a toast."

Sophia reached for her glass and waited anxiously.

"Please do, Robin," his mother sputtered as she motioned for everyone to pick up their glasses.

"Here's to hell freezing over," he said with a straight face. Then he looked directly at Sophia and winked.

❧

"Robin, darling," Ashley's mother crooned. "So, happy you were able to join us," she said as he

motioned for everyone at the table to sit. They all
dropped into their chairs like stones. His mother
turned to the group. "Robin has been under the
weather, you see," she started.

He had? No, he hadn't.

"I explained to everyone when they arrived that
you were not feeling well, and that's why you were
not joining us." She blinked her icy eyes at him.

"It's quite unfortunate that you lied to everyone,
Mother," he said, his voice crisp even to his own
ears. But he refused to compound her lies with any of
his own. Nor would he ever. "I would have thought
better of you. You could have simply told everyone
how much I abhor crowded dinner tables and overstuffed sitting rooms." He clucked his tongue at her.
"Would have been much simpler. And it's not as
though I haven't taken blame for things before."

His mother's face drained of color.

"I hope you're all enjoying your stay," he said to
the table.

Anxious, worried gazes met his. Perhaps he'd been
a little too candid.

"Nice to see you, Robin," Finn said loudly. "And
so nice of you to bring all your parts so they can talk
about yours instead of mine." His brother raised his
glass at Ashley, then took a healthy swallow.

"I've been talked about for years," Ashley said with
a shrug. "It will be nothing new."

Sophia coughed delicately into her fist and said,
"May tonight be a night of new beginnings."

"To new beginnings," chimed the rest of the table.

Twelve

ASHLEY PACED FROM ONE SIDE OF HIS BEDCHAMBER TO the other. Perhaps he'd gone too far when he'd asked Sophia Thorne to visit him the dead of night, risking her reputation, her innocence, and her very life, if the rumors about his homicidal tendencies were true.

In the garden that afternoon, he'd nearly begged her to visit him under the cover of darkness. She'd agreed. Hadn't she? He tried to remember their conversation verbatim. But he'd been so enamored of the way the sunlight played across her hair that he'd probably missed half the words.

Come and visit me tonight?

Will you be playing?

What difference does that make?

If you're playing, I'll have little choice in the matter.

Those weren't the words exactly, but they were close. Yet it was well after midnight. All his mother's guests were safely ensconced in their chambers, or their neighbor's chambers, as the case might be with Finn. And Sophia hadn't arrived.

He stopped to gaze out his window and sighed

heavily. Was it his lot in life to be alone? Was it truly? He'd thought Sophia's arrival heralded the beginning of new things to come for him. He'd attended dinner, for God's sake. Dinner! With his mother and all of her friends. He'd labored through it with a smile on his face. Well, perhaps not a smile, but he'd been present. And he'd done it all for Sophia. She could probably snap her fingers at him and he'd drop to his knees to kiss her slippers—he was that enamored of her.

He groaned aloud. Enamored? Is that what this was? It was something he didn't understand at all. He was two-and-thirty. And he couldn't figure out what his infatuation was with Sophia Thorne. He felt like a green lad who'd had his first kiss. First kiss? Ashley hadn't even had the opportunity to kiss her yet. He could imagine the feel of her in his arms. The taste of her on his lips. He glanced absently around the room and wished she was there to brighten it.

His dressing gown lay draped across the bed. Ashley had run Simmons from the room almost as soon as he'd arrived. Ashley didn't want him to encounter Sophia when she finally did decide to grace him with her presence. He flopped heavily onto the piano bench and plucked lightly at the keys.

Dinner had been painful. His mother's guests all had held their tongues about matters of importance and discussed things like the scandalous clothing young ladies were wearing. It was dreadfully boring. Ashley would rather discuss politics. Or finance. Anything aside from fashion.

To top it all off, he'd been unable to draw his eyes from Sophia Thorne's person the entire night. He'd caught her looking back at him more than once, and not one time did she lower her gaze, shy away from his bold appraisal of her, or even flush when he let his eyes linger too long. She had simply smiled as though they shared a secret. Perhaps they did. Perhaps Sophia knew that Ashley was well and truly out of his league. Perhaps she was humoring an addled old idiot, making his heart and his loins swell with every bold glance she returned.

What if she was?

What if she did, indeed, feel nothing for him? He found that hard to fathom. But it was a possibility. Ashley clunked gently on the keys of the pianoforte. He let his fingers tickle the ivory keys. And it was only once he was engrossed in a song that he heard the door open behind him. His heart leapt into his throat as he turned his head and watched her glide into his room. She looked at him and smiled softly as she closed the door behind her. Into the lion's den goes the lamb.

She was dressed the same way she had been the last time she slipped into his room in the dead of night, in a virginal nightrail with puffy sleeves and a frilly collar. She walked toward him, gazing at the piano until he stopped playing and turned to look at her.

"I thought you'd never arrive," Ashley said hesitantly.

She laughed lightly. "I thought you'd never start playing." She looked down at her state of dress. "Oh, goodness. I've done it again," she said, shaking her head at herself as she drew her lower lip between her teeth and worried it absently.

"Done what again?" Ashley asked.

"I kept on my dress until only moments ago. Because I knew I'd be unable to resist you when you started to play. But then when you didn't, I finally gave up and went to bed." She rubbed the sleep from her eyes and yawned heavily.

"You went to sleep?"

She nodded as she walked closer and sat down on the piano bench and slid closer to him. Ashley parted his thighs so he could feel the length and warmth of her leg through his trousers. She didn't back away.

"I did go to sleep." She looked up at him with a quirky little grin. "Then you began to play." She reached out one delicate little hand and stroked it across the front of the piano. Then she turned to him, smiled broadly, and said, "Thank you for attending dinner."

"I did it for you," he admitted.

"I know," she said softly. "Situations like that must be difficult for you?" she asked hesitantly.

"Quite." He didn't know what else to say about that. It was nearly impossible to voice his thoughts. Even he didn't understand the muddle inside his head. How could he expect her to?

"You did very well, even amid discussions of pantaloons and tall boots." She giggled lightly, and the sound reminded him of the tinkle of the wind chimes he'd given to her. It was happy and melodious and it turned his insides to mush.

"You were worth it," he said as he raised his hand to brush a lock of hair from her face. Her hair hung freely down her back, her combs having been removed. It fell in silky dark waves to land at her waist, and he wanted to gather it in his hands, bury his face in it, and inhale her scent. He shook the thoughts away. They would get him nowhere.

"It's highly unorthodox for a lady to meet a gentleman in his bedchamber, is it not?" she asked hesitantly.

"It is," he admitted.

"Yet you lure me here, anyway," she said with a playful groan.

A grin tugged at his lips. "I believe I am the one who is being lured," Ashley said.

"Directly into my web of deception," she said with a tremulous quake to her voice. She tilted her head from side to side, as though mulling that thought over. "It's not truly deception," she whispered to him. "I'm here to help you."

"You're helping," he croaked out. Dear God, he sounded like a lad of twelve. Only with the urges of a man. It was all he could do to keep his hands off her. He wanted to draw her into his lap and hold her tightly as he explored her body. As he gave her pleasure.

"I'm here for a time," she said with a breezy wave of her hand. "Gone like the wind when my mission is over."

Again with the mission? "Tell me more about this mission you refer to."

She laid a hand on her chest. "Alas, I cannot. It's forbidden, you see?" She blinked her pretty eyes at him, the flakes of gold that rimmed her irises glimmering in the candlelight.

He didn't see. But he wanted to see. He wanted to see her stick her tongue out again to wet her parched lips as she had only a moment ago. He wanted to see her smile. He wanted to see what lay hidden beneath that nightrail. Ashley dragged a hand down his face in an attempt to wipe away his wayward thoughts. He failed. But he gave it a valiant effort.

"You are too innocent for a man like me," he finally breathed instead. Then he hopped up from the piano bench and went to pour himself a glass of whiskey from the sideboard. He immediately felt the loss of her as he moved across the room.

Sophia walked toward his bed and picked up his robe. "Would you mind?" she asked as she slung it around her shoulders. She waited for his nod of acquiescence before she tied the sash. "I feel a bit underdressed," she said.

Ashley glanced down at his own jacket and waistcoat. Simmons had had a wonderful evening putting together his wardrobe. It had been quite some time since he'd been so fancily attired. But she was right. She was in her nightrail. And he was fully dressed. Something about that thrilled him.

Yet he shrugged out of his jacket, anyway. Then he loosened his cravat and tugged it free. And finally, he removed his waistcoat and pulled his shirttail from where it was tucked in his trousers. It was scandalous to be wearing only shirtsleeves and an open collar in front of a lady. "Better?" he asked.

❧

Better? No, that wasn't better. Now he was as poorly dressed as she was. Her eyes lingered at the vee of his shirt, where a sparse dusting of dark hair could be seen. She ached to pull his shirt open and look closer at it. To see what he looked like beneath his clothes. Instead, she said, "I am not here to seduce you, Ashley."

He swallowed hard. So hard she could hear it. "Oh, how I wish you were," he mumbled.

She covered a grin with her hand. "What would people say if anyone knew I was here?"

"They would say all sorts of unkind things. Then they would try to drag you from me before I could cause your demise." He avoided looking at her when he said the last. Now her heart ached for him.

"Yet I do not fear you," she said, watching his face. He sat down on the piano bench facing her, and she dropped into an overstuffed chair beside it. It was probably better to put some space between them. Though she wanted more than anything to touch him. He looked like he needed to be touched. "When was the last time someone embraced you?" she asked quietly.

He looked deep into his whiskey glass instead of at her. "Tonight, when I went to kiss Anne good night."

That was a lovely thought. But it wasn't the kind of embrace she was referring to. "No. I mean a hug from someone other than your daughter."

He shrugged. And avoided her gaze some more.

She stood up and walked closer to him. He sat there on the piano bench until she was within arm's reach. Then he reached out quickly and put his hands on her hips, and dipped his head so that the top of his head lay on her belly.

What an awkward embrace. She put one hand in his hair and one on his shoulder. The hand in his hair stroked along his scalp. He sighed long and loud and drew her even closer. He lifted his head ever so slightly so that his forehead was now on her stomach.

"Sophie," he groaned, the sound vibrating within him.

Sophia impulsively dropped to her knees in front of him. "Ashley," she said as she laid her elbows on his knees and looked at him. He was hurting. She knew it. But she didn't know how to fix it. "I would like to hug you," she said with a smile. "In fact, I would enjoy it immensely."

He shot up quickly from his seat, wrapping his arms around her at the same time as he stood. He nearly lifted her from the ground as he set her on her feet and drew her to him. She fell into him as though she was meant to be there. Her head tucked just beneath his chin as she wound her arms around his waist. She turned her face so that her cheek lay above his heart. She listened to its beat and felt the slow, steady breaths he took in. Only his breaths were not slow and steady. They were quick and tortured. She looked up at him.

"You ask too much of me," he groaned, swiping a hand through his hair in what might be agitation. She couldn't be sure.

"A hug is too much?" she asked hesitantly.

"I made you a promise the last time you were here."

She wracked her brain, trying to remember a promise. "I don't recall." She pulled back from their embrace to look up at him.

"I promised that the next time you found your way to my room in the middle of the night, I would kiss you." He tilted her chin up gently with his crooked finger. His blue eyes were dark and stormy, clouded by something she didn't fully understand.

"Are you angry at me?" she asked, sliding her hands down to hold his forearms.

"God, no," he said with a chuckle. "I'm angry at myself."

"Why?"

"Because I want you with an abandon I haven't felt in quite some time. And I don't know what to do about it," he said softly.

"I think you should kiss me, Your Grace." He lifted a brow at her. "Ashley," she corrected with a laugh.

"You think I should kiss you, Miss Thorne?" he teased. Goodness, he was gorgeous when he smiled. He threaded his hands into the hair at her temples and tilted her head slightly. And then he dipped his head toward hers.

Thirteen

Oh, goodness! He was finally going to kiss her. He looked so hesitant, so unsure of himself as he lowered his head toward hers. His eyes skittered from point to point on her face, as though he searched her closely to see what she was feeling. She couldn't help but wonder how long it had been since he'd kissed a lady. But she wouldn't dare break the spell by asking.

The faint smell of whiskey tickled her nose as his lips finally brushed hers. He stole her breath with that one touch. But the moment his lips grew firm, a heavy knock sounded at the door.

Ashley groaned loudly and raised his head. "Go away," he called out. Then he stood still and listened.

"Robin," a woman's voice called. "I know you're in there. And I know you're awake. I'm coming in." The door handle jiggled. Ashley covered his mouth with his index finger and mouthed the word "quiet" at Sophia. She nodded.

"A moment, Mother. I'm not dressed." The door handle stilled immediately.

Ashley took Sophia's hand in a firm grip and pulled

her over to his dressing room. He shoved her gently through the door and said, "I'll be right back to collect you," with a grin. Then he quickly kissed her forehead and pulled the door shut behind him. He left it cracked barely enough to allow a sliver of light to enter the room. She turned her ear toward the opening and adjusted her body so that she could see through the slit.

Ashley opened the door to his mother and leaned against the casing, effectively keeping his mother out as best he could, with one arm reaching to hold the door. "How lovely to see you, Mother," he said, his voice droll and lifeless.

The dowager duchess ducked beneath his arm and slid into the room. He spun to catch her. "Robin," she began to speak.

He glanced once toward the room where Sophia hid. "This is not an appropriate time, Mother," he tried to interject.

But she would have none of it. "What on earth were you thinking, coming to dinner the way you did tonight?" his mother asked.

Ashley's brows arched and he looked down his nose at his mother. Sophia had never seen him look so imperious. But he certainly could do lofty with the best of them. "The last time I checked, this was my house, that was my dinner table, and that was my food." He scowled at her. "Did you misrepresent yourself? Or did you truly come to my chambers to tell me I'm not welcome at my own table?" The room crackled with energy. His or hers, Sophia wasn't sure. Perhaps it was the two of them bouncing off one another. Goodness.

"You know that's not what I meant," the duchess

said with a heavy sigh. "I was simply surprised, is all." She reached a hand toward his forehead as though to check for a fever. "Are you feeling all right?" Ashley dodged her and sat on the chair Sophia had just vacated.

"I'm feeling quite well, Mother. Thank you for asking." He didn't elaborate. He didn't ask questions. He just looked at her and waited. "Did you have something you wanted to say? Or did you simply come to tuck me in."

Sophia covered a smile with her fingertips.

"I had told everyone you were ill," his mother said quietly.

"I gathered that," Ashley said with a nod.

The duchess began to pace and wring her hands. "So, I believe you should continue to be ill, Robin."

Sophia inhaled harshly at that. Ashley must have heard it because he glanced toward the room where she hid.

"I should continue to be ill?" he asked. His voice was hard as steel.

"Well, yes…" She let her voice trail off. "It's much simpler that way."

Ashley closed one eye, cocked his head, and said, "So you would prefer to use my home, my hospitality, and my staff, but have me not attend the events. I hardly find that to be favorable."

"Robin…" she started to equivocate.

"Spit it out, Mother," he snapped.

"You're a recluse, Robin. Everyone expects you to be recluse."

"Did you not tell me you wanted me to attend your party?"

"Well, yes, but I didn't think you would do it."

Ashley nodded slowly. "I think I understand."

"And what is your relationship with that girl?" his mother spit out. Sophia bristled.

"That girl? You'll need to be more specific."

It was all Sophia could do not to rush from the dressing room and point her finger in the duchess's face. How dare she call her "that girl"?

"Sophia Thorne," his mother said with a roll of her eyes. "You barely took your eyes off her all night."

"You invited her."

"I invited her grandmother. The girl came with her." She waved a breezy hand of dismissal in the air.

"We should discuss this another time, Mother." Ashley glanced toward the door. He obviously didn't want Sophia's feelings to get hurt. But it was very nearly too late.

"She's a nice girl. From a quiet family."

"What do you know of her?" Evidently, he was curious. Too curious to pass up the opportunity.

"I know you spent the night watching her," his mother snapped. "You mustn't be so obvious, Robin."

"What was I obvious about, Mother?"

The duchess sniffed loudly. It wasn't a snort. But close. Duchesses didn't snort, did they?

"You want her. It's easy to see."

"Weren't you just telling me that I needed to find a mistress?" Ashley asked with a laugh. "Which is it, Mother? You can't have it both ways."

A mistress! Over Sophia's dead body. That was her initial reaction. Then her heart twisted within her chest when she realized that her mission would soon be over. She wouldn't be able to fault him if he did turn to a strange woman when she was gone. Or now, for that matter. She was nothing to him. She couldn't be anything to him. Not at all.

His mother didn't answer the question.

"Are we done, Mother?" he asked with a heavy sigh.

"Hardly," the duchess said.

"Then please finish it so I can go to bed." He rubbed at his weary eyes. He did look tired.

"Do you intend to frequent the rest of the party?"

He shrugged. "Perhaps."

"If you do, please don't make reference to homicide, the dead, or… parts!"

He smiled. "I shall just think them to myself, then." He chuckled. "And it wasn't me who brought up parts. You all were discussing that before I arrived."

"Your grandmother is incorrigible," she grunted. But then she did smile at him.

"Are we done yet?"

"I assume we are," she said as she bustled toward the door.

"So, no discussion of homicide, dangly parts, or the dead. I think I can do that." He appeared to mull it over. "But can the rest of your guests?"

"Let's hope so."

"Good night, Mother," Ashley urged.

"Good night, dear." She slipped out as quickly as she had slipped in. Ashley walked slowly toward the dressing room where Sophia hid. Sophia's belly dropped toward her toes when she saw the look on his face.

❧

Ashley could still feel the taste of Sophia on his lips.

He hadn't even kissed her. Not the way he wanted to. He'd brushed his lips against hers and then his mother intruded. Blast and damnation. He had been so close.

He pushed the door open and found Sophia leaning against the wall in the dark room. She looked at him askance, her hazel gaze dark in the night-shaded room. "Would you care to come out of the closet?" he asked her. She drew her bottom lip between her teeth and worried it for a moment. Then she reached for his hand and let him lead her out. He wanted to be the one to nibble that lip.

Ashley stopped suddenly, and Sophia bumped into him. When she would have sprung back, he pulled her to him instead. "Where were we?" he asked.

"I don't think she likes me," Sophia said quickly.

He tipped her chin up with his index finger. "She doesn't have to like you. I like you enough for everyone." Her eyebrows drew together. Evidently, his mother's ramblings worried her more than they should. "Did her comments offend you?" If so, he would fetch his mother right back to the room and make her apologize. Propriety be damned. He would not allow Sophia to be wronged.

"I'm not really offended. Just a little worried." If she tugged on that lip any harder, he would have to kiss it to make it better.

"Don't be," he cajoled. "She means well." Or at least he hoped she did.

Sophia sighed heavily then flopped down into the overstuffed chair. She turned her back to one arm of the chair and dangled her legs over the other. He'd never seen such an awkward yet comfortable pose.

Her bare feet poked out from beneath her nightrail. A grin tugged at his lips at the sight of them.

Her trim ankles were exposed, too. She made no effort to cover them. He liked that. He could almost imagine hours spent in these very chambers with her sitting like that, only she would be naked. His manhood reacted to that thought, and he forced himself to picture Finn in his head instead.

"It appears as though I'll be attending the festivities of the house party after all," he said carefully, watching her face. "If you don't mind spending time with me, that is."

Her smile nearly melted his heart. "I'm only here for three more days," she said with a rueful smile. "Then Grandmother and I must return home."

"Where is home?" he asked as he picked up her foot and absently stroked across the bottom of it. She jerked in his grasp, stiffening her leg so that her nightrail slid even higher up her naked shins and then up over her knee. His gaze was riveted on that knee until she reached down and covered herself with a quick fling of his dressing gown.

"I'm sure you've never heard of the place I'm from." She avoided his gaze.

"Why won't you tell me where you're from?" he asked, realizing how harsh he sounded the minute the words left his mouth.

"It's forbidden," she whispered. Then she sighed heavily and said, "I wish I could change my circumstances, but I can't."

"Tell me you're not already married." She couldn't be. She was too much of an innocent. When he'd kissed her, she hadn't fallen all over him, as a whore or even a tried lady would do.

"I am not married," she said with a smile. She laid her head back against the arm of the chair and looked at him. She didn't say another word. Just looked at him. God, she could undo him with those eyes.

Damn it, he wasn't going to let her slip through his fingers. It had taken him this long to find someone who interested him. "I like you, Sophia," he admitted.

She lowered her feet and turned to face him. "I like you, too."

He sat down in front of her and turned his back to the chair. It was too painful to look at her. And he needed to tell her some things. She laid one hand on his shoulder, and he pulled it lower so he could rub his bristly chin across her hand. She giggled.

"I killed my wife," he blurted out. She stilled behind him. Completely stilled.

"I know everyone thinks you killed her," she said.

"It's true." He turned and looked up at her. "Now I'm sure you want to run screaming from the room."

"I want no such thing." Her voice was soft and not the least bit provocative. Yet it touched his heart. It made a place long dormant within him ache. "If you want to tell me about it, I'd like to listen."

He tucked her hand into the softness of his neck and leaned into it. He'd never felt this need to cuddle. Her suggestion of a hug was at the forefront of his mind. "You do something to me, Sophie," he murmured, his lips now against the back of her hand. "You've enchanted me in some way."

She laughed lightly. "I told you that I don't have the powers to do that."

"And yet you have."

"Then call me fortunate," she said playfully.

"Call *me* fortunate," he corrected.

Sophia leaned down toward him, closer and closer, until her mouth was a hairbreadth away from his. "Call us fortunate," she said. Then she touched her lips to his. Her touch was tentative, and he wanted nothing more than to devour her. To tease his tongue into her mouth and invade her. It had been a long time since he'd had a woman. But this was different. This was her trusting him.

Her lips grew a little firmer and he opened his mouth slightly, then tickled the seam of her lips with the tip of his tongue. She opened for him, and he swept inside. She startled at first, but then she melted. He turned, wanting to be closer to her, and pulled her down to the floor with him, cradling her in his arms as he kissed her. His heart was pounding in his chest at her gentle responses, at the little whimpers she made in her throat. She melted in his arms. And it felt so damn good that he didn't ever want to stop.

Ashley let his hand drift up her side, and she didn't stop him. She didn't react because she was so absorbed in the kiss. So, he took a moment to explore the arch of her back through her robe, but he could not get close enough. Not close enough at all. He pulled one hand down to untie the robe, wanting to press his skin against hers. Her mouth still let him plunder, and those sounds still escaped her throat. He tugged loose the sash of the robe she wore, and spread it open.

But then there was a heavy knock on the door. Ashley lifted his head, groaned loudly, and swore beneath his breath. She giggled in his arms. It made

him want to smile along with her. And tickle her to
make her do it some more.

"Yes!" he called, more than a little bit frustrated.

The door opened slightly and Wilkins poked his
head through the opening. He startled for a moment at
the scene before him, but quickly composed himself.
He looked everywhere but directly at Sophia.

"I didn't say for you to open the door," Ashley
groused as he brought the edges of Sophia's robe
together. She burrowed her face in his neck, and he
liked it immensely.

"Beg your pardon, Your Grace. But it's Lady Anne."

Ashley sat up straighter. "What about her?"

"She's having a night terror," Wilkins said.

Sophia crawled from his lap so he could rise.
Ashley adjusted his trousers and pulled her to her feet.
"Wilkins will see you back to your room."

She nodded, her brows drawn together with worry.
"Do you need some help? With Anne, I mean?"

He shook his head. Anne didn't respond to anyone
but him. "I'll see you tomorrow?" he asked.

"Of course," she said with a soft smile. Then, with
a twinkle in her eye, she stepped up on her tiptoes and
kissed him on the lips. He wanted to drown in her
once again. But Wilkins cleared his throat.

"See Miss Thorne to her room," Ashley barked at
Wilkins. The man merely nodded once. "And your
discretion is warranted." He nodded once more.

With that, Ashley started down the corridor, with
the taste of Sophia Thorne on his lips and the feel of
her in his hands. And all he could think about was
how much he wanted more.

Fourteen

WILKINS SAID NOT A SINGLE WORD TO HER AS HE NAVI-
gated the maze of corridors that led back to her chambers. He walked stone-faced, not showing a hint of
emotion. It made Sophia want to stick her tongue out
at him, or pull her nightrail up around her knees and
dance around him, just to see how he would respond.

The very thought of it brought a smile to her lips.
She probably looked like the cat that ate the canary
when the butler stopped at her door, opened it for her,
and stepped to the side.

"Good night, Wilkins," she murmured.

"Miss Thorne," he said with a serene nod of his head.

Sophia stepped into the room and leaned heavily
against the door. She hugged her arms tightly around
herself and squeezed, a giddy laugh escaping her
throat. Ashley had kissed her. He'd really kissed her.
And it was nothing like Sophia had expected a kiss to
be. She hadn't expected at all for it to be like that. For
him to taste like that. For him to take over her senses
like that. She spun quickly in a circle, his dressing
gown billowing around her.

"Where have you been?" a deep voice barked from the chair beside her bed.

Sophia stopped spinning and turned to face the noise. "Marcus?" she asked. Faint light shone on half of his face, casting the rest of him in shadow. He looked none too pleased, and Sophia raised her chin a notch to stare back at him. "What are you doing here?"

He crossed one foot over the other knee, shifting slightly in the chair in a relaxed pose, a pose Sophia knew well wasn't relaxed at all. "I came to collect my wayward sister," he said. "Both of them."

"Both of us?" What did he mean by that? She'd left Claire at home.

"Claire followed you."

"How did she get past the fish?" Sophia asked. Sophia had bribed them with clothing. Men who could only walk the earth on the night of the full moon desired clothing over all else.

"The same way you did, it appears. When we get home, I'll have to replace my whole blasted wardrobe." His fist struck the arm of the chair with a halfhearted blow. Then he exhaled heavily. "What were you thinking, Soph?" he asked softly.

Sophia crossed to sit gingerly on the edge of the bed, across from her brother. "They wanted to clip my wings," she said hesitantly. She'd completely bungled her last mission. All because of a music box she'd clumsily tripped over. The music had caught her attention for a moment, and then she'd found herself in the clutches of a child. It had taken all of her magic to get out of the situation. And had caused untold amounts of trouble.

"And now they most assuredly will," he said, as he sat forward and looked at her. He looked at her a bit too hard. With too much pity for her comfort. "This mission wasn't meant for you."

"Claire wasn't in trouble. She has nothing to prove. She can stand to lose this one." At least that's what Sophia had told herself all week. Ever since she'd arrived from their land.

"She's not very pleased with you."

Sophia could just imagine Claire stomping her feet and throwing a fit at the very thought of losing to her little sister. "She'll survive it." Sophia dropped to her knees in front of Marcus. "Don't you see, Marcus? This was my last chance. I have to do this right. I can't lose my wings."

"You think the Trusted Few will let you keep your wings if this works out," Marcus said, his face softening with understanding. "Soph, this won't change their minds. If anything, it'll put you in their sights." He rubbed his eyes with his closed fists. He looked tired. Guilt poked at Sophia for a moment.

"Where's Claire?"

Marcus shrugged. "I haven't found her yet. I only arrived today. I suspect she arrived yesterday. But I'm not worried. She'll be here soon, I'm certain." He sighed heavily. "How is the mission going? Have you spent a lot of time with the child?"

She'd spent a lot of time with the child's father. But not necessarily the child. "There are a lot of layers to this mission," Sophia began.

Marcus let his eyes drop to peruse what she was wearing. "Is that a man's dressing gown?" he asked as he jumped to his feet. He looked toward the door. "Just where have you been, Soph?"

"It's not as bad as it looks," she started. But he held up one finger to silence her.

"Tell me you haven't broken any of the Unpardonable Errors."

"I haven't! I haven't broken a single one!" She hadn't let anyone see her in faerie form, not even Anne. Nor had she used her magic to cause harm, even though she wanted to do terrible things to the duke's brother. She had protected her dust. And although she wanted more than anything to tell Ashley what she truly was, she hadn't. And she couldn't fall in love with a human. That would just be tragic. And in opposition to her very nature. "I haven't, Marcus. I swear it."

"Whose robe is that?" Marcus asked.

"It belongs to Anne's father."

"The Duke of Robinsworth?" His brows drew together in consternation. "Were you alone with him, Sophie?"

"Only for a moment," she said hesitantly. A moment each day. Every moment she could steal. "He's out of isolation," she tossed out. "I did accomplish that."

"He's a well-known hermit," Marcus said. "He rarely shows his face in public."

She lifted her nose in the air. "He does now."

"What did you do?"

"He likes me," she whispered. And a grin tugged at her lips despite the fact that she tried to hide it. She couldn't. The fact that he liked her made her supremely happy. "He came out of seclusion. For me."

"And this is a good thing because?" he prompted.

"His daughter is forced into seclusion with him. It won't be until he returns to his rightful place in society that she can take hers. She can't heal with him here in hiding."

"Have you found out the truth of his situation?"

"Not yet." She held her finger and thumb up, and indicated the small space between them. "But I'm this close. This close, I promise."

"Soph, I think you should return this mission to Claire."

"There's no possible way I'll turn Ashley and Anne over to Claire." She shook her head vehemently. "Absolutely not. I will see this mission through to completion." If it was the last thing she ever did before her wings were clipped, it would be worth it.

"Ashley, is it?" Marcus asked, his voice dreadfully heavy.

"That's his name," Sophia quipped back. Then she thought for a moment and jumped to her feet. "There's something I need to see," she said.

"Can it wait until tomorrow?" he asked, his voice weary.

No. Anne's night terror would be over by then. "I need to go and see what upset Anne. Come along or not," she said. "But I'm going."

❧

Ashley strode down the corridor, trying his best to take his mind off the sprightly little lady who'd been in his chambers only moments before. But it was difficult. He could still taste her on his lips and feel her in his arms. But a scream from his daughter's room broke him from his improper thoughts, in somewhat the same fashion a glass of cold water tossed upon his person might.

Ashley quickened his pace. When he entered Anne's room, he found her nurse sitting on the edge of the bed trying to coax Anne from the corner into which she'd retreated. "Excuse me," Ashley muttered as he motioned her to the side and reached for Anne. She scrambled across the bed and into his arms, clinging tightly to his neck as her legs wrapped around his waist.

He rubbed her hair and crooned to her, the way he did every time she suffered a night terror. She sobbed into his bare neck, her hot tears leaving a sticky path in the crease between his shoulder and neck.

"Shhh…" He crooned. "There, now. Is it really that bad?"

She nodded into his neck without lifting her head, but at least her sobs and shaking were beginning to subside.

"Must have been a positively wretched dream," he said softly. He motioned for the nurse with one hand. "Leave us, please," he mouthed to her. When the door was closed firmly behind the nurse, he set Anne slightly away from him so he could look at her to be certain she was truly all right. She drooped onto her pillow with a heavy sigh and a large sniffle.

"Better now?" he asked.

She gave him a tearful nod.

"Do you want to tell me what it was about?" he asked gently as he arranged the bedclothes around her.

"I was falling," she croaked out, her voice still choked by her former tears.

"Falling, as in you tripped?" he questioned. He already knew the answer. It was the same dream she always had.

"No, I was pushed," she said with a hiccup.

It was as he feared. Anne had experienced the same nightmare for weeks after her mother died suddenly. It had lessened through the years, but it was still at the back of her mind. It only resurfaced in times of difficulty. "You're safe in your bed now," he soothed.

"I was falling," she repeated.

"You're not falling now," he said softly. "Are you?"

"No." She sniffled again.

"You're tucked safely into your bed." He brushed her hair back from her forehead. "Would you like for me to tell you a story?"

She gave him a hesitant nod and he crawled higher in the bed to lie beside her, then began his light-hearted tale.

⮜⮞

"He doesn't look very dangerous," Marcus murmured from beside her on the windowsill where he perched precariously beside Sophia. He unbalanced himself on the sill, and Sophia had to reach out to catch him. It was unfortunate that male faeries didn't have wings of their own. "He looks normal," he lamented.

Sophia shook her head, not drawing her gaze from Ashley and his daughter. It felt almost like eavesdropping to observe such an intimate moment. "He's not dangerous. Just misunderstood."

"Did he kill her?" Marcus always did have a way of getting to the meat of a matter.

Sophia whispered. "He says he did."

Marcus nearly fell from the windowsill. "He *did*?" he croaked.

"Shh," Sophia warned, placing a finger against her lips. Ashley's eyes moved toward the window, but then were drawn back to his daughter.

"He did?" Marcus whispered back. "He admitted it?"

She shrugged. "More like he alluded to it."

"Did he or didn't he?" Marcus growled.

"He didn't." She straightened her back and flexed her wings at him. "I'd stake my wings on it."

Marcus whistled low under his breath. "You probably have, Soph," he said quietly.

"I know." She did know. What more could she say? But something told her Ashley was innocent. Now she just had to prove it.

Fifteen

THE NEXT MORNING, SOPHIA WOKE TO FIND THE SUN already peeking over the horizon. She jumped to her feet and made for the washbasin. If she wanted to intercept Ashley and Lady Anne before the rest of the inhabitants of the Hall did, her best bet would be to catch them during the private breakfast they shared each morning.

As Sophia tugged her nightrail over her head, she couldn't help but wonder where Margaret was. She was supposed to be helping her with these confounded human clothes, even if she found the task of waiting on Sophia distasteful. Sophia knew she'd placed Margaret in an awkward situation, but she'd do her best to make it up to the house faerie.

A cough from the window jerked Sophia from her reverie. Actually, it sounded more like someone choking. She spun quickly, not surprised at all to find Ronald perched on the open windowsill. She shivered as the coolness of the morning slipped beneath her nightrail and tickled her ankles. "You could at least close the window," she scolded.

But Ronald just sat there and swung his feet, looking supremely satisfied with himself. Why did that bode poorly for Sophia? She stopped and faced him. He looked much too confident for her pleasure. "I've been given a new post," he said with glee, rubbing his hands together in anticipation.

A new post? "What sort of new post?" Sophia was almost afraid to ask.

He hopped down from the windowsill and turned to pull the pane closed. But his legs were a little too short. Smothering a laugh, Sophia closed it for him.

"I could have done it," he groused.

"Of course, you could," Sophia agreed. Once he got a chair and some books to stand upon, perhaps. But saying so would hurt his feelings. And Ronald with hurt feelings was worse than Ronald on a mission. "Tell me about your new post," she encouraged.

He preened, tugging on his short little waistcoat. "I'm to be your shadow." He grinned with satisfaction.

"By whose orders?" Sophia could already imagine. But she should probably hear him say it before she negated her brother's orders.

"Your brother arrived last night." Ronald didn't say anything else. Just that.

"I'm aware of that."

"He's not very pleased with your situation." Ronald looked much too gleeful. The little tuft of red hair on the top of his head twitched along with his dancing eyebrows. The sight of it made Sophia want to laugh. But she restrained herself. It was difficult, however. He gave a mighty tug to his waistcoat again. "He has dispatched me as your shadow."

So now Ronald would have permission to skulk around behind her. Lovely. He did so, regardless of anyone's orders. Sophia rolled her eyes for show. "He did no such thing."

"He did. He did so. He did require my services. You require my services. Your family requires my services." He began to pace. "Your mission requires my services. He said so."

Sophia sighed heavily. "I'll have him rescind your orders."

Ronald's chest puffed out. "You will do no such thing. I can make a fantastic shadow."

Too fantastic. She'd never be able to get him out from under her feet.

"Shadow… doormat… They're very much the same thing, are they not?"

"Certainly, they're not," he said with a little snort. "I'll be there to protect you. From the dangerous duke. From yourself." He pointed his stubby little finger at her.

"Where is Marcus?" she asked with a huff.

"Below stairs, the last time I spied him. He was on his way to break his fast with the object of your affection."

Sophia dropped the brush she'd been dragging through her hair, and it landed with a clatter on the hardwood floor. "Why would he do that?" she breathed to herself.

"Why, indeed?" Ronald asked. He clucked his tongue at her. "I, for one, am grateful he showed up when he did. It's exhausting keeping up with you all by myself. And now that there are two of you…" He let his voice trail off.

"Me and Marcus?" She spun to face him.

"Claire is here," he said with a wide grin. Blast his hide. He was enjoying his cryptic little game much more than he should, and she was allowing him to get under her skin.

"Where?" Sophia bit out, then worked to calm her temper.

"Below stairs, storing her belongings, the last time I saw her." Below stairs? Why on earth would she be below stairs? But before she could ask, Ronald jerked a chair closer to the window, thrust the pane open, and hurled himself over the side. Sophia ran to the window and looked for him in the shrubbery. Gnomes were surprisingly agile. They could very nearly bounce when vaulted from a great height. That was probably why they were such great climbers. They had no fear of falling.

"Are you all right?" Sophia called softly. Ronald jumped from the shrubbery and began to brush himself off.

"I'm sorry, I can't hear you," he called back with a wide, toothy grin. He cupped a hand around his ear and looked at her expectantly.

Blast his hide. Garden gnomes were insufferable.

A quick knock heralded Margaret's arrival, just before the door was thrust open and the errant maid slipped inside the room. "Where you have been?" Sophia barked.

Margaret just arched a brow at her. "I was returning a lost dressing gown to His Grace." She heaved a disgusted sigh.

"Did you see him? His Grace, I mean?"

Margaret fumbled about the room, picking up here and there. "No. I saw Simmons. I don't think he likes me."

"Since when has that mattered to you?" Sophia mumbled.

"He's a handsome man," Margaret said, her voice somewhat winsome as she stared off into a distance that Sophia couldn't see.

Sophia snapped her fingers in Margaret's face. "Hello," she called.

Margaret jerked herself from her reverie. "You don't have to shout." She took a deep breath. "You need to remain cautious around His Grace." She held up a hand when Sophia started to speak. "I know it's contrary to everything you're feeling…" She narrowed her gaze at Sophia. "But these late-night meetings can come to no good."

Sophia dropped heavily onto the edge of her bed. "I don't know that I can avoid him now." Tears pricked at the backs of her lashes. Somewhere this mission had gone terribly wrong.

Margaret sat down beside her and brushed Sophia's hair from her forehead with gentle fingertips. "I saw your mother go through the same thing. I know it's difficult for you. But you have to stay true to your mission."

Sophia forced herself to focus. "My mother?"

Margaret sighed heavily. "Yes, your mother."

"Tell me what happened to my mother."

"Doing so could taint your current relationships. I cannot." She shook her head. "But know that it causes immeasurable heartache. Avoid it at all costs." She leaned close and looked directly into Sophia's eyes. "Fae marry fae. Humans marry humans. It's the natural order of things. It's only when humans and fae mix and fall in love that things become difficult."

"Why does it have to be difficult?" Sophia groaned. Why couldn't she just enjoy getting to know Ashley and Anne? Why couldn't she fall in love?

"What if it's already too late?" What if she'd already broken Unpardonable Error Number Five? What happened in that case?

"Don't follow in your mother's footsteps," Margaret warned. She stood up and reached for a dress for Sophia. "Let's get you dressed. I fear there will be a small amount of havoc caused by Claire's arrival. You'll need to counter it."

"Are you part soothsayer?" Sophia asked absently.

"No," Margaret said with a chuckle. "I've just lived a long time and have seen a lot of things." She tipped Sophia's chin up to look into her eyes. "Heed my warnings. Falling in love with the duke will only lead to heartbreak."

What if it was much, much too late?

⸏⸎

The Duke of Robinsworth filled a plate for himself and one for his daughter and sat down at the table in their private breakfast room. He'd actually ambled close to the public breakfast room, but no one was up and about yet, aside from two doddering older women who were friends of his grandmother. He wanted to avoid them at all cost. So, he'd settled for another private breakfast, despite his former affirmation that he would be joining the house-party festivities.

He'd make another attempt after he breakfasted. He might join them for archery. But, then again, everyone might fear for their lives if he even looked toward a bow and arrow. Devil take it, anything he picked up would make people fearful, depending on their perspective.

The door to his private dining room opened, and he looked up to find Wilkins, who inclined his head and said, "The new governess for Lady Anne has arrived."

Ashley wiped his mouth and looked at Anne. The little girl's face fell quickly and harshly. "Something wrong?" he asked of her.

"I don't want a governess," she said with a pout.

"If that lip pokes out any farther, someone will step on it," Ashley said as he stood. He addressed Wilkins. "I thought the agency refused to send any more of their referrals."

"That's correct. But this one was brave, evidently." He eyed Anne askance. "I interviewed her and found her qualified."

"By all means, show her in," Ashley said as he sat back and waited.

"She's installing her things in her chambers," Wilkins explained. "But I'll bring her about and introduce her as soon as she's ready."

Ashley dismissed Wilkins with a nod. Then he faced his daughter. "Absolutely no frogs in this one's bed," he warned. "Or insects."

"I know," Anne sighed.

"You'll be on your best behavior," he continued. "And under no circumstances are you to set anyone's hair on fire."

Anne got a little gleam in her eye at the last, almost as though she was proud of doing it.

"Don't even think about it." He shook a finger in

her direction. But with the look on her face, he had to bite back a grin. He reached over and ruffled her hair. She jerked back from him and straightened her locks with stiff, unhappy movements. Perhaps she was getting too old for him to tousle. Another lady he'd love to tousle came to the forefront of his thoughts. A little dark-haired lady with flashing eyes who smelled like bluebells. He would like very much to muss up her hair.

He called to a footman. The man stepped to attention. "Fetch Wilkins for me?" Ashley asked hesitantly. He wasn't at all certain he was making a good decision. But he needed to see her. She was becoming as integral to him as breathing.

Wilkins entered the room a moment later. "Would you find Miss Thorne for me? I'd like to invite her to ride with me this morning."

But a man stepped around Wilkins and directly into his line of sight. "Perhaps you should ask me instead, Your Grace." He bowed slightly. His bow and salutation warred with the annoyed look on his face.

"I don't know you, much less do I want to ride with you," Ashley said, immediately realizing how acerbic his tone was, but he didn't like the way the man looked at him.

"Your Grace," Wilkins began. "This is—"

"I don't particularly want to ride with you either, but as my sister's guardian and the head of our family, you should at least ask for my permission before you take her off alone." The man lifted his nose in the air. "Did you plan to make an offer for her?"

"An offer? Of marriage?" Ashley asked. Wilkins sputtered even more than Ashley did. Poor man. But in the back of Ashley's mind, that didn't sound like such a bad idea.

"Of marriage, yes." He glanced around the room, taking in the startled butler and the still-pouting Anne. "Could you clear the room, Your Grace?" he asked.

"Of all the nerve," Wilkins breathed.

"No need," Ashley said quickly and crisply. "Deliver Anne to the new governess," he said to Wilkins as he strode through the door. He motioned to the stranger. "Follow me, sir. I think my study is a much better place to discuss any slight I may have given you."

"Decidedly so," the man said as he followed Ashley down the hallway. The man was so close on his heels that Ashley didn't even have time to formulate a plan. He breezed into his study and stalked behind his desk. He sat down and began to shuffle through a stack of correspondence while he collected his thoughts.

The man coughed loudly.

"Oh, do sit," Ashley groused with a breezy wave of his hand.

"Thank you, Your Grace."

"You know who I am, but I have not had the pleasure," Ashley said.

"Everyone knows who you are, Robinsworth."

"Quite so," Ashley agreed. He sat back heavily in his chair. "And you are?"

"Marcus Thorne, Your Grace." At what must have been Ashley's blank look, the man continued. "Sophia's brother."

Ashley narrowed his gaze. "When did you arrive?"

"Late last night. I had some matters to catch up on at home before I could join the festivities."

"Late last night…" Ashley repeated.

"Very late." He speared Ashley with a glance. "Late enough to catch my sister returning to her chambers in nothing more than a nightrail and your dressing gown."

If his teeth pressed more tightly together, Ashley feared he would break his jaw. "I see," he said.

The man jumped to his feet. "Do you see? Do you really?"

"I believe I do." Ashley sighed heavily. "What would satisfy you in this situation?" The only thing that would satisfy Ashley would be to marry her. But he didn't want to seem too eager.

"Did you defile her?" Mr. Thorne asked from between gritted teeth.

"You'll have to define the word 'defile,' I'm afraid." Ashley leaned his elbows on the desk to regard the man closely.

"Did you take liberties with my sister?"

"Again, it's all about perspective," Ashley equivocated. *Ask me the right question. Will I marry her? Yes!*

The man put his palms of his hands on Ashley's desk and regarded him closely. "What are your feelings for my sister?"

"Now we get to the meat of the matter. You have finally asked the right question." Ashley tried his best to set his pride aside. And his past. And concentrate only on his future. "I'm quite fond of Sophia," he said hesitantly. He hated the way his head tied his tongue in knots.

"Why was she in your chambers in her nightrail?"

Ashley thought about that for a moment. "I'm not

completely certain. One moment, I was playing the piano, and the next, there she was."

"Oh, dear God," the man groaned, lowering his head into his hands. "Music," he spat. "I should have known." He raised his head, remorse in his gaze. "Shall I assume that you sent her back to her own chambers with haste?"

"You could assume that." Mr. Thorne relaxed with a heavy sigh. "But you would be wrong."

Sophia's brother's head shot up. "Beg your pardon."

"I kept her there in my chambers for as long as I could."

Mr. Thorne turned a little green around the mouth. "What happened?"

"Nothing untoward," Ashley admitted. A few harmless kisses. A few harmless kisses that had rocked his very being. "What matters is that I'm prepared to make it right." He looked directly into his eyes. "I'd like to offer for your sister. I can make a rather generous settlement upon you, if you have need of it."

"I think it's me who's supposed to offer the dowry," Mr. Thorne said, his mouth opening and closing, as though he had words to say but couldn't formulate them.

"I've never stood by society's restrictions," Ashley admitted. "I'm willing to pay handsomely for her."

"I'll not sell my sister." Mr. Thorne heaved a disgusted sigh. Ashley had to give him credit. Many men of undetermined origins would have jumped on the opportunity to get their hands on a wealthy duke's fortune. Even a small portion of it. "Is she still innocent?" Mr. Thorne looked pained by the question.

"She is," Ashley said as he inclined his head.

"I'll be able to tell," the man muttered.

"Appearances can be deceiving," Ashley returned.

"Not where we're from," Mr. Thorne returned quietly.

"And where is that, exactly?" Ashley asked.

"I'm certain you've never heard of it."

That was the same answer Sophia always had. Blast and damn. Would no one tell him details of their heritage? From where they heralded? This one was as tight-lipped as Sophia. "I've only known her for a few days," Ashley admitted. "But she's like a breath of fresh air."

"That's what she's supposed to be," Mr. Thorne said. He sighed heavily. "As long as she's still innocent, my dealings with you are done." He bowed in Ashley's direction. "We'll be taking our leave today. All of us."

Leaving? "Wait!" Ashley called to his retreating back. The man stopped and turned toward him. He arched an inquisitive brow and waited. "She could be carrying my child," Ashley said without even thinking about it first.

Mr. Thorne looked like he needed someone to catch him when he fell. Ashley shot up from his chair and crossed the room. He stopped in front of the man, fully intending to catch him when he collapsed. However, he got a rousing surprise instead when Mr. Throne's right fist cuffed his left jaw.

Ashley took the blow, which was strong enough to knock him slightly off center. What he wasn't expecting was the second punch that hit him directly in the nose. He stumbled, cursed profusely, and then righted himself. He took a deep breath and asked, "Feel better?" as he wiggled his nose to be sure it was still attached. He pulled a handkerchief from his pocket and dabbed at the blood he'd provoked with his own carelessness. If anyone said the same about Anne, he'd be provoked to kill him. If all Ashley got was a bloody nose, he was fortunate.

"Feel better?" Mr. Thorne snorted. "Hardly." He looked devastated. And Ashley's conscience pricked at him a little.

"Do you want to hit me again?" Ashley dabbed at his nose. Damn, but that hurt. It had been a long time since he'd been in a brawl. Well, one couldn't really call taking two punches a brawl. But it still hurt like the devil.

"I want to kill you," Mr. Thorne said as he dropped heavily into a chair. He looked deflated, like a balloon that had lost its air. "This mission wasn't meant for her," he muttered.

Mission? Sophia had mentioned a mission more than once. "Pray tell me about this mission."

Mr. Thorne avoided his question entirely. "She could be with child. This does not bode well." He labored to his feet and tugged at his jacket. "I assume there's only one thing I can do."

"And that would be?" *Let her marry me. Force her to marry me. I'll make her happy with time.*

"She'll have to give up her life as she knows it. And marry you. And face the consequences. There will be consequences, whether her child is born like one of us or you."

Born a murderer. "I don't believe homicidal tendencies are bred into a person," Ashley informed him.

A startled gasp arose from the doorway. "What did you say?" Sophia asked as she barged into the room. She reminded him of a storm cloud heavy with thunder and lightning. Ready to erupt. Her hazel eyes flashed, and her dark brows drew together, her expression stern.

Ashley avoided her gaze. But her brother spoke up. "You should have told me," he said, sounding like an old man, suddenly. A wounded old man. Something inside Ashley twisted. But he schooled his features.

Just then, Sophia noticed Ashley's nose and the bloody handkerchief. She was across the room in a trice. "What happened to you?" she asked as she took the handkerchief and wiped at his nose. Her touch was gentle, but, by God, it hurt. He winced and backed his head up an inch.

"Careful," he murmured. He took her hand in his and held it, looking into her eyes. "I'm sorry," he said. How else could he convey what he was feeling? He couldn't even put word to his thoughts. Much less explain them. "I'm sorry" was a poor substitute.

"Did you hit him?" Sophia asked her brother. She punched her brother in the shoulder, which made him wince loudly. It made Ashley want to chuckle as the man massaged his arm.

"Damn it, Soph, don't do that," he groused. "He had it coming."

"What on earth could he do that would make you want to hit him?" she asked, her voice rising.

"He informed me that you could be with child,"

Mr. Thorne hissed at her. His glance kept moving quickly over to Ashley. But Ashley stayed silent and watched Sophia.

She pressed a hand to her stomach. "With child?" she croaked.

She looked stricken. And Ashley reached for her. She doubled over. This time, he grabbed for her. Dear God, he'd caused her pain. He would undo it.

Sixteen

SOPHIA COULD BARELY CATCH HER BREATH. SHE doubled over in the middle and clutched her stomach. She'd rushed into the room when she'd heard Ashley's muffled curses, never expecting to find him standing there with blood dripping on his cravat and Marcus shaking out his fingers to relieve the pain he'd caused himself. She stayed bent over and took a few deep breaths. With child? A laugh escaped her mouth.

"Sophie, it's all right," Ashley soothed, bending down to her level to look her in the eye. A drop of blood hit the rug they stood on and Sophia looked down at it. They'd come to blows. Over what? She came back upright and he straightened his body along with her.

"You told him I could be with child?" she asked in her most pleasant voice. It sounded a little choked because of all the laughter, and she wiped at her left eye with her knuckle.

"There's no need to cry," Ashley continued. "I'll make this better." She turned to Marcus. Good God, Marcus looked like a wounded man, and he wasn't even the one was bleeding.

"You lied to me, Soph?" Marcus asked. He very slowly tested his grip by opening and closing his fingers.

"I didn't lie," she started, swiping at mirth that overran her other eye.

"There's no need to cry, Sophie," Ashley crooned.

Crying? He thought she was crying.

"Her name is *Sophia*. Miss Thorne to you. And she's not crying, you idiot," Marcus bit out. "She finds this extremely amusing." His gaze moved to Ashley's hand, which still drew light little circles on her back. It felt quite good, actually. "And I would suggest you stop touching my sister." Marcus kept his sight on that hand, which slowed and then stopped. Ashley pulled it back as though it had something vile on it, then let it drop at his side.

"You think this is amusing?" Ashley asked.

Sophia drew her upper lip between her teeth for a moment to keep a loud burst of laughter from escaping. Then she said, "I find it supremely amusing that you think what we did could get me with child. I thought you were a man of the world. Lady Anne was not left under a yew hedge."

Color crept up Ashley's cheeks. He opened his mouth to speak. But no sound came out. He closed it. Then he opened it again. Still nothing.

"Exactly what did you do?" Marcus growled.

Sophia spun to face him. "Nothing that could get me with child, I assure you." She rolled her eyes.

"Be more specific," Marcus said from between gritted teeth.

Marcus would torture himself with this until she told him the truth. "He was playing music," she muttered.

"Beg your pardon, I couldn't hear you," Marcus said, coaxing her with a hand that moved toward him. As though by sheer will alone, he could break her heart open and spill all her secrets. Not likely. "Soph," he warned.

Like a dog with a bone, she thought. He would never let this drop.

"Music!" she yelled. Then she began to pace. "He was playing music. And you know how much I love music."

"He mentioned that. The music is what drew you to his bedchamber?" Marcus asked.

Well, kind of. Ashley himself drew her like a moth to a flame. But the music was what woke her from a dead sleep, a sleep where she dreamed of His Grace doing wicked things to her. But Marcus didn't need to know about that.

"It was very compelling music. More compelling than any I've ever heard. When he stopped playing, I borrowed his robe and went back to my chambers."

Marcus faced Ashley. "Is that the truth?"

Ashley probably hadn't answered to anyone in a very long time. Sophia hoped he wouldn't be too vexed about it. "Yes," he finally bit out. "That's what happened."

"That's why you were dancing in circles when you came back to your room? That's why you looked giddy?"

A grin slid across Ashley's lips. He swiped at it with the back of his hand, but it was still there. He leaned closer to her. "You were happy when you returned to your chambers?" he whispered, a devilish glint in his eye.

She bumped her shoulder into his as heat crept up her face. "Hush," she said, a grin tugging at her own lips. "The point is that," she turned to glare at Marcus, "I am not with child. Nor will I be." She turned to Ashley and said, "Do you need a refresher on how babes are made? Because I assure you that nothing we did would cause it."

"A refresher would be fabulous," the duke said with a wide grin. Blast his hide. He was so easy to like.

"Assure my brother that nothing happened," she coaxed. She should send Ashley's grandmother to him for the education about where babies came from. That was what he deserved.

"Nothing happened," Ashley muttered.

She turned to face Marcus. "And apologize for trying to rearrange his face."

"No," Marcus muttered. "Why should I? He started it."

"You two are worse than children," she sighed. Then she dusted her hands together. "Are we done here?"

"He is," Ashley said with a grunt. But then he straightened and adjusted his coat. "But then there's the matter of my offer."

Marcus opened his eyes wide. "You still want to offer for her?"

Ashley nodded and Sophia's belly flipped over.

She stepped closer to Marcus. "No, Marcus," she said calmly.

"He wants to court you," Marcus said, and she could almost see the machinations of his mind.

"I do," Ashley agreed stoically. All because he didn't know who or what she was. And she couldn't tell him.

"We'd never suit," she said. She felt like a book that had been read over and over, always saying the same thing.

"I think we suit quite nicely," Ashley said smoothly. He winked at her when Marcus turned his head. Her belly did that odd little flip again.

"I'll think about it," Marcus said.

"You'll think about it?" Sophia mimicked, crossing her arms beneath her breasts.

"Yes," Marcus repeated with a nod. "I'll think about it."

"Thank you," Ashley said, extending his hand. Marcus took it with a grunt of dissatisfaction. Or annoyance. Or perhaps he was just dyspeptic. Belatedly, both Sophia and Ashley noted that it was his injured hand. Poor Marcus.

Marcus started for the door. "I'll send your maid to you," he warned as he started down the corridor.

Of course, he would.

❧

Ashley played over the events of the last half hour in his mind. The lady of his interest, and he most certainly had an interest, glared at him from where she stood.

"Why did you tell him that?" she asked, tapping the toe of her slipper on the floor.

"Tell him what?" Ashley stalled.

"You know what," she prompted.

Ashley sighed heavily and rubbed at his forehead. "He said he was taking you away. I spoke on the spur of the moment." He let his voice trail off on the last.

There was so much more he wanted to say. But he wasn't certain she wanted to receive it. He took one step toward her and looked into her eyes. "How do you feel about me, Miss Thorne?" he asked.

She stuttered only a moment when she replied. "I-I like you quite a lot," she finally said. Ashley's heart leapt.

"Do you think that you could love me?" he asked, nearly betraying himself with the softness of his tone. Did he have to seem quite so enamored of her?

Her hazel gaze searched his face. He wondered what she was looking for. He'd thought the important parts worth noticing had died years before. But they hadn't. They'd been sleeping, just waiting for a little slip of a lady to wake him up. If she looked deeply enough, she would see into his heart. "Do you?" he prompted again when she didn't answer. She just appraised him.

"Answering that question won't be beneficial to either of us," she said. Then she reached out a hand to cup his cheek. He pressed his face into it like a cat. God, he loved the way she touched him. The smoothness of her skin as it rubbed over his. He pulled her to him with a gentle tug, and she fell into him with no resistance. He splayed his fingers like a fan on her back, and she let him hold her tight.

"Could you?" he asked, his lips hovering over hers.

"Maybe," she squeaked. She turned her head to clear her throat and pressed firmly against his chest. He didn't let her go. And she didn't continue to push. She softened after a moment. Oh, she gloriously softened.

"I could," she finally breathed. Then her lips touched his, a tentative meeting of mouths. He tilted his head so he could drink her in, and she opened to him. Her tongue tentatively rose to meet his. He growled low in his throat.

A cough arose from the corridor. Ashley lifted his head to find her maid glaring at him, displeasure evident on her face. "Miss?" she said.

Ashley set Sophia away from him a little and smiled at the look of wonder in her eyes. He liked the way he felt when he was in her company. He didn't feel like a jaded old outcast. He felt like he had many, many years ago, when the world was his to conquer.

"Miss?" the maid said again, louder this time.

"Yes, yes," Sophia said, her voice full of irritation. "I heard you."

"Did you, miss?" the maid asked.

She should be sacked for such impertinence.

"Your brother said for me to join you here."

"Of course, he did," Sophia quipped with an eye roll. She stepped back from Ashley and he immediately felt the loss of her.

"I should like to have a word with you," the maid said.

"Of course, you would," Sophia said, her voice glib. She dropped into a playful little curtsy that brought a smile to his lips. She started to brush past him. But he caught her hand.

"Will I see you later?" he asked, allowing his thumb to brush slowly across the back of her hand.

"Will you be playing?" she whispered.

"I will," he affirmed.

"Then I will see you later, I'm certain. Unless my brother locks me in my chamber."

"Which very well may happen," chimed the maid.

Over his dead body. "That would be tragic," he said, instead. She winked at him as she moved toward the door. But almost as soon as she passed, Wilkins appeared. "Did you need something?" Ashley asked.

"The new governess," Wilkins said. "There's already a problem with her."

A problem? The woman had just arrived. "What sort of problem?"

"I took the new governess to make Lady Anne's acquaintance, and Anne refused to come out of the wardrobe."

Good God, would his life ever become normal? Not bloody likely. "So, pull her out of the damn wardrobe."

"The new governess attempted that. And Lady Anne bit her on the arm. Then she dashed from her chambers and now we cannot find her."

Blast and damn. "Did she do much damage to the governess?"

Wilkins shrugged. "Negligible."

Negligible for Anne was not the same negligible as for other children. Anne could do a lot of damage in a short amount of time when she set her mind to it.

Ashley swiped at his nose with his handkerchief as he walked toward the door. "How does it look?" he asked Wilkins, lifting his head a notch and scrunching up his nose.

"Painful," the servant said, wincing a little in sympathy.

"Did I mop up all the blood?"

"Except for what's on your cravat," Wilkins informed him. Simmons would be none too pleased. Wilkins looked across the room and said, "And on the rug." He looked a little perturbed at the latter. "I suppose it couldn't be avoided," he finally acquiesced.

"I suppose not," Ashley said with a grunt, swiping at his nose one more time. Damn but that did hurt. It was no more than he deserved, however. "I should have let you set up an assignation for me, Wilkins." It certainly would have been more convenient than falling for a pretty little lass with flashing eyes, the sweetest lips he'd ever tasted, and a will to match his own. Not to mention her pugilist of a brother. "Remind me where Anne hid last time?" he prompted the butler.

"No one can find Lady Anne when she does not want to be found, Your Grace. We usually have to let her come out on her own."

This time, he wasn't willing to allow Anne to hide and sulk. "Pull all the servants from their posts. Find my daughter."

Wilkins nodded and set about his task.

"Leave no stone unturned. No corner unsearched." He would find her. And then he would... well, he didn't know what he would do. But he would make certain this was the very last time she hid from them in a wardrobe. Or bit a governess. Or ran away.

Seventeen

Sophia wiped a spider's web from her path with gentle fingers. Spiders were cantankerous beasts. They spent hours working on their hunting nets and didn't appreciate it a bit when careless humans destroyed their work. But she had to check the attic. If she was a little girl, it's where she would hide. Sophia swiped at her brow with her forearm as she climbed the dark steps. She held a candle aloft to lighten the gloom, but it simply made the shadows larger and more ominous. Night was about to fall, and Lady Anne was nowhere to be found.

She stepped into the large attic, its slanted roof forcing her to bend at the waist until she was fully in the room. She stretched and looked about. There were stacks of old furniture—chairs, tables, settees, old bed frames. All discarded and left alone. Some were covered with linen bedclothes. But most had withstood the ravages of time despite the dust and grime that coated their surfaces. There were too many places to hide in such a large room. If Anne had decided to hide in the shadows of the great furniture pile, no one would ever find her.

Sophia shoved a linen covering from a pile of furniture, then tugged the covering off another with the flick of her wrist. She would leave no cloth unfurled. No corner unsearched. But then she tugged the covers off a small settee. Standing directly in the middle of the settee was a portrait. Sophia startled for a moment because the woman in the portrait looked so very much like Anne. She held the candle closer and let the shadows dance upon the canvas. It must be Anne's mother.

She didn't even know the woman's name. It wasn't spoken in the household. Not by Ashley, not by Anne, not by the servants, and not by anyone else. It was as though the memory of her had died along with her. Like she'd never existed. But she had. The portrait was proof of it. At the bottom of the portrait was a small brass plate that read, "Lady Diana Trimble, Duchess of Robinsworth."

"Why were you discarded, Your Grace?" Sophia said, her voice trembling a little as she reached into her reticule and withdrew a small vial of shimmering dust. She held it out in front of the painting. Should she do it? It could be disastrous. What if the portrait refused to return to sleep? Everyone knew the duchess had been an obstinate sort. Should she wake the painting to find the truth behind the duchess's death? Only the duchess could tell her story and tell it correctly. But what if the duchess refused to return to sleep?

A haughty smirk graced the lips of the duchess in the painting, as though she knew secrets no one else knew. What Sophia wouldn't give to unlock those secrets. But there simply wasn't time. Anne must be found. She threw the coverlet back over the painting and began to search the recesses of the room for the little girl.

It wasn't until she'd searched every inch of the room that Sophia stopped, sighed heavily, and wiped her brow again. Anne wasn't in this room. And Sophia had wasted valuable time searching it from top to bottom. Where on earth could the girl be?

It was then that she remembered Anne's exuberance at the idea of visiting the village. Would the child have gone on her own? Would she so desperately want to leave the confines of the Hall? She probably would.

Sophia raced down the stairs, shaking the dust from her skirts as she went. She met Marcus at the bottom of the stairs. "Has she been found yet?"

"Not yet. The duke is beside himself. Perhaps you should go to him, Soph," he said reluctantly.

"I think I know where she is," Sophia said, trying to catch her breath. "Follow me."

❧

Ashley barked orders from the foyer of the manor, pointing this way and that, and snapping at all those who stopped to inform Wilkins about the areas they'd searched. The maids and footmen had been dispatched along with the rest of the household, and even the dowager duchesses, both the younger and the older, were searching, along with the guests of the house party. Anne's name reverberated off the walls of the Duke's ancestral home and for the first time ever, Ashley wished he lived in a small cottage in the middle of town. Yet despite all the searching, the child had not been found.

A shiver crept up Ashley's spine. What if they couldn't find her? What if she was injured? What if someone had taken her? Fear squeezed at his heart, and Ashley realized he wasn't concerned at all with her behavior or her surliness or her poor attitude; he simply wanted her. He wanted to hold his daughter and assure himself that she was all right.

Out of the corner of his eye, he saw Sophia Thorne update Wilkins on the areas she'd searched. The butler placed a large mark over the area she'd indicated on the quickly drawn map, and then she turned to continue searching. But instead of going back toward the mazes and corridors that were the Hall, she made for the front door. And she took her brother with her. Where on earth was she going?

Ashley followed them at a discreet distance as they went out the front door, their heads pressed closely together. They continued down the steps, and at the bottom, Sophia's maid waited with two horses. They pranced and danced in their places, tugging at their leads until Mr. Thorne boosted Sophia up into her saddle and climbed upon his own trusty mount. Then with a gentle kick and an easy touch, they sped through the gates toward the village. Ashley searched the dim light of twilight, but the maid had vanished as quickly as she'd arrived. He scratched his head. Then he turned toward the door and bellowed, "Someone get me a mount."

⁓

"Just where are we going, Soph?" Marcus asked.

"To get Lady Anne," Sophia said, not taking her eyes from the road. Her horse was sure-footed, but even her filly couldn't predict how rutted the road would be. "I should have gotten a lantern."

But then Marcus reached into his inner pocket and retrieved some pixie dust. Pixie dust was a glorified name for it. It was actually firefly bait. They loved the sugary crystals that were coated in fae magic. He tossed a light sampling of them into their horses's manes. Within moments, hundreds of fireflies surrounded them, lighting their way.

He shrugged at Sophia, a look of chagrin on his face. "For the horses," he said lightly.

"You always were afraid of the dark," she teased.

He rolled his eyes at her. "Pray tell me what has you in such a hurry to go to the village?"

"I think that's where Lady Anne has gone."

"What indicated that to you?"

"Intuition," she explained with a breezy wave of her hand.

"Just how deeply are you involved with this family, Soph?" he asked, a troubled look on his face.

"Deeply enough," she said quietly. Then she slowed her mount as they approached the village. The fireflies dispersed almost as quickly as they'd arrived. A boy ran out of the stables and took their leads, and one helped Sophia to dismount as Marcus did the same.

"There's not enough magic in the world to help you locate that child," Marcus warned.

But then Sophia heard it. She heard a series of taunts and leering jeers. And a shrill shriek as a small girl child screamed as though tormented by the devil himself. Sophia's heart stopped beating for a moment. Then she ran toward the sound.

When she turned the corner into a dark alleyway, she found Lady Anne standing with her back to a rubbish pile. Before her stood four taunting, teasing boys, each brandishing weapons of their own making. None of them would allow Anne to pass.

Anne stomped her foot and screamed in her most unladylike voice as tears streamed down her reddened cheeks. "My father will make you pay. All of you."

One boy snorted loudly. "Your father the murderer? What will he do? Kill us?"

Another boy chimed in with a crude jest. "He'll throw us from the tower of the castle, the same way he did his duchess."

Anne's eyes grew round. "He did no such thing!" Tears poured down her cheeks. "My father didn't kill anyone."

"Your father killed your mother. But since he's a duke, he didn't have to pay for it. He should have been hanged." The other boys agreed with even louder jests.

"Take it back!" Anne yelled, barely able to get the words out over her tears.

Sophia approached on slow feet, not daring to make a sound. But Anne saw her and made a move toward her. Sophia held up her hand to stop her. With her other hand, she reached into her reticule and drew forth a vial of shimmery dust.

"Don't, Soph," Marcus warned, reaching for the vial, but Sophia had already poured the dust in her palm, and with one heavy breath, she blew it into the air. The boys didn't even know she was there behind them, until she said the words:

"The truth be too difficult to bear,
yet with this spell you will wear,
the truth as though it were a cloak,
giving meaning to the words you spoke."

The dust shimmered in the air like a great glittery ball until it formed over the heads of each of the boys. Above each boy, the particles glimmered and formed a moving picture, a memory of each boy's weakness.

"Pay close attention, Anne," Sophia instructed. The boys froze, each looking at the great bubbles of shimmering dust with fear and trepidation. Then the dust began to take shape. "Each of us has insecurities, and it's the most insecure of us all who would tease and torment a girl you don't even know." The dust painted a portrait, yet the pieces of the portrait moved like living, breathing people in the shimmering lights above the boys' heads.

The biggest boy's portrait was of himself, cowering in a cupboard as a man slapped a woman across her face. The woman's eyes shone with tears, as did the boy's. It was a scene the boy saw often at home perhaps. He ducked his head in shame. Then Sophia poked a finger into his bubble and it burst like shooting sparks. He kicked at a stone at his feet, confusion on his face. But she sensed something awakening in him as well.

The other boys had similar thoughts in their heads, but of different proportions. One had a drunken father who spent more time with the bottle than he did his family. And another had a father who spent more time with his mistress and their children than he did his wife and theirs. And another was born on the wrong side of the blanket, yet no one knew.

"I'll not ask you to apologize, but I'll ask you not to condemn a girl for something you know nothing of, for we all have secrets, do we not?" Sophia asked in her most stern voice.

"Yes, miss," the boys chimed as one.

Sophia swirled her finger in the air, making all the images disappear and, with them, the dust. Along with that went the memory of what each boy had just seen, except for the boy's own self-portrait. The glittering images would remind each of them that their own truths could easily be distorted.

"Apologize," Sophia ordered.

"I'm sorry," they all chimed at once.

"You may go," Sophia said as she stepped to the side to let the boys pass. But they took two steps and stopped, their eyes growing wide.

"Your Grace," the oldest boy said as he dropped into a clumsy bow. The other boys followed suit. The Duke of Robinsworth stepped to the side and they all scurried past him.

"Ashley," Sophia began. The duke held up one finger to shush her. He was one with his ducal greatness in that moment, commanding and dominant. It was the first time he'd ever looked dangerous to her. Sophia bit her lip to keep from speaking. He motioned to Anne and she ran forward. Then he caught her up in his arms and turned away without a word, murmuring soft words to her.

"How much did he see?" Sophia asked softly of Marcus.

"All of it, I'm afraid."

Eighteen

ASHLEY CRADLED HIS SLEEPING DAUGHTER'S HEAD ON his shoulder as he dismounted. He could have passed her off to the groom who met him, but he would have to give her up to do so. He would have to lose the warmth that was her and give it to someone else, and he wasn't prepared to do so. Not when he'd just found her.

His mind was a muddle of thoughts. He must be a bacon-brained idiot to believe what he'd just seen was real. He'd watched as Sophia, his Sophia, blew some sparks into the air. Then, with a simple command, she'd made them come to life. It was like watching glimmery, shiny actors upon a stage. Yet they were depictions of what was in the children's heads. Or thoughts she was putting into their heads. He couldn't tell which. He must be bound for Bedlam. There was no way that what he'd seen could have been real. Maybe it was a manifestation of his worried mind.

Anne snorted and drooled upon his shoulder as he walked up the steps of the Hall. He glanced down at her. Her face was streaked with dirty tear tracks, and her hair was a scraggly mess. She desperately needed a wash and a pretty, clean dress.

Ashley walked through the door and was immediately accosted by the sight of his mother arguing with Wilkins. Arguing. A duchess and a butler barking at one another without a care for their positions or their consequence. Perhaps Ashley had slipped into some other realm where things weren't as they were supposed to be. His mother he could understand. Wilkins did things to intentionally provoke her. But Sophia... He didn't understand what had just happened with Sophia at all.

"I will have the two of you thrown into the dungeons if you don't stop that bickering." The duchess's mouth dropped open. "Together," he barked. "I will force the two of you to share a space not more than eight paces wide until you learn to get along." His mother opened her mouth to contradict him, but then she saw Anne there on his shoulder.

"You found her!" she cried, as her eyes filled with tears. His mother could provoke tears at will, but perhaps these were genuine? It was impossible to tell. "Is she all right?"

"A little dirty, but otherwise fine," Ashley said. "Wilkins, call for a bath for her," he instructed as he started for the stairs.

"Yes, Your Grace," the stoic older man said with a bow.

"*Yes, Your Grace,*" his mother mimicked in a singsong voice. "Why does he get 'Yes, Your Grace' while I get no respect at all?" She pointed a finger at the butler and jabbed it into his chest.

Wilkins grabbed the offending finger and opened his mouth to snipe back, but Ashley interjected, "The dungeons, I vow."

They both pursed their lips tightly together and regarded one another with annoyed expressions. The duchess jerked her hand from the butler's grip, and Wilkins colored slightly to find that he'd still been holding it.

"The bath?" Ashley called behind him.

The duchess bustled up the stairs toward him and held out her arms. "Let me take her. I'll see to her bath and put her to bed. The poor thing is exhausted." Ashley reluctantly handed her over. His mother had never shown a spark of maternal kindness toward Anne. He feared rebuking her for the mere fact that she might never offer again. He eased Anne into her arms. And smiled as she nestled into his mother's warm grasp.

Ashley had several matters to attend to. First, there was a governess who'd allowed Anne to run away. Then, there was the matter of Sophia and the nonsensical happenings with her. Lastly, but not least, he had to find Finn. Finn had a head for riddles and finding lost truths. He'd wanted to research Sophia Thorne since he'd met her. Ashley would finally let him.

A startled maid jumped back against the wall as he stormed past in the corridor. He didn't slow his stride.

"Wilkins!" he called as he stormed through the door to his study.

The servant appeared within moments.

"Find Lord Phineas and send him to me. And find Miss Thorne and send her to me as well."

"Yes, Your Grace," Wilkins said with a nod and he slipped soundlessly out the door.

Ashley sat back and rubbed the bridge of his sore nose. Damn, but that did hurt. He tried to recount the events of the evening. He'd made an offer of marriage to Sophia Thorne. Then his daughter had run away. Then he'd witnessed some unbelievable act that was too ludicrous to be explained in any rational manner. He rubbed across his nose again without any thought and grimaced. That bloody well hurt, by God.

A moment later, Finn strode into the room. "You bellowed?" he said, his voice droll and lifeless as he dropped into a chair across from Ashley.

"I did not bellow," Ashley groused.

"I dare to differ, Robin," Finn contradicted. "I happen to have been bellowed at enough that I can tell a bellow from a friendly call."

"I'll be friendly with you later. Good God, you'd think I were a bit o' muslin you wanted to coerce into spending time with you. I'm not. I'm the bloody Duke of Robinsworth, for God's sake." His voice slashed like a whip across the room. A whip that moved too quickly for him to call it back. He reached for his nose in frustration and bit out a curse when it hurt.

Finn's eyes opened wide. "Well, by God, Robin, it's about time." His brother began to clap his hands in a very sarcastic manner.

"About time for what?" Ashley asked, air escaping him like from a great big balloon when he sighed.

"You've worn the willow long enough. About time you found your stones and began to order people about again! It's fabulous." Finn jumped to his feet.

"Bloody well brilliant." Then he narrowed his eyes at Ashley. "Does this have anything to do with Miss Thorne?" Then he swiped at the air with his hand as though wiping his comments away. "Never mind, it's not important. I hear you found Anne."

"I did."

"Where was she?"

"In the village, of all places," Ashley said. He wouldn't tell Finn about the odd circumstances he'd encountered when he found her. Finn would never believe him, anyway. "She was being teased by some of the lower orders."

"She wasn't harmed, was she?" Finn's sandy-colored brows drew together with concern.

"Not harmed, but she was rather frightened." Ashley took a deep breath and regarded his brother.

"Why do I feel like you need to tell me something?" He reached for his own nose. "Do I have snot on my nose?" He swiped at his upper lip.

"Shut it," Ashley ground out, but he couldn't stop the grin that pulled at his lips. Finally, he admitted, "I need your help."

"With?" Finn suddenly looked serious.

"Miss Thorne." That was all he said. Then he met Finn's gaze, which danced with humor. Blast his hide. He balled up a piece of parchment on his desk and threw it at his brother's thick head. "Just what do you find so amusing?"

"My big brother, the dangerous Duke of Robinsworth, needs help getting a chit into his bed?"

"Not into my bed, you idiot." Ashley swore beneath his breath. He could get her into his bed all by himself. Couldn't he? It wasn't important. "You offered to research her past. I'd like to take you up on your offer."

Finn sat forward with his elbows on his knees. Ashley had his full attention.

"I want to know everything you can find out. About her, her brother, Marcus, and even her grandmother."

"Answer one question for me," Finn said with a grin. "Are you in love with her?"

Was he? He'd been fairly certain he was, until tonight. Now he didn't know what to think. "Just put your snout to the ground and dig up whatever you can."

"Only Miss Thorne is allowed to compare me to a dog," Finn said.

"Why is Miss Thorne allowed to do so?"

A lopsided grin crossed Finn's face. "Because she's much prettier than you are."

A cough sounded from the doorway. Ashley looked up to find Wilkins standing at attention. "Don't cough up any vital organs, Wilkins. Just speak."

The butler looked more than perturbed at Ashley's comment, which was almost amusing. "I have never 'coughed up any vital organs,' Your Grace. Nor would I." He raised his nose in the air.

"Of course not. It would be much too messy," Finn tossed out.

"Quite," Wilkins replied. Then he cleared his throat. And grimaced at Finn's grin. The man would probably never cough again. "You asked me to send Miss Thorne to you."

Ashley raised a brow in encouragement and rolled his hand in the air. "And?"

"I'm afraid that would be impossible, Your Grace."

Ashley jumped to his feet. "Has she refused to see me?" He started for the door. By God, she would see him. How dare she refuse him? A little part of his heart began to ache at the very thought of her not wanting to see him. Blast her.

Finn grabbed his shoulder. "Wait, Robin," he said quietly.

"I cannot bring her to you because she is not in residence." Wilkins looked decidedly uncomfortable.

"Not in residence?" Ashley knew he probably sounded like a dolt, but he didn't understand.

"Not in residence," the butler repeated. "She has left. And she took her grandmother and Mr. Thorne with her." So, she'd gone and taken her whole family. What a dreadful turn of events.

"Their belongings?" Ashley asked.

"Gone, Your Grace."

"Their horses?"

"Gone, Your Grace."

The only woman who'd stirred anything within him in what seemed like ages? *Gone, Your Grace.* Ashley rubbed at his nose again and swore profusely.

"One would think you'd learn that it hurts to rub your nose when someone has punched it. Leave it alone for at least a fortnight," Finn said.

Ashley arched a brow at him. If anyone knew anything about brawling, it was his brother. "A fortnight, you say?"

"At least."

"He's correct, sir. Shall I pour you a whiskey to dull the pain?"

Did he want to drink the thoughts of her away? Not particularly. "That won't be necessary." He turned to Wilkins. "Thank you. If you hear of her whereabouts, please do let me know."

Wilkins bowed quickly and slipped from the room.

"How deeply shall I dig?" Finn asked.

"To the other side of the known world if that's what it takes," Ashley said. He would find her. She would not disappear from his life. Not until he had some answers.

Finn squeezed Ashley's shoulder gently. "You really care about the chit, don't you? Or has she swindled you?"

"She's not a chit," Ashley grumbled.

Finn chuckled. "There's my answer."

"Do you need any funds?"

"I'm fairly plump in the pockets at the moment. I'll send you a bill, should any exorbitant expenses arise."

"You know where I live."

"And I will find out where Miss Sophia Thorne lives as well."

God, Ashley hoped he could.

❧

Marcus would wear a hole in the Aubusson rug if he didn't stop his incessant pacing. And his hair had seen better days. He'd run his hands through it in frustration to the point that Sophia was afraid he would rip it right from his head.

"How could you, Soph?" he groaned.

He'd asked the same question every hour on the hour since they'd arrived at the Slipper and Stocking, a tiny little inn they'd stumbled across when they'd left the Hall. When they'd left Ashley. And Anne. Sophia's heart twisted within her chest. She'd left her charge. With the mission incomplete. She may as well clip her wings herself and present them to the Trusted Few on a silver salver. She'd just ruined any chance she'd had of saving them.

Marcus began to tick items off on his fingers. "One: Never share the existence of the fae. Two: Never use your magic to cause harm. Three—"

Sophia held up a finger to stop him. "That's actually three and four. See, I know the Errors as well as you do, Marcus." She jumped to her feet. "Do you think I'm an idiot?" She rarely raised her voice at her brother. But he was insinuating that this was avoidable. That any of it was avoidable. It wasn't. Not a bit.

His voice softened. "Do I think you're an idiot?" he asked. He shook his head. "I think you're in love. That is Error Number Five." He ran his hands through his hair again and stopped to yank ineffectually at the strands. "Three out of five Errors, Soph," he growled. Then he flopped back onto the bed and covered his eyes with his forearm. "What am I going to do?" He raised his arm and looked up at her. "What if I can't solve this for you?"

Sophia sighed. "Then they'll take my wings." She shrugged. There was nothing more to say. Then her eyes filled with tears. "When the moon is full, we'll go back. I'll throw myself upon their mercy."

"They'll turn you into a blasted house faerie, Soph," he said. "No powers. The only bit of fae magic you'll possess is intuition."

"Nothing wrong with intuition, Mr. Thorne,"

Margaret grumbled from in front of the wardrobe where she unpacked their belongings.

Marcus winced. "No offense intended, Margaret."

"None taken. It's a trying time," she said breezily.

Sophia looked over at her grandmother, who sat knitting quietly in a rocking chair, completely unconcerned, apparently, with the state of affairs. Sophia dropped at her feet and laid her head on her grandmother's knee. "Tell me the answer?" she asked softly.

Her grandmother gently pushed a curl from Sophia's forehead and looked deeply into her eyes. "You'll appreciate it more if you come to it on your own."

"What if I never come to it?"

Her grandmother laughed, a rich sound that made Sophia's heart feel lighter. "You'll come to it. You are enough like your mother that you'll do the right thing."

That made Sophia pause. Her mother hadn't done the right thing. "She was banished from our world." Her grandmother suddenly refused to look her in the eye. "Wasn't she?"

"She is no longer permitted in the land of the fae. If you want to know how that came about, you'll have to ask your mother."

Ask her mother? She didn't even know where her mother was.

Just then, a harsh, incessant rapping noise began on the windowpane. "Better let him in," Sophia grumbled.

Marcus crossed to the window and thrust open the pane, allowing Ronald to climb over the sill. The gnome landed on his feet and bowed in front of Marcus. "I bring a missive, Mr. Thorne." Ronald always sounded very proper when Marcus was present. Not at all like he did when Marcus wasn't in attendance. There was none of the wringing of hands or cryptic speeches.

"From whom?" Marcus asked absently as he turned the envelope over and regarded the seal. "The Trusted Few?"

"Indeed," Ronald replied, his nose rising a little in the air.

"Did you go back to the fae?" Marcus asked.

Ronald held up one finger and began. "That is neither here nor there…" but Marcus cut him off.

"Did you or did you not?" he ground out.

Ronald flushed and kicked at a speck of dust with the toe of his slipper. "It was my duty," he informed them all.

Sophia jumped to her feet. "You've been spying for the Trusted Few."

Ronald looked decidedly uncomfortable. "Not exactly."

"You went back through the portal," Marcus said, his voice deathly quiet. It made the hair on Sophia's arms stand up. And it made Ronald blanch even more. "For what purpose?"

Garden gnomes could come and go at will through the portal, unlike the fae. The fae could only pass on the night of the full moon, unless they bribed the fish. "I was bid to bring reports."

"Of our actions." Sophia flopped onto the bed, mimicking Marcus's earlier pose. She talked from beneath her puffy sleeve. "Pray tell what the Trusted Few have to say. Open the blasted missive, Marcus."

"Language, miss," Margaret warned.

"Language, my arse," Sophia retorted, but unshed tears burned the backs of her lashes. This hadn't turned out at all like she'd planned.

She heard Marcus break the seal with his fingertip and then heard his long exhale. It sounded heavy enough that it should have ruffled her skirts. But she looked up to find Ronald sitting on them. "Get up," she ordered, yanking on her skirts. Ronald rolled and toppled to the floor with an oath.

"That wasn't very nice," he grumbled as he dusted himself off.

"Neither is spying," she replied hotly. "What does it say, Marcus?"

"We have a new mission." Marcus held the parchment out to her.

"Certainly, you're not being serious." She took the paper from him and read it quickly. "We're to deliver a present to Viscount Ramsdale and his wife." She looked at Ronald. "What sort of present?"

Ronald reached into his pocket and pulled out a small silver casket. "It's sealed by magic," he informed her as he passed it over to her. That meant he'd tried to open it and been unable.

"We're to deliver it in a sennight?" Sophia looked up from the missive to find Marcus's watchful gaze on hers. "Why must we wait a sennight? Can't we just deliver it now and be done with it?"

"Our instructions are to deliver it at the ball. A sennight from today."

"Oh, I do love a good ball," her grandmother chimed in, not even looking up from her knitting. "We shall all attend."

"But we'll miss the moonful. We won't be able to return home for more than a fortnight after that."

"Nevertheless, those are our instructions." Marcus

tossed the missive into the fire, where it shattered like the sparks of flint on steel.

"Well, that's an interesting turn of events," Sophia breathed. "I thought they'd never send me on another mission. Perhaps they'll let me keep my wings, after all?" She arched a brow at Marcus.

"I highly doubt it."

Sophia raised a finger to her mouth and absently worried a nail, until Margaret shot her a scolding glance for her actions. She huffed and settled onto the bed. Another sennight to prepare for the ball. Then more than another fortnight before she'd leave Ashley's land. A lifetime without her wings. And without Ashley and Anne.

"I have more time to complete my mission with Lady Anne," Sophia mused aloud.

But Marcus disagreed. "That mission has been passed on to Claire."

Sophia jumped to her feet. "You can't do that."

He dusted his hands together as he said, "We're finished with this conversation, Soph. I know you don't like it. But that mission was always meant for Claire. She's installed as the girl's governess, which gives her more access than you currently have."

"But," Sophia floundered.

"And no one saw her use her fae magic," Marcus interjected, his voice harsh enough to break stone. "She's in a better position than you are."

Yes, yes, Claire was in a better position than Sophia. She was with the Duke of Robinsworth. And Sophia never would be again.

Nineteen

ASHLEY CLOSED HIS LEDGER AND LAID HIS HAND FLAT upon it. He couldn't come up with one more task that needed doing. Nothing else was pending his approval. No one needed to be paid. No one needed his counsel. He'd avoided bed until the wee hours of the morning, knowing that he'd feel lonelier than ever when he went into his empty bedchamber.

It had been six days since she'd left. Sophia had only visited him there twice, but he could still smell her in the room. Still feel her pressed against his side as he played. Still hear the cadence of her wicked little breaths as the music excited her.

He scrubbed a hand down his face in frustration. He'd learned to avoid his nose, which was healing much nicer than he'd anticipated. No bruising and very little inflammation. But his nose just made him think about Sophia again. Everything made him think about her.

He groaned to himself and settled deeper into his chair.

But then heavy, quick footsteps sounded in the corridor. Finn burst into his study as though the hounds of hell were upon his heels. His hair stuck out in every direction, and his clothes were covered with trail dust. He was missing his cravat.

Ashley leapt to his feet. "Who died?"

Finn crossed to the sideboard and poured himself a healthy shot of whiskey, tossed it back, grimaced for a moment, then shook his head and grinned. "I found her."

Ashley crossed to stand in front of his desk, hitching his hip upon the edge as he crossed his arms over his chest.

"Oh, stop trying to look so imposing," Finn groused as he poured another shot of whiskey. "It took nearly a sennight, but I found the Thornes. All of them. They're at the Slipper and Stocking."

They were less than a half day's ride away? "Are you quite certain it was them?"

"More than quite," Finn said. Ashley crossed the room and put the whiskey away. Finn scowled at him. "I bring you good tidings and you hide the whiskey? How dare you?"

"If you drink much more, you won't be able to tell me what you've learned." Ashley settled into a chair and reached out one foot to kick a chair closer to Finn. "Sit. Pray tell me everything."

Ashley waited with bated breath for news of Sophia and her whereabouts.

"I followed them all the way to town," Finn said. "And then out of town. And then back to town. I got a little turned around. But then a man approached me on the street and walked by me singing this little song about a lass with eyes the color of honey and molasses, and he was speaking of a girl named Sophia. I wish I could remember the words." He began to sing softly to himself.

Finn had obviously had more to drink than Ashley had originally thought when he arrived. "Go to bed, Finn. Sleep it off." He got up to go to bed himself, but Finn jumped up to follow him.

"I asked him where he'd heard that song. He said a little man with a round head who was about two feet tall was singing it in the bushes by him, and he'd been so enamored of it that he'd learned every word." Finn groaned at what must have been the ungodly amusement that was sure to be on Ashley's face. "I know, it sounds quite farcical, but I swear it's true." He laid a hand upon his heart. "The little man was singing of your Sophia Thorne."

Ashley snorted. "She's not my Sophia."

"But she will be, if you have any say in the matter."

Yes, she would.

Finn swished his hands in the air, as though to wipe away any obstruction. "So, this man was singing about Sophia and talking about the little man. And I thought how odd the whole situation was." He reached out to grab Ashley. "You'll never believe this, Robin." He looked like he was about to burst.

"I'm certain I won't."

"I asked him where he saw the little man. I felt certain he'd say he met him during his stay at Bedlam, but he didn't. He pointed down the road. So, I walked down the road, and guess what I found?"

It was only then that Ashley realized Finn had dropped a burlap sack as he'd walked into the room. And the sack was moving. "Tell me that's not..."

"I caught him, Robin. I caught the little man. He told me all about the Thornes."

"Was this before or after you shoved him in the sack?"

Finn appeared to think it over. "Before."

"You have a little man in the little sack." Ashley was quite certain his mouth was hanging open. But he couldn't help it. It was too ridiculous for words. Finn looked like the cat that ate the canary. "What's really in the bag, Finn?"

Finn rolled his eyes and then crossed to the bag and upended it. And from the bag rolled a little man, who, when unfurled, stood about two feet tall. Finn had the man's hands tied in front of him and his feet bound, and Finn's cravat poked out of the man's mouth. Ashley heard what he thought sounded like an oath from the little lad. He wore a yellow waistcoat and a black jacket, with a red cravat of his own.

The little fellow murmured something at him from behind the wad of fabric shoved into his mouth. "What did you say?" Ashley prompted. The little man motioned to his mouth with his hands. "Oh, quite right."

"Don't do that, Robin!" Finn shouted, just as Ashley tugged the plug from the little man's mouth. But it was too late. The red-faced little creature leaned forward and sank its teeth into Ashley's finger. "It bites," Finn said belatedly.

"Bloody hell," Ashley murmured to himself as he took a step back from the creature. "You could have told me it bites before you let me free its mouth."

Finn shrugged. "I tried."

"Try harder next time."

"Untie me," the little man said.

"It speaks," Finn said, sinking down onto his knees to regard the little man more closely.

"Of course, I speak, you dolt," the little fellow said. "You and I had a whole conversation before you stuffed me in the sack."

A grin tugged at the corners of Ashley's lips.

"You don't have to call me names," Finn returned.

The man held up his hands. "You don't have to tie me up."

Ashley snorted. He couldn't help it. It was too hard not to laugh.

The little man held out his hands to Ashley. "Your Grace, would you untie me, please?"

"You know who I am?"

The little man looked at Ashley like he was the worst sort of idiot. "Doesn't everyone?"

Ashley supposed that was true. "I'd like to talk to you," Ashley said, as he approached slowly. He reached out a tentative hand. "You're not going to bite me again, are you?"

"Not unless you make me," the man said with a sudden jovial grin. "And to think, I thought you were the dangerous one."

"A misnomer, I assure you," Ashley replied.

Once Ashley cut through his bonds, the little man clambered into a chair and turned to face Finn. "Tell me your wish, sir, so I can go back to my duties."

Ashley could think of only one wish he would wish. "A wish?" he asked, as he settled in a chair across from the little man.

"You freed a garden gnome. You get a wish." The little man regarded him with a slow smile.

"Wait. I should be the one to get the wish. I caught you."

"Exactly." The gnome shook his head as though he was talking to an addled man. "You caught the gnome." He pointed to Ashley. "He freed the gnome." He pointed to his left ear. "Use these for something other than holding up your spectacles, won't you?"

"I don't wear spectacles," Finn muttered.

"Then you don't use them for a single thing, do you?" the gnome taunted.

Ashley chuckled into his fist. Finn cursed behind him and pulled up a chair. "The little lad knows Miss Thorne," Finn reminded Ashley.

"Little lad?" the man said with a snort. "I'll have you know that I'm two hundred and ten years old." He snorted again. "Little lad," he murmured, disgust in his voice.

"What are you?" Ashley asked.

"Is that your wish? To know what I am?"

"Absolutely not," Finn interjected.

The gnome sighed heavily. "Can you make it go away?" He pointed to Finn. "It makes me nervous."

Finn bristled at the "it" reference. "Why you little…" But Ashley held up a hand.

The little man grinned broadly and appraised his fingernails closely for a moment. Then said, "You humans certainly are a foolish lot. I am a garden gnome."

"I never thought garden gnomes were real. Next you'll tell that the gargoyles guarding my garden gates are real."

The gnome arched a brow at him.

"Good God," Ashley swore. "They are?"

The gnome shrugged.

"I have to get back to my post. Sophia can get herself into some serious messes when I'm not around to watch her. I'm her shadow, you know?" the gnome said, his chest puffing out with pride.

"I'm certain you make a wonderful shadow."

"Until someone catches him," Finn tossed out.

The gnome stood up in the chair and looked for a moment like he would launch himself at Finn. Ashley was almost ready to let him. But Finn held up two hands to fend him off. The little man huffed and settled back into the chair. "Your wish, Your Grace," the gnome prompted.

"How long have you known Miss Thorne?" Ashley asked casually.

"Since the day she was born. And her mother before her," the man said with pride. He narrowed his eyes at Ashley. "You get one wish, Your Grace."

"I bet Miss Thorne will be looking for you."

"She has an upcoming mission. And I must be nearby in case she needs me."

"Exactly where are you all from?" Ashley asked, trying not to seem too concerned.

"I'm certain you've never heard of it."

Bloody hell. Why was it that they all replied with the same answer?

"Your wish, Your Grace?" he asked, his foot wiggling impatiently.

"I believe you should stay the night," Ashley suddenly said. "A man of your importance gets the best bedchamber and a fine meal." Ashley rang for a servant. The little man preened under Ashley's praise and was practically licking his lips at the thought of a good meal.

"The best bedchamber?" he asked, his chest puffing up with pride.

"I hope you'll do me the honor of being my guest." Ashley had to find out where Sophia was. He wanted to know everything there was to know about her. He could probably get more out of the man with simple kindness and flattery, but he'd have that wish now. Then ask for more of the man on the morrow. "My wish is to have Miss Thorne." Ashley knew she'd been at the Slipper and Stocking, but was that where she still resided?

The gnome appeared to mull it over for a moment, scratching his chin. "Which one?"

There was more than one? "Miss Sophia Thorne."

"You can find Miss Sophia Thorne at the Ramsdales' ball tomorrow night."

"Ramsdale, you say?"

Ashley bellowed loudly and Wilkins poked his head into the room. Even in the middle of the night, the butler was still at his post. "Wilkins, do you think you can secure an invitation to the Ramsdales' ball tomorrow night?"

Wilkins looked slightly taken aback. But the servants had a way of getting things done that Ashley had never understood. "For whom, Your Grace?"

Ashley fought not to roll his eyes. "For me."

Wilkins looked started for a moment but recovered quickly. "I believe I can." He nodded once at Ashley.

Then he noticed the gnome, who sat with his chin resting on his upturned hand, his feet swinging a foot off the floor. The butler barely blinked. There was barely a twitch. He looked less startled to see a little man, fancily dressed, than he had when Ashley asked for an invitation to the ball.

"Good. Secure an invitation for me. And find a bedchamber—"

A cough from the gnome cut Ashley off.

"Take Mr...?" He waited for the gnome to fill in the blank.

"Just Ronald," the gnome said with pride. As though it were his heritage rather than a single, ordinary name.

"Please take Ronald to our best bedchamber. And be sure he's settled for the night." Ashley reached out to shake hands with the little man. His grip was surprisingly firm. "I hope you rest well, sir," Ashley said.

The man preceded Wilkins from the room, so Ashley called to his retreating back. "Wilkins?"

"Yes, Your Grace?" he said as he came back around the corner.

"Secure his door and his windows," Ashley said quietly.

The butler smiled and nodded. "Yes, Your Grace."

Twenty

SOPHIA STEPPED OUT INTO THE DARKNESS OF THE NIGHT and shook the lethargy from her brain. She'd been engaged by the music since she'd arrived. Pulled toward it as though some invisible string connected her and it. She'd been listening intently ever since the moment she'd heard the lilting sound of the orchestra. Since the very moment she'd walked through the blasted doors.

It was a good thing her dance partners hadn't expected her to converse, or she'd have been labeled a bumbling idiot the moment she opened her mouth. Certainly, they'd tried to talk with her, but she'd been so enamored by the music that she couldn't put two rational thoughts together. Still couldn't. It was much like being foxed. Drunk on the rhythm of the music. Yet it didn't reach her the same way Ashley's music did. It didn't jar her very soul. It didn't call to her the way his music did.

She leaned heavily against the cold exterior wall of the Ramsdales' monstrous home and let the chill seep through her gown to scorch her skin. It felt quite nice, having something to think about, aside from the music. But then the door beside her opened and a man stepped into the shadows. "Miss Thorne?" the interloper called.

Sophia shuffled farther into the darkness, just as the music seeped around the door to greet her as well. She huddled farther in the shadows.

"I could have sworn I saw her leave through that door," a second voice said.

"Quite an odd piece of baggage, is she not?" the first man asked. She could vaguely place his voice but couldn't remember his name. She'd danced a minuet with him. How dare he compare her to baggage!

"Pretty as a picture, though." He guffawed loudly. And unattractively. His laugh was almost as big as his hooked nose. And it was huge. "It's too bad she has bats in the belfry."

"What do you mean?"

Indeed? What did he mean?

"She couldn't put two words together if her life depended on it. It was like talking to the marble statue outside my father's hunting lodge."

"Since when have you cared one bit about *talking* to a lady?"

Unable to take any more, Sophia stepped from the shadows into the light that filtered out the window-panes. "Since when have either of you become such grand individuals that you can speak so callously of someone you've only just met?" She dusted at her skirt.

Even in the darkness, Sophia could see them both flush. "Miss Thorne." The hooked-nosed one had the nerve to speak.

Indeed. She was of a good mind to throw some dust above their heads and bring their own insecurities to light. But then Marcus popped his head around the corner and into the darkness as well. He looked at the two men, who fidgeted from foot to foot.

"Is everything all right out here?" he asked of the men. Then he raised a brow at Sophia.

"Everything is fine. These two gentlemen here have decided that I'm dumb as a rock, however. Since I can't put two words together, perhaps you should take me home."

Marcus gave them both a scathing glare. They blanched even more, and the hook-nosed one opened his mouth to speak. "Save it for someone who cares to hear it," Marcus bit out before the man could do so. Marcus held his elbow out to Sophia, and she took it with no hesitation.

As he led her back into the ballroom, she steeled herself against the music, but it infiltrated her senses regardless, making her brain feel like mush. "Please tell me you delivered the package. Can we go home now?" Sophia asked of her brother.

"I would have delivered it, but I don't know who it's for yet." He reached into his pocket and retrieved the small silver casket. Then he opened her reticule and dropped it inside. "But I do know it's for you to deliver."

Blast and damn. Of course, it couldn't be simple. It had to be difficult.

Marcus looked down at Sophia's dance card and noted that she had an empty space. "I'll take this waltz," he said absently, as he led her out onto the floor.

"Better you than some unsuspecting peer who will

expect me to converse." Sophia placed her hand in his, and he stepped toward her. But then the music screeched to a halt. Every eye in the room looked toward the orchestra. And the orchestra members stared openmouthed at the entrance of the ballroom.

Sophia feared she looked as dumbstruck as the rest of the occupants of the room. But she was finding it difficult to draw in a deep breath. There, at the top of the stairs, stood the dangerous Duke of Robinsworth in all his splendid glory. He wore all black, except for the gleaming, icy-blue diamond pin that winked at her from the center of his cravat. It matched his eyes almost perfectly. A wayward lock of hair fell across his forehead and she wanted to rush to him to brush it back. But Marcus's hand tightened on her arm. "Don't even think about it," he breathed.

It was all she could think about. It had been days since she'd laid eyes on Ashley Trimble. Days since she'd seem his smile. Since he'd made her heart trip within her chest. Since he'd looked at her as though she were the only person in the room. And he was doing so now. Every eye in the room turned toward her when his gaze landed upon her. And then an audible gasp echoed around the room as the corners of his mouth lifted in a small smile.

He turned and greeted his hosts quickly and efficiently. They looked a bit more than surprised. But were obviously honored to have a duke in their presence. Even if he was the dangerous duke, he was still of the upper orders of the peerage, and it was an honor for him to set foot across their threshold. Much less linger for a moment in their home.

The orchestra took the cue from the butler, who motioned for them to begin again. They did so, but their eyes were on the duke, rather than on their music. Nevertheless, a lilting minuet began.

"Breathe, Soph," Marcus urged.

Oh, dear, that would probably help her stay upright, wouldn't it? She inhaled deeply through her nose.

"That's better," Marcus said soothingly.

"Perhaps for you. Because now you won't have to catch me as I fall."

He nudged her toe with his. "You need to take a step, Soph."

Sophia looked around her and saw that people were moving with the music. But all she wanted to do was look at Ashley. She looked to the place where she'd last seen him. He wasn't there. Her heart lurched.

"Stay with me, Soph," Marcus urged. He squeezed her hand so tightly that it almost hurt, but it snapped her back to the present.

"I'm here," she muttered. "Under protest." She took a deep breath and looked up at Marcus from under heavy-lidded lashes. "Why do you think he's here?" Sophia asked as they separated.

"You know why he's here," Marcus said under his breath as the music brought them back together.

She hoped she did, but it would be nice to hear someone say it. "You think he's here for me?" Her voice quavered a little. She looked around the room, but Ashley's dark suit was nowhere to be seen.

Marcus circled around a grinning girl and came back to her. "I think he's here for you. We should probably get you out of harm's way."

Sophia tripped over his toe. Out of harm's way? "Not on your life," she breathed.

"Soph," he warned, his voice a low growl.

The music slowed to a halt, and Marcus led her off the dance floor. He stood with her on the outskirts of the room and looked down at her dance card. The rest of her dances were filled. And her next partner should be coming to greet her any moment. She looked around. Captain Perkins was a red-haired man with a kind smile. He stood over six feet tall and was lean and lanky. She saw him approach from across the room to collect her. He had a swagger to his step that was almost cockish. He had none of Ashley's grace.

Would she compare every man she met to Ashley? Probably. For the rest of her life.

But Captain Perkins stepped up to her side at the same time Ashley did. One on her right and the other on her left. Ashley looked somber as he raised her dance card to see what was next. He looked up at the captain and arched a brow. "You won't mind if I take your dance, will you, Perky?"

Sophia never would have assumed the red-haired captain's face could grow any redder, but it did. "Perkins," he corrected. "And, actually, I believe my name is written in for this dance." He squared his shoulders and stared Ashley down.

Ashley took the card in his hands and tore it in half. He handed the other half to Captain Perkins. "There, that should do it." Then he held out his elbow to Sophia as though daring her to take it.

She slipped her hand into the crook of his arm

and let him lead her onto the floor. It wasn't until his
hand landed on her waist that she realized his power
over her. The music held no power at all. Ashley
commanded every second of her attention.

⤴⤵

It was all Ashley could do not to grin like a bacon-
brained ninnyhammer. However, since every eye in
the room was upon him, he couldn't possibly tell her
how damn happy he was to see her. He settled his
hand at her waist and squeezed gently.

"How are you?" he asked softly enough that only
she could hear him.

Her gaze didn't rise above his cravat when she
spoke. "I'm well."

The soft sound of her voice hit him like a bolt of
lightning. He had Sophia Thorne in his arms. In a
crowded ballroom, he reminded himself. He forced
his feet to move. It had been years since he'd waltzed.
Since he'd graced a ballroom.

"How is Lady Anne?" she asked, her voice rolling
across him like silk. He fought a shiver.

"She's well."

He turned with her in his arms, tugging her closer
than was allowed, but he couldn't help it. She still
smelled like the bluebells of summer, a smell he would
have in his mind forever. He'd missed her. He wanted
nothing more than to pick her up and carry her from
the room. To set his lips upon hers and taste her. To
be with her. He supposed he would have to settle for
what he could get.

"She asked about you."

A heavy sigh left her lips. "Why are you here?" she asked. Her hand trembled within his.

"For you." He didn't say more than that. Just those two words.

She inhaled deeply, causing her bodice to swell, and the fullness of her breasts teased his chest. Walking, much less dancing, would soon become impossible. Ashley waltzed her to the edge of the room and out the side entrance, down a long corridor, and into a small parlor. He closed the door behind them. Then he opened it again. "For propriety's sake," he said with a grin.

The lilting sound of the music was little more than a memory. But Sophia Thorne was real. Flesh and blood in front of him.

"Propriety?" Sophia scoffed. "You should know by now that I don't give a rat's arse about propriety." She turned her back to him and walked slowly toward the window.

"A rat's arse," he repeated with a chuckle. God, she was delightful.

"Why are you here, Ashley?"

He cocked his head at her sideways. "You asked me that a moment ago. I already answered."

She raised her fingertips to massage her forehead. "I remember."

"I have a long-standing history with music," Sophia said with a sad shake of her head. "It makes me forget things. And it has gotten me into more than one predicament."

"Like finding your way into my chambers in the dead of night?" he prompted.

"Exactly." She raised a fingernail to her mouth and began to nibble it. "Yet the music here doesn't affect me like yours does." She stepped toward him and laid a hand upon his chest. "I don't understand it, but you do strange things to me."

He didn't understand it, either. "The feeling is mutual, I assure you." He covered her hand with his and didn't let it go even when she tugged it. She softened against him.

"You know what I am," she said as she laid her cheek against his chest, right over his heart.

"I can assure you that I know nothing." He raised a hand and gently teased the tendrils of hair that had escaped her coiffure.

"You're a dangerous man," she said quietly, raising her head to look him in the eye, finally. He stiffened. He couldn't help it. In this moment, with this lady, he didn't want to be the dangerous Duke of Robinsworth. He wanted to be Ashley Trimble, there to court Sophia Thorne. But that was not to be, evidently.

"I'm no more dangerous than I was those nights you stole into my room. No more dangerous than I was when we shared time in the garden." He didn't want to beg for her favor and, in fact, refused to do so.

"But you are, because now you know my secret."

Ashley snorted. He knew nothing. Absolutely nothing. "Something happened in the village," he began.

"Yes, it did," she said, cutting his words short. "Something that never should have happened. You were not to know."

He chuckled, a self-deprecating sound if he'd ever

heard one. "I can assure you that what I know is just enough to leave me flummoxed."

"I won't be here much longer. In your world," she began. Her pretty hazel eyes welled with unshed tears, and a piece of Ashley's heart might as well have broken in two.

"My world is your world," he tried. "It doesn't matter that I'm a duke. Society means nothing to me."

She shook her head. "You saw me use my magic with your very own eyes. And yet you still think I'm from your world." She spun away from him. "I'm not. And I cannot be."

"Magic."

She spun quickly to face him. "Magic!" she said loudly, raising her hands in the air as though calling him forward to brawl with her. "I am magical."

He chuckled. "Yes, you are."

A grin tugged at her lips. God, she was pretty when she smiled. "You are incorrigible." She waved at him in dismissal and turned back to face the window. "I don't know what you want from me," she said on a long exhale.

"I want to spend time with you."

"I don't have time to give you. I must return home soon."

"Where is home?"

Both he and she said at the same time, "I'm certain you've never heard of it."

She laughed and shook her head. "We have had this conversation before."

"I vaguely remember that it didn't scare me from your side the first few times we had it." He probably looked like a green lad, begging for a lass's favor. He swiped a hand down his face and grunted at the lingering pain in his nose.

"How is your nose?" she asked quickly, approaching him from across the room. She stopped and looked up at him, appraising his nose a mite too closely.

"Healing."

She nodded. "Good."

"You can trust me with your secrets, Sophie," he said quietly.

"You can trust me with yours," she retorted. One dark brow arched at him. An invitation? It was like waving a red flag in front of a bull.

"When can I see you?"

She held her hands out to the sides. "You see me now."

He wanted the intimate setting they'd had when she visited his bedchamber. Not like this.

"When can I see you?" he repeated, his voice harsh-sounding even to his own ears. *When will you tell me your secrets? When will I get to tell you mine?* He didn't say the last. But he thought it.

"I can't, Ashley." When he began to mutter a protest, she held up a finger and shushed him. "I simply cannot live in your world."

The door to the room opened slowly, making a creaking noise that made Sophia look over his shoulder toward it. "Is everything all right in here?" a male voice asked.

"Viscount Ramsdale," Sophia chirped as she stepped around Ashley. "I was feeling a little faint and the good duke brought me for some air."

"Are you well now?" The man's gaze flicked from one of them to the other. "I would be a poor host if I didn't offer my assistance."

"I'm well." Sophia looked at Ashley. "I think you owe me a waltz since we didn't get to complete the last one." She looked down at the torn dance card that dangled from her wrist. "And I just happen to have some free dances." Her eyes twinkled at him.

If a dance was all he could get, he would take it.

Ashley held out his elbow and she slid her hand inside, squeezing gently as she did so. "Ramsdale," Ashley muttered as they walked past the man.

Suddenly, Sophia pulled him to a halt. She reached into her reticule and retrieved a small silver box. She held it out to Viscount Ramsdale. "Do give this to your wife for me," she said. Then she slid her arm back into Ashley's and he towed her back toward the ball. He wanted to tow her toward his carriage. Or toward his bed. But he assumed a crowded ball was all he would get.

"Dance with me this night, Ashley," Sophia said quietly as he led her onto the floor. "As though it's our last."

"It's not," he assured her.

Her eyes didn't meet his when she replied softly, "We shall see."

Twenty-One

ASHLEY WATCHED SOPHIA FROM BEHIND THE PALM fronds in the corner of the ballroom, keeping check on her location even after he had to give her up to a new partner. It would ruin her reputation if she danced every dance with him. She didn't seem to give a care about her reputation, but he did. He knew what it was like to have a bad one, a really bad one, and he didn't want her to suffer the same fate.

Devil take it, just being seen dancing with him would give her more than a bad reputation. It would cause a scandal.

"Were you thinking of asking that frond to dance, Robinsworth?" a male voice asked from behind him. Ashley turned to find Mr. Marcus Thorne lounging comfortably against the wall, his arms crossed in front of his chest. One foot was raised so that the heel of his slipper pressed against the wall. "You've become quite cozy with the palms while I watched. Such a loving touch you have." He made a snort beneath his breath. "And I thought it was just my sister you liked to get cozy with."

"Your sister. A palm frond." Ashley shrugged. "I am not choosy."

"Been alone too long, have you?" Thorne asked. "I could find someone for you, aside from my sister, that is, if you just have need of a tumble."

Did the whole blasted world think he couldn't find a whore if he wanted a whore? He didn't want a whore. He wanted Sophia Thorne. "Thank you, but I'll pass." He shoved the palm frond to the side and looked for her on the dance floor. She wasn't there. A moment before, she'd been in Perky's arms. A respectable distance from him, but still in the man's arms. But now they were gone.

"You won't catch her unless she wants to be caught."

Ashley let that comment rumble around in his mind for a moment. Then he steeled his features, looked down his nose at Thorne, and said, "I already caught her. In the village."

Sophia's brother scoffed. "You caught nothing."

Ashley forced himself to chuckle, although it was the last thing he wanted to do. He stepped closer to Thorne. "I most definitely caught her. And you are well aware of it. In fact, I imagine that's why you came to find me in the foliage."

Thorne straightened his back. "Perhaps I like palm fronds as much as you do."

"Perhaps you think I'm an idiot."

"Perhaps you give yourself too much credit."

Touché.

Thorne sighed heavily. "What do you plan to do with the knowledge you obtained?"

Ashley shrugged. "I haven't decided."

"She can't be in your world. Not permanently. Not if she wants to remain in ours."

Again with the world? His world and her world weren't that different. She was obviously a cultured lady. She had a tongue sharp enough to cut glass, but her manners were perfect, her dress divine. She didn't lack funds or education. Not that he could tell.

"How much of it is a ruse?" he asked.

"All of it," Sophia's brother replied without even blinking. "Nothing about her is as she's led you to believe."

Ashley grunted. He didn't know what to say to that. But something about the lady called to him. That wasn't entirely in his head, was it? It couldn't be. There had to be a reason for it.

"Another will come along, Robinsworth. One who can be what you need."

Another wouldn't be Sophia.

Thorne's hand landed on his shoulder and squeezed it. Ashley fought the urge to shrug him off. "I don't offer marriage lightly," Ashley informed him.

"I don't warn you off marriage lightly," Thorne responded. He was difficult to read, but Ashley almost sensed that he regretted his words. The whole situation. "I warn you for your own good. She's not of your world. She can't stay in it."

"Try to take her from it, and you'll regret it," Ashley finally bit out.

Thorne's face softened. "No, I'm afraid you will."

❧

Sophia fanned her face as Captain Perkins led her from

the dance floor. It was growing warm enough that she felt moist in the crowded room.

"Can I get you some punch?" the captain asked.

"Punch would be heavenly," Sophia sighed with a smile. He was a nice man. Not everyone had insides that matched their outsides, and vice versa, but she sensed that his did. He led her over to the punch bowl, allowed a servant to prepare a glass for her, and placed it in her hand. She took a healthy sip. "Thank you."

He looked toward her torn dance card and grinned. "It appears as though no one has taken the next few sets."

Sophia laughed. "I wouldn't have a clue if someone did or not. Perhaps someone will remember me and come to claim their due." She shrugged. She really didn't care if no one arrived to claim her. She enjoyed talking with Captain Perkins. She'd rather be with Ashley, but the captain was a nice man.

"I'm surprised Robinsworth hasn't come to claim you, yet." He glanced about them. "Perhaps he left?"

Sophia highly doubted it. She scrunched up her face.

Captain Perkins laughed. "Yes, I doubt it as well. He seems rather intrigued with you."

Sophia didn't know what to say to that.

"Will you accept a friendly warning about him?" He looked down at her, his gaze serious and concerned.

"Something tells me I do not have a choice in the matter." Then she squeezed his arm. "Pray continue. It will do me good to hear the truth about the man." She batted her lashes at him. "You did intend to tell me the truth, did you not?"

He chuckled and leaned close to her. "When you do that flirty little thing with your eyelashes, it makes me want to lie to you just to see if I can coerce you to do it again." He sighed dramatically. "But, truthfully, Robinsworth is a dangerous man."

"So I have heard." She clucked her tongue at him. "What evidence do you have of this?" She tugged the top of her glove toward her elbow and didn't look at him. She didn't want to give too much credence to his words. No more than they deserved.

"His wife falling from the tower of their ancestral home is not evidence enough?"

"I don't believe he pushed her." Sophia would not believe that. Not for a second.

"Nor do I," Perkins said quickly.

"Then why on earth are we having this conversation?"

"Because someone did push her. She did fall from the tower."

"You don't think she could have tossed herself from the turret?"

"Not very likely, since she was confined to a wheeled chair. She could barely move herself from the bed to the conveyance."

Sophia's gaze shot up to meet his. She had heard none of this. Not once had anyone mentioned that the late duchess was disabled. "What was her ailment?"

"That's not common knowledge."

"Of course, it's not." Sophia drank the last of her punch and passed the glass to a waiting footman. "Nothing about the Duke of Robinsworth is common knowledge."

"One thing is well known, Miss Thorne. He's dangerous. Do take care around him."

Sophia nodded. What more could she do? It wasn't as though she would be alone with the duke any time in the near future. Her mission had been given to Claire.

The next set began and no one came to claim Sophia for a dance. Sophia was relieved. But the music began to steal her wits.

"Are you all right, Miss Thorne?" Captain Perkins asked, taking her elbow in his palm to steady her.

"The music," she said, raising a hand to rub her temple.

"Would you care to walk with me to the card room? I'd like to check on my sister. The last time I saw her, she was heavily involved in a game of whist."

She tucked her hand into his arm and inclined her head. They started down the long corridor, but as they walked farther toward the noisy, voice-packed room at the end of the passage, Sophia heard a melodious voice coming from a nearby room. "Who is that?" she asked of the captain.

He inclined his head toward the sound and concentrated. "Sounds like Lady Ramsdale, maybe?" He shrugged. "I'm not certain."

"Lady Ramsdale sings?"

"Like a songbird," the captain said. "She has the most beautiful voice I've ever heard." He shook his head. "But she only sings by special request for special guests. It's rather rare to hear her break into song in this type of setting."

They continued down the corridor toward what Sophia assumed must be the music room, and the words become clearer and clearer, as did the tone. It struck her heart like an anvil strikes metal. Like the kick of a horse. Like the tick of a clock that ticked at her very being. Like Ashley's music. She inhaled deeply and tried to steady herself.

The captain stepped to the side and motioned for her to precede him into the room. She did so, skirting around the room to stand in the rear. There were fewer than a dozen people in the room, but it seemed crowded. Sophia let the sound of Lady Ramsdale's voice wash over her, closing her eyes as the lady hit the high notes, feeling them all the way to her soul. In that moment, it was almost as though a piece of her cracked into two pieces.

Unfounded tears suddenly burned the backs of her lashes, and she found it nearly impossible to commit to a full breath. She blinked hard and studied the woman standing beside the piano. Lady Ramsdale's auburn hair tumbled from her upsweep to tease her bare shoulders. Bare shoulders that were riddled with freckles. Freckles she obviously didn't feel the need to hide. She had them across the bridge of her nose as well. Her nose was narrow and her cheekbones high. She looked quite fae, truth be told.

Sophia's lungs began to burn with every inhale. She laid a hand on her chest and tried to steady herself. But the lady's song was tantamount in her mind. Then Lady Ramsdale reached one hand to adjust the pewter comb that held her hair in place, and as she adjusted, Sophia thought she saw the edge of a pointy ear present itself from behind her hair. Lord Ramsdale was beside her in a trice, adjusting her comb and patting her hair back into its place. She smiled softly at him, a wicked little smile that made him blush. She ran a fingertip slowly down his upper arm. He shot her a playful look and stepped away from her.

She continued to sing, never breaking her stride, the music rising and falling over Sophia like water over the falls. And just as harshly. Her knees began to tremble. She reached out one hand toward Captain Perkins as a tear traced a hot path down her left cheek. But suddenly, the captain wasn't there. Sophia stumbled into a hard object. She looked up, her vision blurred by her tears, and saw the man she needed. The only one she needed.

"Ashley," she said aloud. The music in the room stopped. Every eye turned toward them.

"Sophie," he said, his brow furrowing as he caught her to him. "What's the matter?"

She stretched her arms about his neck and held on, but her arms quivered under her own weight, and her knees refused to support her. She collapsed against him. He swept her up into his arms and looked down into her face.

"Sophie," he cried, his voice harsh and jarring. "Tell me what's wrong?"

He lowered his face close to hers, as though he could give her the breaths that left his mouth to replace her own, which refused to support her. "I think she's my mother," Sophia whispered. Then darkness overtook her, and she let it.

❦

Ashley looked down into Sophia's face and took in her pale countenance, her closed eyes, and the weakness of her body, and his heart lurched within his chest. "Sophie," he called to her, gently jostling her within his arms. "Come on, Soph," he urged.

Sophia's brother approached him and attempted to take her from his arms. "Let me have her, Robinsworth," he said, shooting Ashley a glance that could have stopped a charging elephant in its tracks.

"Not on your life," Ashley replied, turning her body away from her brother. It was terribly selfish of him, he knew. But he wasn't about to put Sophia in anyone else's arms.

Suddenly, her grandmother was at his side. "Come this way," she urged, as she bustled out the door and down a long corridor. She stopped at a small yellow parlor and stepped to the side to allow him in. Ashley lowered Sophia's inert body onto a settee and dropped to his knees beside her.

"Did she grow overwarm?" Ramsdale asked from the doorway. But then his wife shoved her way into the room and moved Ashley to the side with a gentle push. He made way for her. He didn't want to, but he did. He'd never felt quite so lost. Quite so desperate for help.

Lady Ramsdale took Sophia's hand in hers and squeezed it gently. She touched the side of Sophia's face with gentle fingertips, as though looking for something even Ashley couldn't see. When she looked up, tears welled in her eyes. "Mine," she breathed. Then a sob tore from her throat, and she pressed a hand to her mouth and rose. She dashed across the room and flew into Sophia's grandmother's arms.

Lord Ramsdale looked about as discomfited as

Ashley felt. He watched his wife with horror on his face. Lady Ramsdale cried into Sophia's grandmother's shoulder until her sobs became small hiccups. Then the older lady pushed Lady Ramsdale from her with her hands upon her shoulders and said, "It took you long enough to recognize us." She grinned an impudent and unrepentant grin.

"Exactly what is going on, here?" Thorne asked.

Lord Ramsdale shrugged. Ashley couldn't answer either. And Sophia still lay on the settee with her eyes closed, her breaths falling naturally and comfortably in her stupor. Only Sophia's grandmother and Lady Ramsdale had a clue as to what was transpiring, it seemed.

"I never thought she'd find me," Lady Ramsdale breathed. Then she looked at Thorne and covered her mouth again. "Marcus," she said. She crossed the floor and tried to envelop him in her arms. He stepped to the side, incredulity still written on his face. Thorne looked to Ramsdale as though begging for assistance with his wife.

"He doesn't recognize me," she said with wonder, as another sob hiccupped from her.

"Have we met, Lady Ramsdale?" Thorne asked.

"Once upon a time, yes," she said. A lone tear trickled down her cheek. She didn't reach for him again. Not yet.

Suddenly it was clear to Ashley. The flashing hazel eyes. The dark auburn hair, with more curl than was fashionable. The high cheekbones and pixie-like appearance. But it wasn't his story to tell. It was hers. And Ramsdale appeared to be in the dark as well. The poor man's gaze was flashing from one person to the next.

"Let's move Sophia above stairs, shall we?" Lady Ramsdale said with a wave of her hand. Ashley moved forward to pick her up, but Ramsdale moved faster.

"I can carry my daughter above stairs, thank you, Your Grace," he said, his voice cracking at the last. Then he speared Ashley with a glance. "Can I leave it to you, Your Grace, to handle the festivities while I take care of familial obligations?"

Meaning, could he give Ashley a meaningless task to take his mind off the fact that Sophia was about to meet her parents for the first time? To keep him from hearing their deepest secrets? To permit them some dignity during this trying time? He supposed he owed them that much. "May I call upon her when the guests have departed?"

Ramsdale glanced down into Sophia's sleeping face, and he coughed to clear the lump from his throat. "Perhaps tomorrow?"

Ashley shook his head. "Today."

Ramsdale sighed heavily. Ashley feared he had some explaining to do. And so did they.

Twenty-Two

SOPHIA WOKE TO THE NOTES OF A GENTLY HUMMED song. The sound of it washed over her like a warm blanket, comforting and snug. She blinked her eyes open, not entirely sure of where she was, and took in the sunny bedchamber with the reddish-purple hues of the sunrise visible out the window. She stretched broadly and looked for the source of the hum.

At her side, a woman sat with an embroidery hoop in her hand. She pulled a piece of gossamer thread through the sheerest of fabrics. She hummed softly to herself as she did so, a small smile tugging at the corners of her lips. Her hazel eyes suddenly rose to meet Sophia's and she startled. Her grin widened. "Oh, you're finally awake."

Sophia sat up on her elbows. "Where am I?" she asked. Then vague recollections of the night before clouded her senses. She closed her eyes tightly and tried to remember. But it was all cloudy. One thing she did remember, however, was falling into Ashley's arms just after she'd recognized her mother.

Her mother.

Her mother sat before her. There was no doubt in Sophia's mind that the woman smiling at her was her mother. The lady brushed her hair back over her ear and Sophia noticed the small pointy crest of it, evidence that she was fae. She let her gaze linger on the woman's features. So much like her own.

"I know this is all a shock to you," Lady Ramsdale said, reaching a hand toward Sophia. But Sophia scuttled outside of her grasp in the big bed. Lady Ramsdale tilted her head to the side and sighed heavily. "I understand your reticence. Really I do." Tears welled in her eyes, and she blinked them back, and then swiped quickly at her nose. "I have a lot to tell you," she said.

"You've had twenty-six years to tell me anything I needed to know." Sophia knew the words were harsh. They made *her* wince, and she was the one who said them.

"I couldn't go back," her mother said with a quick shake of her head. As though her affirmations could explain it all. "I had no magic. No dust. I tried. I couldn't find the portal. Time after time, I tried. I even made your father go with me. He has compared me to a Bedlamite on more than one occasion." She began to fidget with the bedclothes. She took a deep breath. A breath heavy enough Sophia was surprised that she didn't suck all the air from the room. "I never thought they would be able to take you from me."

"Where is Grandmother?"

"Sleeping. I sent them all to bed. Even Marcus. He's quite confused."

If he was half as confused as Sophia, he was nearly insane.

"Only your duke is still awake. He's probably still standing vigil at the door." Her hazel eyes twinkled. "He's the one, isn't he?" She leaned forward and propped her chin in her hand, blinking those pretty eyes at Sophia. It was like looking into a mirror.

Sophia shook her head. "He can't be the one. He's not of my world."

Lady Ramsdale snorted lightly. But she didn't say anything else. She reached into her pocket and pulled forth the silver casket Sophia had given to Lord Ramsdale the night before. "I believe this is for you."

Sophia sputtered. "I gave that to your husband last night. It was our mission."

The lady chuckled heartily, tears welling again in her eyes. "My father's machinations, I imagine. I am so glad he finally came to his senses. I thought he'd never do this."

Sophia shoved her hands back as her mother tried to give the casket to her. "But it's sealed by magic. I can't open it."

"I have already opened it. It filled in a lot of blanks for me. I imagine there's one for Marcus, too." She held it out again.

Sophia shook her head. "What's in it?"

Lady Ramsdale shrugged. "My memories of you." She shook her head quickly and got up to face the window. She kept talking. And Sophia let her. "I thought my magic would be strong enough. I thought I could keep you. I cast a few spells, enchanted some charms. I even enchanted you. Your love for music? Have you ever wondered where it came from?"

Sophia had always wondered.

"It's a token I planted within you. A memory of me. One of my greatest loves, aside from my husband and children, is music. In case my spells didn't keep you here with me, I wanted you to be able to find me someday." She shrugged. "It worked."

"You tried to keep me with you." Sophia sat forward, fully absorbed in the tale.

"With my very being," she said, clutching a fist to her chest. "I'm the daughter of one of the Trusted Few, for goodness sake. A renowned mission faerie. A thing of legend and lore. I thought my magic would be strong enough. It wasn't." She equivocated. "Well, it was. But it was a little too late."

She sat down on the edge of Sophia's bed and continued her tale, her words frantic and hurried and barely comprehensible. "When someone of the fae falls in love with a human, he or she must make a choice. A lady must choose between his world and hers, you see? I had to choose to stay with your father and go forward with him in this world, knowing full well that any children I had who were born fae would be taken from me just after their birth. Along with my memories."

Sophia opened her mouth to speak but closed it quickly when her mother rushed on.

"It's an ending we expect, but I thought I would be able to keep you. I took every opportunity I had to break the fae hold upon you." She held up both hands as though offering something to Sophia. "It didn't work. They came and took you, and they took my memories of you. Of all that I did." She reached for the silver casket. "That's what's in this box."

Sophia didn't take it.

"I tried something different with each of you. With you and Marcus, it didn't work. I didn't know until I laid eyes upon you that you even existed. But I knew you with my heart the moment I saw you." She clutched a fist to her chest again.

What about Claire? She didn't mention Claire.

A quick rap at the door grabbed her attention. The door opened a crack, and a lovely young woman entered the room. "I just couldn't wait any longer," she said, a grin upon her face. Lady Ramsdale sighed, smiled, and beckoned her closer. "Sophia, this is Rose. Rose is my youngest daughter." Lady Ramsdale reached up and tucked a lock of hair behind the girl's ear. It was pointed, just like hers. "She's fae, too. But I finally found a way to keep one of my children."

"You have more children." Sophia suddenly felt like her heart was being ripped from her chest. She'd let the Trusted Few take three of her children. And had kept the fourth. "Did you just try harder with the fourth one?"

Lady Ramsdale's brows knit. "Fourth?" She shook her head as though to clear it. "I have two daughters and a son of this world. One of my daughters, Rose, was born fae. The other two were not. The two who were not born fae—there was never any question about them remaining with me. The fae didn't want them. They would have wanted Rose. They would have taken her from me. But something I did worked with this one. I don't know why." She stroked a hand down Rose's hair. "It's not her fault she was allowed to stay with me," she said succinctly, as though warning Sophia to treat her sister with kindness.

Of course, it wasn't the girl's fault she was the one her parents had kept.

Sophia rubbed at her temples. A dull thump began behind her brows.

"I know this is difficult for you," her mother said. "It's a lot to take in at once."

"I need some time to digest all of this." Sophia shoved the counterpane back and got to her feet. "I'd like to talk to the Duke of Robinsworth. If he's still here, as you mentioned."

Her mother's eyes softened. "Of course, you would. Your head must be spinning with all this new information."

She had no idea.

⁓

Ashley pulled his watch fob from his inner pocket by its golden chain and flipped it open. He'd been up all night, waiting for Sophia to wake. But within the room, all had been quiet since Lady Ramsdale had sent everyone else to their chambers for rest several hours before. As the clock struck six, he heard low mumbling from within the room.

He got to his feet and crept closer to the door. He desperately wanted to know what was going on inside that room. He yawned into his cupped hand. Despite the fact that a butler had brought him a chair and tea during the night, he'd been waiting diligently for hours. Perhaps now he would get some answers.

"I didn't know dukes listened at keyholes," a voice chirped from beside him. Ashley looked down into hazel eyes much like Sophia's. The girl's unbound hair had the same curl but was much lighter, more like Lord Ramsdale's.

Ashley inclined his head at her. "In my experience, dukes can do whatever they please, within reason." He probably sounded like a sanctimonious arse, but he didn't care.

The girl giggled. Then she rapped lightly on the door and slipped inside. More conversation happened for a moment and then she left the room, with Lady Ramsdale at her side. The lady stopped in front of him. "She's asking for you."

Ashley's heart leapt.

"This is a lot for her to absorb in a very short time. I told her things I didn't even remember until I saw her." She looked at him closely. "How do you feel about my daughter?"

"Pardon me, my lady, but I think I should discuss that with your daughter before I discuss it with you." He adopted his most imperious duke's scowl. She didn't seem intimidated. Perhaps Sophia had learned her impertinence from her mother.

Her eyes twinkled. "Yes, I believe you should." She stepped to the side and motioned him into the room.

He entered to find Sophia staring out the window, wearing a dressing gown with the frilly white collar of her nightrail peeping from the neckline. "I'm a little underdressed," she said, holding her hands out to the sides.

He did the same. "Perhaps it's me who's over-dressed." He smiled at her. "Are you all right?"

Suddenly, she rushed forward and hurled herself into his arms. He caught her to him and let her embrace him tightly as sobs wracked her body. His heart broke for her, yet he still held her close to his heart and let her vent her frustrations, her anger. He just let her cry. When she settled a bit, he carried her over to a chair and settled into it and arranged her in his lap so that her head rested on his shoulder.

"Feel better?" he asked as he brushed her hair from her eyes.

"No. Not really." She sniffed.

"Do you want to talk about it?"

She pointed to a silver casket that rested on the bed. "I suppose the answers are in that box."

Ashley didn't fully understand. Or understand at all.

She went on to explain. "It contains my mother's memories. Apparently, when they took me from her, they took her memory of me as well."

"When who took you?"

"The Trusted Few." He must have looked confused because she continued. "The governing body of my world." Her eyes danced from his mouth to his lips to his chin. "You know I'm not of this world."

"I'm beginning to understand that. But it scares the hell out of me," he admitted.

"Me, too," she said on a heavy exhale. Then she got up and retrieved the casket. "Open it with me?"

He would do anything she asked of him. "Of course."

She flicked the lid with her thumb and it flew open, as though some force inside was clambering to get out. Glitter shimmered and shone in the air until it began to take shape, and then, like the golden pictures she'd played over the boys' heads in the village, it took the shape of shadowy, shimmery people who acted out the most prominent of her mother's memories. But these pictures were accompanied by emotions. Emotions so strong they nearly stole Ashley's breath. Regret. Pain. Longing. Agony. All tempered by love, compassion, and caring. He reached for Sophia's hand and squeezed it tightly.

Her mouth fell open as the truth became known to her, and a tear ran down her cheek. But a smile was also tugging at her lips, and she looked at him, her eyes shimmering almost as much as the glittery pictures did. "I never would have dreamed…"

"Nor would I." Was he dreaming? Would he wake from this and find it a figment of his imagination? Machinations of too much time spent alone? He looked down at her. She still clutched tightly to his hand. "Does this resolve things for you?"

She snorted. "Not by half."

"Good, because I am mightily confused," he admitted.

"I don't know what happens next," she said, and he wanted to draw her to him and protect her with a sword and shield from all the things that were coming at her. But he didn't have either. Nor would she welcome his interference.

The glitter began to dissipate from the air, shooting like stars flying across the sky and then dissolving like the morning dew on his garden.

He thought about it a moment. "Come back to the Hall with me. Take some time to absorb it all. To come to terms with it."

"I'm not certain that's a good idea," she said, and he could tell she wasn't sold on the idea.

His heart sank. "Marry me and then come home with me."

She shook her head and the corners of her mouth turned down. "I cannot." That was all she said. Just that she could not. She could if she wanted to. Perhaps she just didn't want to. Didn't want to enough. He tried to come up with a reason for her to leave the family she'd never known. It was selfish of him, he knew, but he wanted her. He needed her. If only for a few days.

"I have something that will make you change your mind." He adjusted the fit of his rumpled coat and steeled himself. "I have someone who belongs to you within my walls."

She startled. "Claire?" she asked. "Claire can take care of herself."

Who the devil was Claire? "No. Who is Claire?"

Her brows knit together. "Then who?"

"You will have to visit me to find out. But I will tell you that this person will be incredibly happy when you come to stake your claim."

"Stake my claim?" She looked confused. And a little vexed.

"You will want what I have."

"Did I forget my dust?"

He shrugged his shoulders. "With all the dust at my estate, I doubt I would notice any you left behind." He paused and took a deep breath. "But no, it's living and breathing. A little fellow about two feet tall."

"You caught Ronald!" she cried. She put her hands on her hips and stomped her foot. "How the devil did you do that?"

"Finn did it, actually. Then I freed him. And he bit me. And then I caught him again. I'd like to untie him, but he has really sharp teeth."

Sophia laughed and leaned forward, pressing her cheek over his heart for a moment, as though he alone could bolster her. He took a deep breath at the same time she did. "Set him free, Ashley. I cannot come to you."

"Why not?" He began to feel like a lost child at a carnival, desperate to find his way to the person to whom he belonged.

She turned to face the window. "It will only prolong the hurt." She spun back to face him. "Set him free."

"No."

Her eyes narrowed. She was quite adorable when she was vexed. "You'll only do us both harm by keeping him."

"You can put a stop to it. Simply come and retrieve him." He bent and kissed her forehead, despite the fact that it was wrinkled with what he supposed was worry. Or anger. He wasn't certain which. But he forced himself to turn and leave the room.

❧

Sophia plucked a flower from a plant in Lord Ramsdale's lovely garden and brought it to her nose, deeply inhaling its lavender scent. She let it envelop her as she tilted her head up toward the sun and let its warmth shine upon her skin.

"You look just like your mother when you do that," a voice said from a few feet away from her.

Sophia startled and dropped the flower, which fell to the cobbled walk beneath her feet. "Allow me," Lord Ramsdale said as he bent to retrieve it. He held it out to her, allowing it to twist and twirl between his fingers.

"Thank you," Sophia croaked. She reached out a tentative hand to take it from him.

"It's not that bad, now is it?" he asked suddenly, his voice sounding like he'd swallowed an apple and was choking on it with every word.

"I suppose it could be worse," Sophia twittered nervously.

"I can assure you there's nothing worse than finding out you have children you've never known, Sophia." His voice grew stronger. "Absolutely nothing."

She raised her eyes to meet his. "Yes, there is. It's living for twenty-six years without parents at all."

He took a moment to clear his throat and collect his wits. Then he sighed heavily. "If I could have changed it, I would."

"Did you not know the dangers going into it?" she asked. Her tone was sharp and she was well aware of it.

He nodded slowly, as though he held some reticence about answering. "I knew the dangers. But your mother and I thought our love would transcend the odds. We were youthful. Full of folly. Ridiculously naive."

"What made you think you were that special?" she snorted.

He plucked a flower of his own and spun it between his fingertips. "I couldn't live in her world. I would have left this one in one beat of my heart. I swear it." He looked into Sophia's eyes, and she felt almost as though she could see into his soul. "But I couldn't. So, it was your mother who had to sacrifice.

We went a few years with no children at all. We planned it that way."

Warmth crept up Sophia's cheeks.

He chuckled at her discomfiture. "Perhaps your mother should have this discussion with you."

"Pray continue," she said. "You tried not to have children."

He nodded. "But then we found out Amelia was expecting. She was over the moon with happiness." He motioned toward a garden bench and encouraged Sophia to sit with him. She did so with hesitance, not certain whether or not she was prepared to let down her guard. When he was settled beside her, he continued his tale.

"She began to use her magic again. She had no dust—they'd taken that from her when they clipped her wings." He shook his head, sadness clouding his features. "I think it would have been easier for them to take her life than her wings. But that is not the point of this conversation." He pressed on. "They clipped her wings. And took her dust. But she still had magic within her. She used every spare bit of it to protect you. But it wasn't enough."

"There was nothing anyone could do," Sophia said. "You'd made the choice for her to leave the fae. You must accept the consequences." She hoped she didn't sound as bitter as she felt. She probably did. More the pity.

"They took our memories of you. It was like you never existed. Not until your mother laid eyes upon you last night." He reached out one hand and covered Sophia's with his. "The moment she saw you and

Marcus, she knew you were ours. And so did I. It took some time for the memories to return. But now they're there, like they'd never left." He patted her hand. "Please accept my apology for letting them take you."

His voice was choked again, and he got up from the bench, looked out over his garden, and didn't look in Sophia's direction. Perhaps he was trying to compose himself.

"Have you seen Marcus?" Sophia asked.

Lord Ramsdale, her father, nodded. "He feels very much the same way you did, I'm afraid. I spoke to him briefly, but we need to talk more."

"It will take some time," Sophia tried. Time. It would take a millennium. "I'm willing to try."

He spun quickly to face her. "I'm so happy to hear that."

"I'm not of this world, however, so I cannot stay here."

"But you can come and go at will." He looked… hopeful.

"Not quite at will. But on the night of the moonful, I can pass through the portal. Unless they oust me from the land of the fae, too. That is still to be determined."

"The Duke of Robinsworth?" he asked.

She nodded.

"What is your relationship with him?"

"Do you plan to play the role of father now?" she asked.

"I plan to do more than play at it," he said. Sophia's heart leapt.

"He was my mission. Or at least his daughter was."

"Were you able to help them?"

She shrugged. Had she? She wasn't certain. She hadn't solved the mystery of his wife's death. "He plays the pianoforte. So, I was inexplicably drawn to him." Although, now that she thought about it, the token her mother had left within her was so she could find her parents. Why did Ashley's music affect her so heartily as well?

"The spell was to bring you to a loved one. One who has the power to love you with heart and soul, my dear," he informed her, his eyes softening as understanding seeped into her. "Perhaps there's more to your duke than you think."

"There's no such thing as predestation," she bit out. She refused to believe that she was predestined to find Ashley and forced to love him. Forced to leave her land the way her mother had. Forced to give up any children she and Ashley created. Anger grew and grew within her.

"I don't think it has anything to do with predestination. I think it's a spell gone awry. I'm certain your mother didn't think that you would find us and find a man who loved you all at once when she cast the spell."

"The very thought is a little absurd, is it not?"

He chuckled. "Nothing is absurd when you're dealing with the fae."

Wasn't it? "I have to go and see Ashley at some point. He has my garden gnome."

Her father looked perplexed. "Ronald?" he finally asked. "I haven't seen him in ages."

"I suppose not," Sophia said. If he hadn't seen his children, he certainly wouldn't have seen Ronald.

"Hateful little creature. Attacked me once in the garden when your mother and I were courting.

Thought God had loosed the hounds of hell upon me, and then the little nuisance bit my ankle. I still have a scar." A grin tipped the corners of his lips despite the vehemence of his tale.

"He's loyal to a fault."

"How did Robinsworth end up with him?"

"I'm not certain. But he bade me retrieve him."

"I'll accompany you, if you like."

She smiled at him and shook her head. "I should probably do it myself. I have some things I need to say to him." She patted his hand this time. "Don't worry. I'll take Margaret with me."

"Margaret wasn't very adept at keeping your mother out of trouble, if I remember correctly. Perhaps she has gotten more cautious as she has aged."

"Perhaps."

"If you don't mind, I'd like to have a conversation with Marcus similar to the one that we just had. If I can locate him, that is." He lumbered to his feet and smiled down at her. "Shall I escort you inside?"

"No, thank you, Lord Ramsdale," she began. His face fell.

"Will you ever call me Father? Or did we botch things up too badly?"

"I don't even know how long I'll be in this world."

"For quite some time, if your duke has anything to do with it."

"He's not my duke," Sophia began.

"Certainly, he's not," he said with a chuckle. Then he bent and placed a chaste, comforting kiss on her forehead. "I'll see you in a bit."

"Yes." Yes, he would.

Twenty-Three

"IT WOULD SERVE THE LITTLE BEGGAR RIGHT IF YOU left him there until the end of time," Margaret groused from where she was bent over Sophia's valise, packing her belongings.

She absolutely could not leave Ronald with Ashley while they all went back to the land of the fae. He had to be retrieved, and it looked like Sophia would be the one who had to retrieve him. She wanted a moment alone with Lady Anne, regardless. More than a moment. She wanted to solve the puzzle that was her mother's death for the girl and for Ashley. She couldn't do any of those things without going to the Hall. "I will retrieve him. Then I will return and we can go back to the fae on the rising-dawn wind, just as we had planned."

The midnight wind was already swirling. She could feel it in the air. All she had to do was step aboard and she would be back in the land of the fae. They all would. Well, Sophia, Marcus, and Margaret would. Sophia had very little time to say her good-byes to Ashley, speak with Anne, and retrieve Ronald.

Say good-bye to Ashley... She'd be leaving the biggest part of her heart behind when she did. But it couldn't be avoided. She couldn't live in his world. And he couldn't live in hers. When she returned, they would all step aboard the rising-dawn wind and it would be as though they'd never been in the human world.

Sophia picked up her reticule and looked inside. Her vials of dust, in their clear glass bottles, shimmered like diamonds. She might need them. Heaven forefend, she might need all of them. She might also need none of them.

"Stop fretting, Sophia," her mother said from her chair by the wall. "Everything will work out as it should. You'll see."

"I'm not fretting. It's only Ashley I'm going to visit. Not some mad killer who will chop off my head."

The corners of her mother's lips tipped up in a smile. "It's not your head I'm worried about."

Margaret grunted from her corner of the room. Nothing more was heard from her. Just a grunt.

Her mother pretended to look affronted. "Now, Margaret, do speak up if you have something to say." She cupped a hand around her mouth and pretended to whisper, "I never knew Margaret to withhold her feelings on any matter. Has she gotten soft in her old age?"

"She has gotten wise," Margaret piped up. She shook a finger at Mother. "And you should not encourage her."

"Not encourage my daughter to follow her heart?" Lady Ramsdale placed a hand upon her chest. "What kind of a mother would I be if I did that?"

Margaret pursed her lips, as though she wanted to say something but withheld it.

"Say it," Sophia's mother prompted, her eyes narrowing in challenge. "I dare you."

Margaret opened her mouth as though to rush into speech but closed it quickly. Then she opened it again and said, "You of all people should recognize the folly in this."

"The folly in falling in love?" Sophia could tell that her mother was purposefully goading Margaret into speech.

"The folly of giving your love to a man who's not meant for you."

"Like I did?" her mother questioned softly.

"The fireflies tell tall tales about you," Sophia said, trying to break the tension in the room.

Her mother scoffed. "They do love to prattle on about nothing. Always have." She speared Sophia with a glance. "Pray tell me what they have to say."

Sophia shrugged. "Just that you committed some heinous crimes and were banished from the fae."

"It's a crime to fall in love," her mother said.

Margaret took a deep breath and then her mouth opened. And words Sophia had never expected to hear tumbled forth. "The crime, my lady, is that your children were raised without a mother and a father."

Sophia interjected, "Margaret, please hold your tongue."

But her mother overrode her. "Margaret, please let loose your tongue. It always was razor sharp and viciously wicked. What has changed you, I wonder?"

"You knew the dangers when you chose him."

Her mother finally jumped to her feet. "Don't you see? There was never a choice. Not for me. He is the other half of my soul. I gave up my life as I knew it for love. And if offered the same opportunity, I would do it again."

"You'd abandon them again." The words slashed like a whip across the room, harsh and painful.

"I. Never. Abandoned. Anyone." Her mother said the words slowly, and her voice choked with emotion.

Sophia sighed heavily and pinched the bridge of her nose between her thumb and forefinger. "We have already determined the previous course of events. Must we rehash it?"

"Only as a lesson to you, because you're about to make the same mistake," Margaret said.

Sophia stepped forward and clutched Margaret's hands in hers. "I choose the land of the fae, now and always. I choose it over Ashley. Over any life I could have had with him."

"Yet you go to him for one night."

Would one night sustain her for a lifetime? Maybe it would.

Sophia sighed heavily and opened the door. She stepped through it and looked back over her shoulder. "I will meet you tomorrow on the rising-dawn wind. We'll complete our journey together."

Margaret snorted. "I will believe that when I see you step back into our world."

"I never left our world. I'm still firmly planted there."

"You will return one day, Sophia. Won't you?" her mother asked. Her voice was hopeful and almost afraid.

"To visit you, yes. Of course. Now that I have a mother, I do not plan to stay away from her for long." Sophia tried to offer an encouraging smile. But returning would be difficult.

"Are you certain you don't want to take Margaret with you tonight? To keep you from being distracted by his beauty and charm? Or his need for you?"

Perhaps she wanted to be distracted by it. She didn't answer, and simply hooked her reticule around her wrist and walked down the corridor. Away from her mother. Away from Margaret's scolding look. Away from her conscience. Away from the land of the fae for one night. When moon sank low in the sky, she would have to leave. There was no other way.

❧

Ashley tossed a card onto the growing pile in front of him. Who would have thought a garden gnome could best both him and Finn in a game of whist? He never would have believed it in a million years. Yet the little fellow smirked at them both from across the table, his feet pumping back and forth in front of him, high off the floor.

Finn ran a hand through his hair and tugged it gently. "I can't believe I let a garden gnome beat me."

Ronald said, "Pfft! Let me? I think not."

Finn laid his hands flat on the table and leaned forward toward Ronald. "You are an odious little man."

"Better to be odious than odiferous," Ronald replied as he pinched his nose. "You smell like the horse you rode in on."

"Just because your legs are too short to allow you to mount a horse," Finn snarled back.

"Too short?" Ronald cried as he jumped to his feet. If Ashley didn't put a stop to it, they would be at fisticuffs within moments. The same way it had been for the last few days.

"Stop it, both of you," Ashley snapped. "Watching the two of you is like caring for unruly children. The pair of you need a governess."

"I'll take that one you hired for Anne off your hands, Ashley," Finn said with a rakish grin.

The gnome raised his fists. "You will do no such thing." He rushed toward Finn.

"Bloody hell," his brother growled as he stepped to the side to avoid the gnome. "Keep that thing away from me, Robin," he bellowed.

"Ronald," Ashley called, using his most imperious tone. The gnome stopped, with Finn's hand upon the top of his head, holding him back. "Stop tormenting Finn."

The little fellow adjusted his waistcoat with all the dignity he could muster. "Is that your wish?"

"You know it's not."

The gnome growled low beneath his breath. "Blast and damn," he said. "You have to set me free so I can meet the midnight wind with Sophia. She needs an escort back to the fae."

"Sophia has been notified that she will have to retrieve you herself if she would like to see you. Two days ago." Two days of pure hell. Two days of being unable to go to her. Two days doing nothing but look for her arrival. Wishing for it.

Dreading it.

He had a feeling it would be the last time he saw her.

Finn glanced at his watch fob. "It doesn't look as though she's coming tonight, either, Robin," he said with a look of pity on his face. "Shall I escort it back to its chambers?"

Finn had quickly learned that nothing ruffled Ronald's feathers more than being called "it." Ashley shot Finn a quelling glance. But Finn just smirked at him.

A soft scratch sounded at the door and Wilkins stepped inside the threshold. Ashley jumped to his feet.

"You could at least try to play hard to get, Robin," Finn said.

"What is it, Wilkins?" Ashley asked.

"You have a visitor, Your Grace."

"Who is it?"

"It's her, Your Grace."

There were a good many hers he could be referring to. But only one Ashley would give his last breath to see.

"It's Miss Thorne." Wilkins looked like he was almost happy about it.

"Thank God," Finn roared. "Finally, he can stop pacing and looking at the clock. Bring the lady in, Wilkins. Don't just stand there."

Ashley really wanted to see her alone. But he had the whole night to do that, didn't he?

"Your Grace?" Wilkins questioned. He lifted his nose higher in the air and ignored Finn. Finn was better left ignored in most situations.

"By all means, show her in," Ashley finally choked out.

Sophia preceded Wilkins down the corridor and
toward Ashley's study. Her heart beat like mad within
her chest, and her lungs refused to take in a full
breath of air. Yet, still, she went where the butler led.
Because Ashley was at the other end of the journey.
She stepped into his library and the room fell silent.
He stood with his back to her, looking down at a
piece of parchment on his desk. He did not look up.
Not when Finn bowed over her fingertips nor when
Ronald took her hand and brought it to his lips to
greet her.

She forced herself to look down at Ronald. "Are
you well?" she asked.

"As well as can be expected after being imprisoned
by the dangerous Duke of Robinsworth." He played
with a loose thread on the sleeve of his coat.

Sophia ruffled the tiny tuft of hair on the top of the
gnome's head. "You're lucky he didn't consume you
in one bite, as small as you are."

Finally, Ashley looked up, and storm clouds brewed
behind his sky-blue eyes. "I save the big bites for those
who are not innocent," he said, his voice low. A
shiver walked down her spine. She remembered him
saying those very same words to her in his garden the
first time they were alone.

She could barely find her tongue. But she forced
herself to scoff. "And you think he is innocent? You
couldn't be further from the truth."

Ronald puffed out his chest with pride. He worked
hard at being a libertine at times.

"Wilkins, could you see Ronald to his chambers?"
Ashley asked. He still hadn't greeted her. He still

hadn't touched her hand. She wanted desperately for him to say or do something.

"Back to my chambers," the gnome grumbled.

"Don't worry," Sophia assured him. "I'll be along to collect you shortly."

He skulked away with Wilkins at his side. Wilkins poked a finger at him in warning. "Don't even consider trying to trip me. You remember who won the last time."

When they were gone, Sophia looked from Ashley to Finn. Finn appeared as though he had no intention of leaving.

"Good night, Finn," Ashley said loudly, not taking his eyes from Sophia's. His gaze was locked with hers.

Finn started for the door, mumbling, "I can tell when I'm not wanted."

It wasn't until the door clicked shut behind him that Ashley reached for her.

Twenty-Four

SOPHIA LET HIM JERK HER CLOSE, HARSH AND UNYIELDING in his need for her. A laugh escaped her throat as he bent his head and nuzzled his stubbly jaw into the sensitive skin at her throat. Winding her arms around his neck, she threaded her fingers into the hair at the base of his skull and tugged gently, forcing his head up so she could look at him. Instead, he pressed his forehead against hers, gulping in large breaths of air, his eyes tightly shut as though he was in pain.

"I thought you'd never arrive," he whispered, his words harsh enough to shatter glass yet soft enough to rub over her skin like a caress.

She touched her mouth to his quickly and tried to pull her head back so she could talk to him, but his fingers threaded through hers, locking her in his grasp with her arms behind her back as his lips chased hers in her retreat.

"You knew I would come for Ronald," she said against his lips. But it was nearly impossible to think with him kissing her in such a manner, much less speak.

Suddenly, he jerked his head back from her. "Tell me you're not here just for Ronald," he growled, looking at her face as though he'd never seen her before.

Sophia forced herself to take a deep breath before she said, "No. I'm here for us, too."

"For how long?" he ground out. His breaths heaved from him in huge, gasping bursts.

"For tonight." It nearly broke her heart to say it. But it must be said.

"I'll have tonight to change your mind," he whispered, almost reverently.

"You can try," was all she could offer.

He laughed softly, raising her hands to put them back around his neck, and then his fingertips slid down her arms until she was caught within his grasp, her belly against the hardness of him. "Oh, dear," she whispered, unable to say more.

"I need you," he said, raising trembling fingers to brush her hair back from her face, tucking it behind her ear. His eyes lingered on the pointy tip of her ear. He stopped short and stared at it.

"This is the first time you've noticed it." She tilted her head to look at him, watching for his reaction as he studied her ear. "It's always been like that."

"How could I have missed seeing that?"

"You were more concerned with other parts of my body?" she asked, feeling particularly wicked.

"What else do you have?" he suddenly blurted out.

"Beg your pardon?"

"What else marks you as… what are you, exactly?"

"I doubt you want to know all the details." She tried to laugh, but it was nearly impossible.

"I want to know everything about you," he said, his lips touching hers again, softly this time.

"I am fae," she said, taking a deep breath to bolster herself. She disentangled herself from his arms and stepped back from him. "I can't think when you touch me like that," she admitted. He nodded and crossed to the sideboard to pour himself a drink.

"Would you like one?" he asked and then raised his glass to his lips for a quick swallow. She nodded and stepped toward him, but before he could pour a glass for her, she took his from his hand and raised it to her own lips. He made a noise in his throat when her lips touched the place where his had been.

"Thank you," she said, passing it back. The liquor traced a fiery path down her throat, nearly stealing her breath. He raised it back to his own mouth and took a swallow, regarding her over the rim of the glass as he drained it dry.

"Where is the land of the fae?" he asked.

"Somewhere you've never heard of."

"Again with the cryptic comments?" he groaned as he dropped into an overstuffed chair. He crooked a finger at her, and she went without even deciding to do so. He tugged her so that he could lace his fingers with hers. "Don't lie to me, Sophie. I deserve more than that."

"You saw what I did in the village."

"I'm not certain what I saw," he said, laying his head back against the chair to regard her from beneath heavy-lidded lashes. He pulled her down to sit on his lap and jostled her lightly with a bump of his knees. "Explain it to me."

She brushed a wayward lock of hair from his fore-head. "Please know that it's forbidden."

"Ballocks, Sophie," he said quietly, his hand resting on her hip, his thumb drawing tiny circles that threatened to disarm her.

"I can't think when you touch me," she scolded.

He chuckled. "Yet, I can't seem to be able to stop."

"I have this final night," she began. But her voice cracked and she forced herself to stop. She squeezed her eyes shut tightly for a moment, then opened them and looked directly into his. "I have this final night. Then I must catch the rising-dawn wind in the morning."

"Must you?" he whispered.

She nodded. "I must."

He stood up and swept her into his arms. He tossed her for a firmer hold and she squealed. "What are you doing?"

"If I have you for one night, I want to spend it in my bedchamber." He started for the door.

～❧～

"Wait!" she cried as he started down the corridor. He didn't even stop to look down at her, afraid he would see rejection on her face. Ashley didn't stop walking until he reached his chambers. He stomped past one flustered maid who plastered herself against the wall in fear, closing her eyes tightly as he passed, as though by doing so, she could erase the idea of where they were going. Because it was quite obvious he was taking Sophia to his bed.

When he entered his rooms, he dropped her feet and let her slide slowly down his body until she hit the floor.

"Wait," she muttered against his lips as he bent his head with the sole purpose of devouring her. But she giggled into his mouth at the same time and didn't act like she wanted him to stop at all. So, he didn't. But then her hands smacked playfully against his chest. "A moment, Ashley," she finally said, lifting her lips from his.

Some little part of her hesitance must have finally seeped into his brain because he realized she wasn't nearly as amorously involved as he was. Damn his eyes. He forced himself to lift his hands from her body and walked across the room, then dropped onto the bench beside his pianoforte.

"Will you play for me?" she asked tentatively.

He harrumphed. "Isn't that what I have been doing since I met you?"

Her eyes narrowed and she regarded him stoically for a moment. "Is it?" she asked. "I certainly wasn't playing."

"Never?" he asked. He probably sounded like an untried adolescent.

"Not even once," she replied, her voice crisp enough to cut through the air like a knife. "How dare you diminish the feelings I have for you by accusing me of toying with you?" Her cheeks flushed scarlet and a blush crept up her neck. He'd never seen her angry. She was quite lovely. And a force to be reckoned with when she was truly in a temper, he'd wager. But in this case, he would bet he'd hurt her feelings more than angered her. And that made his heart ache.

"You have feelings for me?" He studied her face while he asked the question.

"Would I be here if I didn't?"

"I was holding Ronald for ransom."

She crossed to sit beside him on the bench. "I'd have come here even if you weren't."

He took her hand in his. "I want to marry you."

She shook her head, negating his words as soon as they left his lips. "I can't live in your world. I can visit it from time to time, but that's all."

"Do you plan to do that?" He brought her fingers to his lips and kissed the backs of them.

"Now that I have parents here, and they remember me, I suppose I'll visit. But it won't be enough to suit either you or me." She shrugged. "It simply cannot be managed."

"Tell me your secrets," he prompted.

She laughed. "You tell me yours."

He nudged her knee with his. "A compromise? I'll trade you one of my secrets for one of yours."

She looked at him askance, her gaze skeptical. But slowly she nodded.

"Why did you come to me that first night?"

Her face softened. "You think it was a plan, don't you? To seduce you?"

He didn't answer. He just watched her.

"It wasn't. I was completely drawn to you."

Was that a good thing or a bad thing?

"I know now that it was my mother's fae machinations that drew me to you." She grimaced. "That's probably going to get too close for comfort, if we discuss it, however. May we move on to the next subject?"

He shook his head. "No. Let's finish this one."

"Her spell was for me to recognize the song of someone who loved me. To be drawn by it so I could find her. But in her spell-casting, she neglected to think that someone else may love me, as well."

Ashley felt like hiding his head. He hadn't even known how he felt until recently. How on earth could she know?

"It's all right. You needn't tell me." She squeezed his hand. "I already know." She tipped his face up to hers and touched her lips lightly to his. "And the feeling is mutual."

"Your mother's spell…" he began.

But she cut him off. "My mother's spell drew me to you. It didn't make me fall in love with you." She laughed, a self-deprecating sound. "You did that all on your own."

Ashley's head spun with the news.

"My turn," she said, interrupting his thoughts. "Did you love your wife?"

"Don't you want to know if I killed her?"

"No." She batted those dark lashes at him. "Not yet."

He sighed heavily, taking a breath to bolster himself. "Did I love her?" He thought for a moment. "No. I never did."

"Not ever?"

"No. She and I had nothing in common. We married to suit our families. She was frail from the day I met her. And only came to my bed because she was obligated to give me an heir."

She tilted her head and listened to him. He'd never spoken of this to anyone. Ever.

"She was relieved when she found out she was expecting."

"I would have been ecstatic," she whispered softly.

"She was relieved because she no longer had to share my bed, you see. For nine months, she would be free of my affections. And, if we conceived a boy, she could be free of me forever."

"You wanted more." She didn't ask a question. She just knew he'd always dreamed of more.

"I wanted a wife I could touch and talk to when I wanted, and not just when she was breeding. I wanted a wife I could tell my secrets to. Someone who would hold them dear." Ashley shook his head. "It wasn't until much later that I realized what was going on with her."

"What was it?" Sophia's brows drew together.

"She loathed my touch so much that she became ill whenever I was around. She got so weak that she took to a wheeled chair, so she could get about. She never left her bed unless someone forced her to do so." He crossed to the sideboard to pour a drink. "I tried to be intimate with her. I tried to tell her things. I tried to talk to her. I spoke with her about my business ventures. About the investments I made. I would leave home to take care of business matters and always returned to her. She was so frail that I didn't stay away for long, you see."

"I do see…" she began. "You felt obligated to her care. Of course, you would."

"She played me for a fool."

"What do you mean?"

"There was a gentleman. A peer who approached me. He'd done quite well, and he often invested in schemes I was invested in. He was also seen in the company of my wife on occasion. I began to get suspicious. I planted some false information with my duchess to see if it would get back to him. It did. Every bit of it. He lost his shirt in the deal. And his stockings. And everything else."

"He came to see me. Accused me of all sorts of foul things. Tried to blackmail me into paying him when he realized what I'd done. I refused. He threatened to harm my wife if I didn't pay him. I never expected him to follow through."

"Where is he now?"

Ashley finally looked up from his glass. "In Parliament. He serves his duties as though he's not penniless and homicidal." He shrugged. "I never could prove he did it. But I'm certain of it. I would bet my fortune and my family on it."

"You didn't kill her."

❧

Ashley looked wounded at her question. He chuckled, a sound without any mirth at all as he drained the last swallow of his drink. "Oh, I wanted to kill her. On more than one occasion. When I found out she'd been sharing a bed with this gentleman throughout most of our marriage. When I learned that she'd shared my business secrets with him. When I found out her illness was all a ruse to keep me from her bed. When he tried to blackmail me. I wanted to kill her. And I may as well have."

"That's why you never disavowed it." She pressed her fingertips to her lips. "Because you felt guilty."

"If I'd done as he asked, he wouldn't have carried through with his threat. I thought he loved her a little." He made that chuckling sound again. "I was quite wrong.

"The dangerous Duke of Robinsworth did cause his wife's death," he said with a grimace. "But not in a way anyone would have ever expected."

"You are not to blame for her folly."

"I may as well have tossed her from the tower myself."

"That's not true," she started. But he just shook his head.

"Enough with my secret. I'll have another of yours now."

She tapped her chin for a moment, trying to figure out what to tell him next. She may as well show him. She turned her back to him and pulled her hair over her shoulder. "Would you unfasten my gown for me, please?"

He gulped and stared at her for a moment. But not for long. He rose and began to work the fastenings on the back of her gown. When her gown was loose, he stepped back and away from her, and ran a hand quickly through his hair. "Don't worry," she teased. "I simply want to show you something."

"Show me everything," he groaned as a grin stole across his face.

She pointed to a nearby chair. "Sit," she commanded.

He did so with no hesitation, aside from sweeping a hand down over his mouth, as though he wanted to wipe the silly grin from his face. It didn't work. He regarded her closely, leaning forward with his elbows upon his knees.

"Would you close your eyes for a moment?" she asked.

He groaned, his grin growing even wider. "Must I?"

She couldn't keep from laughing at his stricken look. "You must."

"All right," he acquiesced and he squeezed his eyes tightly together.

Sophia shoved her gown from her shoulders and untied her chemise at the neck, letting it fall to the floor. She wore nothing else, aside from stockings and garters. She turned her back to him and called forth her magic, letting her wings appear. It wasn't often she summoned her wings when she was of average size. She fluttered them lightly, satisfied when she stirred the air just a little bit around her. She peered over her shoulder and saw that she made the lock of hair on his forehead lift.

"What was that?" he asked.

"You may open your eyes and see," she said.

"Bloody hell," he gasped.

Twenty-Five

ASHLEY HAD TO REMIND HIMSELF TO BREATHE. IT WAS as though she'd stolen all the air from the room when she removed her clothes. There she stood, naked in front of him. But from her back arched pretty wings that matched the flushed color of her skin. They stood up taller than her shoulders. And dropped down low enough to cover her bottom. All he could see were her wings, the back of her head, and her pink garters and white stockings. Dear God, she was beautiful.

He forced himself to exhale and took a step toward her. "By the saints, you're a faerie," he breathed. Her hands were in front of her, one cupping each of her breasts, shielding them from his gaze. "Don't come any closer," she said, when he moved to walk around her. Her wing bent, wrapping around her enough to block his view. He stopped. "I'm not decent," she went on.

"I'll say," he gritted out.

She fluttered her wings lightly, and the breeze she created washed over his skin, making his manhood spring to immediate attention. Or perhaps it was the sight of her naked that did that. He couldn't be certain.

"What do you think?" she asked.

He reached out one tentative hand to touch her. But she jerked forward. "They're very sensitive," she warned. A slow flush crept up her body, and her wings blushed as well. Good God, she was the most beautiful thing he'd ever seen, flushing scarlet there the way she was. He pulled his hand back.

"I want to touch you," he said, recognizing the hoarseness of his own voice.

"Could you get me your dressing gown?" she asked, turning her body so that her front faced away from him as he stepped toward the wardrobe to retrieve it. But as she turned, she faced his full-length mirror that stood on the floor by his dressing table. Her eyes met his in the looking glass, and she blushed scarlet. Her wings took an even brighter hue, turning a soft but startling pink. He turned his head, though doing so was the most difficult thing he'd ever done, and held his dressing gown out to her on a crooked finger. He felt it fall away from his hand and heard it rustle as she put it on.

"You can open your eyes now," she said.

He slowly opened his eyes to her and wanted to cry with despair when he saw her wrapped in his gown, her pretty pink wings gone. "Where did they go?"

"I can make them come and go at will," she informed him with a shrug. "They're a little unwieldy beneath clothing."

"They're beautiful," he said. He couldn't come up with anything better than that. Just "they're beautiful." He probably sounded like a complete dolt.

"Thank you." Another pretty blush crept up

her cheeks. A clock down the corridor chimed the midnight hour, and she said, "My time here is drawing to a close."

"You can't go yet," he complained. There had to be something he could do to make her stay. There had to be something.

"I have a few more hours," she said quietly as she crossed to his bed and climbed atop it. "Let me sleep with you for one night."

He dragged a hand down his face. He nodded.

She turned down the linens and the counterpane and settled herself against his pillows. He went to join her. "What shall we do to occupy the night?" she asked, a grin tugging at her lips.

He could think of plenty of things to keep them occupied. But he started with her stockings. Ashley picked her tiny foot up in his hand and tickled the bottom of it. She giggled and tried to jerk back from him, but he held fast. God, she made him feel like was an adolescent again. But then she suddenly stilled, her eyes hot and limpid.

♣

Ashley trailed his hand up the back of her calf, sending tingles to every single part of her body, from her head to her toes. Her breaths were already shallow, and she could barely concentrate on anything but him. He tugged at her garter and rolled her stocking down her leg. Then proceeded to do the same with the other.

"Will you douse the lights?" she asked, hating to hear the quiver of her own voice. But she was frightened. He doused every light in the room but a single candle, his chambers growing darker and darker until there was a single dancing shadow playing upon the wall—his. She watched his graceful form as he began to shrug out of his jacket and waistcoat, and then tugged his shirt from his trousers and over his head. He sat down on the edge of the bed and tugged off his boots, laughing as he tossed them one by one to the floor with gentle thuds. He sounded more carefree than she'd ever heard him.

"Are you happy?" she asked. She could sense that he was. But her senses had been wrong in the past.

"Happy to have you in my bed?" he said as he shucked his trousers and crawled across the bed toward her wearing nothing but his smallclothes. "I'm bloody ecstatic."

He reached for her in one quick move and she shrieked as he drew her beneath him. "Ashley," she cried.

"Sophie," he crooned in retort, as he reached between them and tugged open his dressing gown, which she still wore. He devoured her with his gaze as her skin was revealed, and he lowered his head to tease her belly with his stubbly chin.

"God, you're exquisite," he growled. His mouth traced a fiery path across her stomach and up to the swells of her breasts. He uncovered them with reticence, his breath leaving his mouth in a hot rush of air when he'd uncovered her. Sophia shrugged her shoulders from the dressing gown and reached for his hair. She threaded her fingers through his dark locks, pulling him tightly to her as he explored her stomach and the line beneath her breasts with his tongue.

He didn't go any higher, seeming content to caress her, but her nipples were aching for his touch. She very gently tugged his head toward an aching peak, and he raised his gaze to meet hers for a moment as he drew the tip of her breast into his mouth.

"Oh," she cried out, arching her back to get closer to him.

He very gently licked across her nipple, watching her face as he did so, and then closed his eyes tightly as he burrowed more closely to her, seating himself between her thighs. She spread her legs for him, and he settled there.

"I'm afraid," she whispered to him, her breath hitching in her throat as he moved from one breast to the other.

"I won't harm you, Sophie. I promise." He stopped his ministrations and looked up at her, as though he needed her permission to continue. She nodded, drawing her bottom lip between her teeth to worry it. He dipped his head again, taking her nipple back into his mouth as his hands played up and down her sides. He began to rock against the center of her, and she could feel the raspy coarseness of his smallclothes against her tender skin.

"Take those off?" she asked.

He lifted himself briefly to slide them down and over his feet. Then he came back to her and she could feel the length of him pressed against her. "Please tell me that you'll be mine," he whispered fiercely, looking into her eyes as he rolled her nipple between his thumb and forefinger. She could do nothing more than nod as sensation swamped her. The pulse between her thighs grew more and more strong, and she had to remind herself to breathe.

Between them, his hand drifted lower as his lips met hers, and he slid his tongue very tenderly and softly into her mouth as his fingers found that little nub at the top of her sex that was pounding so strongly. She cried out at his tender ministrations, his mouth taking in her mewling little sounds as he breathed her in with every stroke of his fingers against her. Her hips began to arch to meet him. But then he replaced his fingers with his thumb and slid one finger inside her. Sophia nearly exploded. He stilled above her. "Tell me to stop and I will."

She jerked his hair. "If you stop now, I will use all of my fae magic to do something terrible to you."

He pretended to think it over. "Could it be that bad?"

"Oh, it most certainly can," she ground out.

He shifted his hips so that the tip of him pressed against her center. "You're an innocent, are you not?"

She nodded quickly against his shoulder, squeezing her eyes tightly shut as he pressed a little harder, sliding through her wetness and lodging just barely inside her. She felt the pain of his entrance for no more than a moment. He stilled when she cried out. "Are you all right?" he asked, his breath hot and heavy against her ear.

Her answer was a tug to his backside, and he slid farther inside her. The burning pain of it was over almost as quickly as it arrived. And with one thrust, Ashley seated himself fully inside her.

His breath-filled grunt as he stopped startled her. "I

need but a moment," he said quickly. "Or this will be over before it has begun."

He stayed still inside her as he let his fingers creep back down her belly and slide into the molten heat between them, and he began to rub that aching nub again. Sophia pressed her lips against his, drinking him in as he began to move his hips in time with his fingers. He pressed her legs a little wider apart and slid ever so much deeper inside her with every thrust. She began to arch to meet him, and he tilted her hips so he could take even more of her, so he could go even deeper. He touched a magical place inside her she hadn't even known existed. And something she didn't understand at all began to build within her.

"Ashley!" she cried against his lips.

"Sophie," he grunted in response. He said her name in small whispers again and again as she felt a wave beginning within her. It threatened to crest and smash her to pieces, and finally it did. Sophia broke, crying out as her climax ripped through her. He grew even harder inside her, thrusting slowly in and out of her as she fluttered around him. And when she was done and returning to earth, he stilled inside her, his arms shaking on each side of her, then thrust once more and groaned her name. He spilled himself within her, soaking her walls, making her even wetter than she was. His last thrusts were so pleasurable they neared pain. But then he stopped. He stopped and brushed her sweaty hair from her face. He looked down at her, her blue eyes almost black in the darkness of the room.

A tear fell from the corner of her eye. "Oh, God, Sophie," he said, still hard within her. "Did I harm you?"

She squeezed her eyes shut tightly, and a hot tear slid a warm trail down toward the linens, nearly scalding as it traced its path down toward her ear. "You didn't harm me," she admitted.

"You're certain?" he asked. He looked so worried. She brought his face down to hers and kissed him softly.

"I just didn't know it would be like that."

"Neither did I," he said as he slid himself from her still-aching sheath and lay down beside her. He rolled to the edge of the bed and crossed to the nightstand, where he wet a cloth with water and cleaned her. She would have flushed scarlet, if he the room weren't so dark. He took a moment to clean himself, and then he joined her in the bed. He pulled the counterpane over them both and tugged her into the crook of his arm.

"Promise you'll never leave me," he said as he yawned widely and placed a kiss into the hair at her temple.

She couldn't promise that, so she said nothing. She nuzzled her face in closer to his heart and closed her eyes. She would enjoy these final moments, for they would be her last.

Twenty-Six

SOPHIA WOKE TO A SOFT SCRATCH AT THE DOOR. SHE rolled over and halted for a moment because a heavy weight was wrapped around her. She forced her eyes open and smiled as she realized the weight that had her so effectively pinned to the bed was Ashley. His arm draped over her even in sleep. He tugged her to him, and she went willingly, laying her head upon his chest. "You all right?" he asked, his voice groggy from sleep.

"Shh…" she whispered to him. "Go back to sleep."

He nodded sleepily and pressed a kiss into her hair. A soft snore erupted from him, making her smile. But the scratch sounded at the door again. Sophia slid gingerly from beneath his arm and retrieved her chemise. She tugged it over her head quickly and went to the door. She opened it only a crack and looked into Wilkins's very disapproving face. "Miss," he said, his voice as cold as a midmorning wind in winter.

"What is it, Wilkins?" she whispered. She didn't particularly care if he disapproved of her. But it did sting just a bit to know he didn't regard her very well.

"His Grace is needed," the butler said haughtily.

"Needed for what?" she hissed back.

"That would be a discussion for His Grace, miss," he clipped out.

"His Grace is sleeping." She could sound just as haughty as the butler, couldn't she, if she were of a mind to? "If I feel like it's worth his waking, I'll tell him." She made a come-hither motion with her hands. "Out with it, now."

"It's Lady Anne. She's having a night terror," he finally admitted.

Anne? A night terror. She looked back at Ashley, who slept peacefully. "A moment," she said and she turned to get Ashley's dressing gown. She shrugged into it and followed the butler into the corridor, closing the door to Ashley's chambers quietly behind her. "You'll have to show me the way," she warned.

He looked down his nose at her for a moment, and then gave her a brisk nod. He began to walk, and she followed. She couldn't help but wonder why Anne's rooms were so far from His Grace's, when she seemed to need him so often. But it was not her riddle to solve.

When they reached Anne's chambers, Wilkins stepped to the side and bade her to precede him. She did so with no hesitation at all.

But what surprised her was the voice of her sister Claire as she entered the room. Claire sat in a rocking chair in the corner of the room. "It was rather difficult to convince Wilkins that Lady Anne had need of her father," Claire bit out. She held a sobbing Anne in her arms. "Now I can see why he didn't want to disturb him." Her gaze was full of censure. "Did you enjoy yourself?" she asked, her tone harsh enough to cut glass.

"Oh, do shut it," Sophia barked as she held her

arms open to Anne. The girl flew across the room and directly into her grasp. She hugged the girl to her and sat back on the bed, drawing her across her lap.

"There now," Sophia crooned. "It can't be that bad, can it?" She very gently brushed the girl's wet hair from her face. "Has your naughty governess been telling you stories of trolls and snails?"

"I did," Claire said, raising her nose high in the air. "But I doubt that's what brought on this bout of tears," she clarified.

"I was falling," Anne said, her face pressed into Sophia's shoulder.

"Well, now you're not," Sophia crooned to her. "You're tight within my arms. All safe and sound."

Lady Anne hiccupped against her shoulder and began to quiet.

"She has night terrors often," Claire said.

"Yes, I know. I'm fairly certain she was there when her mother's accident happened."

"It wasn't an accident," Anne sniffled. "She was thrown."

"I know," Sophia said quietly, rocking the child back and forth.

"How do you know?" Claire asked quietly.

"Her father told me the details," Sophia explained. "Could you pass me the music box, please?" Sophia held out her hand for the small box and waited patiently for Claire to put it in her hand.

"That's the oldest trick in the book," Claire snorted.

"And it works," Sophia sniped back.

Sophia jostled Anne within her arms very softly. "Anne, I need for you to do something for me," she said.

Anne nodded against her chest but didn't loosen her frantic grip on Sophia.

"I need for you to remember what happened to your mother, only for a moment."

Anne closed her eyes tightly.

"Then I want you to take that memory and put it in this box. We'll lock it up, and you never have to open it again if you don't want to."

"Fool's magic," Claire barked.

"Shut it," Sophia warned.

Sophia nudged Anne. "Go ahead. Put it away."

"I can't," Anne cried.

Claire opened her palm and blew across it, and magical dust stirred within the air. It swirled until it formed a picture in the air, a shimmery portrait of a woman with long golden hair falling from the tower. Anne closed her eyes tightly and refused to look at it.

Sophia reached out and caught the picture in the air, crumpling it between her fists like a piece of parchment. She placed the bit of memory in the music box and closed the lid with a resounding thwack.

"Take it away," Sophia ordered.

With a loud harrumph, Claire got up, sprinkled some dust over the music box to seal it, and placed it upon a high shelf. "You must leave the memories for her for later," Claire warned. "She may have need of them."

"I highly doubt it," Sophia snorted.

"You've become too attached to this family," Claire said, her gaze direct and cutting.

"I know," Sophia whispered, tears pricking at the backs of her lashes as she hugged Anne to her and held her close. The girl began to drift off to sleep in her arms.

Sophia looked up at Claire. "I leave on the rising-dawn wind."

Claire nodded.

"Will you stay long enough to be certain the memories are gone?"

"For the girl or for the duke?" Claire asked.

"For them both," Sophia whispered.

"Do you want me to take his memory of you as well?"

Sophia bit her bottom lip hard enough to draw pain. "Yes," she whispered.

❦

Ashley woke with a jerk, reached across the bed, and felt for Sophia. Her side of the bed was cold. He bolted upright. Only moments before, she's been nestled softly within his arms. And moments before that, he'd been inside her. He'd taken her innocence, and she'd taken his. He'd never known a feeling like the way he felt for Sophia, and parts of it scared him to death. But the rest of it felt so right.

Ashley jumped from the bed and searched for his dressing gown. When he couldn't find it, he pulled his shirt over his head and donned his trousers, then stepped out into the corridor in his bare feet. He stormed down the hallway, and didn't stop until he saw Wilkins coming in his direction. "Your Grace," the butler began.

"Where is she?" Ashley snapped.

The butler blanched. "To whom are you referring, Your Grace?"

To whom did Wilkins think he was referring? "Miss Thorne, man. Where is she?"

"Which one, Your Grace?"

Ashley stumbled for a moment over his own thoughts. "How many are there?"

"Two, Your Grace. The governess. And... yours."

His. Yes, indeed. She was his. "Mine," he bit out.

"She's in with Lady Anne." He nodded down the corridor. Ashley started in that direction.

As he continued down the corridor, he spotted a lady leaving Anne's chambers. "Sophie," he called. Thank God. He thought she'd left him. His heart beat a staccato rhythm within his chest. But the chit looked up and it wasn't Sophia. She looked a lot like Sophia, however. He tilted her head and regarded her closely.

"You're one of them, aren't you?" he asked.

She dipped into a quick curtsy. "You'd have to define one of them, Your Grace." She raised a brow at him.

"Later," he murmured. "Where is Sophie?"

She nodded toward his daughter's closed door.

"She hasn't gone then?" His heart was hammering, as though it desperately wanted to jump from his body.

"Not yet," she said cryptically. She turned to walk away. He reached for her arm, loosening his grip when she winced at his hold.

"How can I make her stay?" he asked.

"You can't. She has to want it." She looked almost sorry for him. He didn't like it. Not one bit.

"I believe she does."

"Not enough." She looked down at where he still gripped her arm and he set her free.

"Apologies," he murmured.

"No offense taken," she said. Then she started down the corridor. Ashley pressed his forehead against the door of his daughter's chambers, inhaling and exhaling there in the cold corridor, as though those breaths could be his last. Finally, he eased the door open.

The scene that greeted him made his heart twist within his chest. Sophia lay beside his daughter in her tiny bed, her body close to Anne's but not touching her, except where her fingertips played lightly down Anne's hair. His daughter slept, and Sophia looked at him with a tear in her eye.

"So lovely," he breathed, a lump forming in his throat. This was what he wanted. He wanted her in his life forever. In their lives forever.

"Yes, she is," Sophia agreed.

"I was referring to the both of you," he said, not taking his eyes off her. "Did she have a night terror?"

"She did," Sophia said. "But she won't have them any longer." She nodded toward a music box perched high upon a shelf. "The memories are in there. When she's ready, she can open it and it will be like they never left."

"She's not ready for memories such as those."

Sophia smiled softly. "Which is why I took them from her. They'll no longer plague her."

"I'm not ready for memories such as those, either," he admitted.

"No one is," she agreed, her hand still stroking down Anne's hair. "She sleeps well."

"Better than I have seen her sleep in a very long time."

Sophia gave him a quirky grin. "My mission is complete," she said with a shrug. Very carefully, she got to her feet, careful not to disturb Anne. "Helping your daughter was my mission," she reminded him.

"But what about me?" he asked, his voice cracking on the last as he drew her into his arms.

Twenty-Seven

ASHLEY LIFTED HIS HEAD AND LOOKED INTO HER EYES.

"You were never my mission, Your Grace," she whispered to him as she brushed that wayward lock of hair from his forehead. She would miss that lock with all her heart. A sob nearly welled from the center of her, but she forced it back. She tried to smile at him, but it was a watery, disastrous effort.

He inhaled deeply, as though he could breathe her in and make her stay. "You have some time before the morning dawn wind," he remarked, his eyes moving to the window, where the moon still hung high in the sky.

"I do," she said with a nod.

"Spend it with me. In my arms." He didn't ask her. It was a command. One she didn't intend to fight. She nodded.

Ashley smiled and brushed her hair from her face, then took her hand in his and tugged her toward the doorway. She protested lightly, taking one more moment to look down at Anne. She looked into Ashley's face. "She will remember me for a time. But not for long."

"Then I shall remind her of you," he said, his fingers twining with hers, holding her tighter, even with that small grasp. "For you shall never be far from my thoughts."

"I'll be a world away from you." So close, yet so far away.

He tugged her into the corridor, as though he was anxious to get her alone. "Exactly how far away?" he asked, a sly grin crossing his face.

She shook her head. It was not meant to be. "The Trusted Few may never give me leave again. They may never grant me leave from my world to visit this one."

"Your wings?" he asked.

"At their discretion," she said with a shrug. "I'd wager that they'll take them from me. The same way they took my mother's."

"If they do, you can come back to me?" He looked hopeful. Too hopeful.

She shook her head. "No. I cannot." She could be carrying his child. If she was, she would never, ever leave the land of the fae again. She would never take the risk her mother had. She would never, ever lose her child. She would live in her land without Ashley and with any child they created, or she would do so alone. If she wasn't with child, she would still remain there. She would live her life as though she'd never met him. But she had. Oh, yes, she had. She let him draw her into his arms as they entered his bedchamber.

Ashley tugged at the ties of his dressing gown and shoved it from her shoulders in one quick move. She stumbled against his haste to disrobe her, laughing as he lifted her chemise over her head, and then she stood there, dressed in nothing more than moonlight.

His eyes grew darker, almost black in the dimly lit room. He reached for her, and she stopped him only momentarily, long enough to disrobe him as quickly as he had taken her clothes off. Within seconds, he was as naked as she, and she led him to the bed with a forceful tug of his fingers.

With her hands upon his shoulders, she took a step toward the bed, forcing him backward with a gentle shove until he sank into the bed of his own accord. His mouth immediately moved to her breasts, as his arms snaked around her waist and drew her to him. She flung her head back with a laugh, and pushed him to the bed, climbing over him. When they were nose to nose, he cupped the back of her head in his hand, forcing her to look at him. "What can I do to make you stay?" he breathed.

"Nothing," she said. She stopped moving. Stopped laughing, stopped loving. Just stopped. "I am not of your world. We were never meant to be."

With a quick roll, he drew her beneath him, smothering her gasp with his lips as he growled against them. "Tell me we're not meant to be," he said, settling between her thighs. He rocked against her center but didn't lodge himself inside her. Instead, he stole her breath as he pressed the head of his shaft against that little bundle of nerves that thumped so loudly and made her cry out. "Tell me," he growled. "Tell me you don't love me." He rocked against her center again, small noises leaving his throat as he narrowed his eyes. It was almost as though he could look into her very being.

"You know I can't," she cried out as the head of his shaft lodged inside her.

"Tell me you love me," he ground out as he filled her completely in one harsh stroke. His arms shook on either side of her head, quavering as he looked down at her.

"You know I can't."

He pushed himself even farther inside her, farther than she'd known he could go. "You can't love me, or you can't tell me?" he growled.

"It's forbidden," she whispered on a rush of pleasure as he moved inside her. He withdrew in one long, slow stroke. And then he vanished. He didn't surge within her again. He fell beside her on the bed and covered his eyes with his arm. He inhaled deeply. In and out. She watched the rise and fall of his chest. His manhood jutted up, standing between them, shimmery with her wetness. "Don't push me away," she whispered, reaching to pull his arm down from where it covered his eyes. "Not tonight. Don't push me away." She tugged harder and he finally relented. "I leave on the rising-dawn wind."

He laughed. It was a sound without any mirth at all. "I've a mind to lock you in the tower and keep you there."

Her heart leapt at the thought. But they would come for any children she and he conceived. They would take them. It would never work.

"I could go with you," he offered. "Anne and I. We could leave everything and come with you."

"You would do that for me?" she whispered.

"I would do it for us," he said. He rose up on his

elbow and looked at her, as though a light had just flickered to life for him.

"There has never been a human in our world."

"Ever?" He looked shocked. Everything he'd learned and *that* shocked him?

"Ever," she affirmed.

"There's a first time for everything."

She shook her head. "No."

He refused to beg her to love him. He had too much pride. She would leave with the morning wind, as though she'd never existed. "You will forget me in time," she said.

"Never," he vowed as he rolled to cover her with his body again. If she thought he would ever forget her, she was due for a stay at Bedlam, rather than her land. He brushed her curls back from her face. "Tell me you love me. Leave me with the knowledge of that."

"Do you doubt it?" she croaked out. A tear rolled from the corner of her eye. "I wouldn't be here if I didn't. For God's sake, Ashley, I lost the color of my wings tonight. I'll forever be known in the land of the fae as one of lost innocence, provided that they let me keep my wings at all."

He didn't understand. Not at all.

"I wanted one night with you," she growled, tugging at his hair in frustration.

Something she said finally sunk in. "I have ruined you," he said.

She nodded. "Ruined me for anyone else." She

heaved a sigh. "In your world, innocence is something that can be kept a secret. In mine, it's not."

"Yet you let me have it anyway."

"One night," she declared, tugging his hair to make him look into her eyes. "I needed one night."

"One night," he repeated. He probably sounded like an idiot.

"One night," she whispered. Then she parted her thighs beneath him and rocked her hips. "Make it a wonderful night. One I'll always remember."

He lodged the head of his shaft inside her. But then he swiped a hand down his face and withdrew from her. She cried out beneath him, "Blast it, Ashley," she groused.

"You'll be ashamed of the time you spent with me," he guessed. He rolled to his back and she climbed over him, looking down into his face.

"If you get a case of the vapors over this, Robinsworth, I will never forgive you." Her hair hung down, draping them both in her auburn curls. Then she smiled at him and spread her thighs, settling over his manhood, rocking against his length. "Who would have thought you would be prone to fainting at the thought of taking a lass's innocence?"

"When all my blood rages away from this head," he said, pointing to his hair, "I suppose I could be prone to fainting." He forced himself to match her playful mood.

"I like the path your blood has traveled," she said as she lifted herself, straightening her arms, her breasts bare and high. He reached for one and tweaked her nipple. She spread her thighs farther, and the heat of her touched his shaft. He rocked his hips and slid his hands down her sides until he could reach between them and lodge his shaft at her entrance. She drew her bottom lip between her teeth and worried it.

"Since I have already ruined you, I see no need to repent at this point," he growled, as he raised his hips and pulled her down to sheathe him in one solid stroke. She gasped, the noise rocking his very soul.

"My dangerous duke," she cried out.

He was about as dangerous as a mouse, except to her, it seemed. To her, he *was* dangerous. He'd ruined her life. And now he insisted on taking even more from her. "Tell me you love me, again," he ordered, rolling her beneath him.

"I can't," she cried out as he thrust inside her and retreated slowly, watching her face as he brought her pleasure.

"You can," he urged. "Tell me. Just once more." He reached a hand between them and began to rub that little nub he knew would take her over the top, while he moved slowly inside her wetness. She arched and cried out, drawing his mouth down to her breast. He teased her with his tongue against her nipple.

"Tell me," he said. Then he drew her nipple into his mouth and sucked it harshly, laving it with his tongue as he continued to torment her, continued to stroke within her. Continued to love her.

"I do," she cried out. He hastened his fingers and sped his thrusts, and she wrapped her legs around him, locking her feet behind him.

"Tell me how you feel," he grunted, ready to spill himself inside her, but he needed more from her before he could. He needed to know. He needed to know she loved him. Because, by God, he loved her with everything he had.

Sophia's legs began to shake around him, and her arms quivered where she held tightly to his forearms.

"Tell me," he grunted by her ear, thrusting in and out of her.

It wasn't until a moment later, when she finally broke with the force of him loving her, that she screamed it. "I do love you," she cried. Her lips touched his forearm, and then he felt her wicked little teeth nip at him. She squeezed his manhood in her quivering sheath, yet he forced himself to continue stroking her, determined to wring every ounce of pleasure she had from her very being. She lunged within his arms, the force of completion rocking them both as he came inside her, as he gave her everything he was, making them one in his heart and his mind.

When she stilled within his arms, and her arms fell away from him, and her legs lowered from around his waist, she stilled against the mattress as though he'd taken her very life. But then her eyes opened and she smiled at him, a sleepy little smile full of wicked intention.

"I do love you, you ninnyhammer," she said with a grin. Then she tucked herself into his side and fell into an immediate and peaceful slumber. He drew her to him, ready to join her, but he couldn't sleep yet. There was still too much to do. He had to keep her with him. And he had a mere few hours to figure out how to do so.

Twenty-Eight

A NOISE, SOFT AND BLUNTED, BUT LOUD AND dangerous at the same time, jarred Sophia from sleep. She lay wrapped around Ashley's long and lanky body, one naked calf tangled with his. She sat up on her elbow and looked down at him. Goodness, the man was beautiful in sleep. His face held none of the weariness that usually provoked a scowl. Sophia pulled her body back from his, and he reached for her in sleep.

"Shh," she whispered. "Sleep."

He grinned without opening his eyes. "You're still here."

"For a few more moments," she whispered back.

"How much longer?" he murmured.

"She must be ready to catch the rising-dawn wind," a voice said from the side of the bed. Sophia reached to jerk the counterpane over her and Ashley.

"What the devil is that?" Ashley asked, raising his head to look toward the foot of the bed.

"Ronald," Sophia groaned. "A moment of privacy," she scolded.

"You've had more than a moment," he said, his tone acerbic.

"How did you get out of your chambers?" Ashley asked.

"It takes more than a lock and key to keep one of my nature confined," Ronald said with a smirk.

"Finn," Ashley groaned.

"Indeed," the garden gnome said. "He should use his head for more than a hat rack."

"I have been telling him that for years," Ashley groaned. He drew Sophia further into his arms and nuzzled his morning stubble against her throat. "Go away, Ronald," he said, lifting his head only for a moment.

The room was dark, but the cold morning light that filtered through the curtains warned of the coming dawn. Sophia giggled. "Yes, Ronald," she agreed. "Do go away." Ashley cupped her breast, making her want to squirm within his grasp.

"We must go," Ronald warned.

"A moment," Ashley growled, his lips nipping at hers as he rolled her beneath him.

"You have no more than a moment," Ronald warned. "The wind will leave without you if you don't get out of that bed, get dressed, and get ready to go."

Ashley scooted himself to the edge of the bed, still on top of her, but crooked, which made her want to laugh with the impropriety of it all. "Give us two minutes alone, Ronald. Then we'll be along."

"Do you promise?"

Ashley brushed at the lock of hair that hung down across his forehead. "On my honor."

"Do you have any?" the gnome snorted.

Ashley made a move to grab for him. "You little curmudgeon." The gnome's feet scuttled across the floor, moving out of his reach. Ashley sighed heavily, "A moment, Ronald."

"Margaret and Mr. Thorne left with the earlier wind," Ronald said. "I convinced your brother to let me come and fetch you."

That was very fortuitous for him.

"So, Your Grace, if you will be so kind as to get off her…" Ronald cleared his throat loudly, letting that finish his sentence.

Ashley pushed his upper back toward the center of the bed. "I believe Ronald has caught Wilkins's illness."

"Illness?" She laughed as Ashley growled low in his throat and tossed the counterpane higher over his head, and began to kiss his way down her body. She heard a click as Ronald slipped out the door. Sophia shoved the counterpane down and reached for his shoulders. "What illness?" she asked, tapping the top of his head lightly with her fingertips.

He looked up between her naked breasts. "The one that causes them to begin and end sentences with a clearing of their throats. I often think they're choking." Ashley lightly tickled her sides.

Sophia shoved at his shoulders. "I have to get up and get dressed." She looked toward the window at the purple shades of sky that were appearing. "If I miss the morning wind, I'll be stuck here."

"That sounds like a good plan," he said with a chuckle, as he kissed her lips quickly.

She pushed at his shoulder again and he stopped to look down at her.

"You're not going to stay, no matter what I do." It wasn't a question. It was just a statement. A true one. She shook her head. Tears pricked at the backs of her lashes. He rolled off her and to the edge of the bed, where he sat for a moment. Then he sighed heavily and reached for his trousers. He pulled them up over his hips and tugged his shirt over his head. He held her dress out to her. "May I at least walk with you out to the wind?"

He didn't think he could jump aboard, did he? "The wind won't recognize you as a traveler."

"Why does that sound so sensible to me?" he said with a laugh. He pulled on his boots and jacket. He looked rumpled, but she had never thought him more handsome. "I don't have Anne with me. I wouldn't try to jump aboard."

That tugged at Sophia's heart. "Will you tell her I said good-bye?" she whispered.

"No."

Oh, that hurt. "Why not?"

"I'll tell her you said 'see you later.'"

"But that will probably never happen."

He pretended to pull a mock knife from his chest. "Let me have my dreams, will you?"

She sighed heavily and forced herself to rise from the warmth of his bed. "Tell her whatever will ease the way for her."

Ashley helped her dress, taking a moment to trail his lips over her shoulder and the back of her neck, sending a shiver down her spine as he fastened the back of her gown. "Thank you," she said softly.

He spun her around and tipped her head up to his. "Thank you."

"I don't regret falling in love with you."

"Good," he said, and he drew her into his arms.

⚜

Ashley didn't have any regrets, either. Not about meeting her, falling in love with her, or continuing to love her. His only regret was that she had to leave him. But he would soon do all he could to fix that. He patted his coat pocket. Perhaps he had some leverage that might help him to get her back. He would have to wait and see.

Her fingers tangled with his as she leaned forward and lay her head on his chest. "I love to listen to your heart beat," she murmured into his shoulder.

"Keep listening and you might hear it break into a million pieces," he warned. He took her by the shoulders and pushed her back from him. He protested with a murmur. He looked toward the window. The sun was rising.

"We must go," he said.

She nodded and tugged him by the fingertips toward the door. He followed her, his arm around her as they traversed the corridors of his home. And then they came to the door of his secret garden. "May I have entrance to your garden?" she asked with a silly smile.

"You always have had leave," he said. He shoved the door open and found Ronald waiting on the other side.

The gnome looked at his pocket watch and scowled. He closed the fob and tapped it lightly. "Time, it is a-wasting."

"Your parents?" Ashley asked.

"I already told them good-bye," she said as she wrapped her arms around him and inhaled deeply. "I want to take the scent of you with me," she murmured.

"Give me a moment to collect Anne, and you could take all of me," he laughed.

A gentle wind lifted his hair and a shiver crept up his spine. "The morning wind?" he asked.

"It has come to collect me, I'm afraid." She stepped onto her tiptoes and pulled his head down to hers, touching his lips softly but fully. He would remember that kiss always. Then she stepped back and took a deep breath, and the wind began to blow harder. It blew leaves around his garden, and caused the plants to shiver and shake so hard that they slung the morning dew about like a gentle rainfall. Yet there wasn't a cloud in the sky.

Her hair lifted, blowing about her face, and she moved to brush it aside. "I will not forget you," she said, speaking over the gusts. Suddenly, the gusting wind stopped, and Sophia's maid appeared as though out of the mist. "I caught the wind at your parents'," she said with a shrug. "Your brother and grandmother have gone ahead of us." She held out a hand to Sophia. "Let me help you, Sophia," she said, her voice kind. Sophia took a deep breath and put her hand into the maid's.

Ashley wanted to reach for her. He wanted to call her back to him, but he couldn't. He brushed his hair from his eyes and watched the gentle wind as it seemed to absorb her. It swirled around her, and it looked almost as though her dress became part of it, billowing in the wind. Her hair swirled about, and he feared for her safety. But then she raised a finger to her lips and blew him a kiss.

It was quite ridiculous to do so, but he reached out to catch it. He knew when she was leaving, when he could no longer see her maid. When he could no longer see the color of her dress or the glimmer in her eye.

The garden gnome bowed low before him. "Your Grace," he said. "Many thanks for your hospitality." Ashley moved to pay his respects to the little gnome, but at the last moment, he reached for Ronald's jacket and snatched him from the path of the wind. He held him by the neck of his jacket and watched as his feet kicked in the air. The little man's hands flailed.

"Put me down," he snarled.

Ashley chuckled. "I think not." He held the gnome out farther from his own body to eliminate the blows that he could have sustained. "Finn!" Ashley called out. His brother stepped from the bushes and held open a burlap sack.

"You," the gnome snarled.

"Yes, me," Finn taunted.

"Let me go." The gnome was red with rage. The wind was beginning to slow. "I can still catch the wind, but not for much longer," he warned.

"I'll have my wish," Ashley said as he stuffed the gnome into the burlap sack. "I would consider you well and truly caught," he said as he helped Finn to tie a knot into the top of the bag.

"What do you intend to do with me?" the gnome asked, his voice muffled by the sack.

"I intend to get my wish," Ashley said. But first,

he needed to talk with Sophia's parents. He turned to Finn. "Can you keep that thing under control long enough to put it in the coach?"

"With pleasure," Finn smirked as he tossed the bag over his shoulder. Finn grunted when Ronald kicked him in the back through the bag.

❧

Sophia felt as though the wind was taking her breath, and she'd never been so strangled, not in all the many times she'd ridden the wind back to the land of the fae. She held tightly to Margaret's fingertips until a sob welled within her. The woman reached for her and drew Sophia into her arms.

"I was wondering how long you could maintain," the maid murmured. She stroked Sophia's back gently. But then Sophia looked up. Ronald was there in the wind with them for a moment. But suddenly, a darkly clad arm reached into the mist and jerked him from it. Ronald let out an oath and disappeared from sight.

"What the devil?" Margaret breathed.

"He pulled him back." Sophia's heart leapt. "Why would he do such a thing?"

"Your duke knows the gnome is the keeper of wishes." Margaret didn't look very pleased.

"You don't think..." Sophia began. But it was too ludicrous to even consider.

"I do think," Margaret said. She shook her head. "He's a fool if he thinks he can get to the land of the fae using a wish."

Suddenly, Sophia reached for her reticule. She opened it quickly and pressed a hand to her heart when she saw what was inside. She tipped it over and not a thing fell out.

"Where is your dust?" Margaret cried. Her face blanched white.

"I don't know," Sophia said, suddenly unable to take a full breath.

"You're going to be in big trouble, miss," Margaret said, shaking her head.

Yes, she was.

Twenty-Nine

SOPHIA STEPPED OFF THE WIND WHEN IT STOPPED swirling, still clutching tightly to Margaret's hand. The grass always seemed greener in the land of the fae. But aside from that, it was no different from Ashley's land. Aside from the magic, that is. For once, the grass didn't look greener. It didn't smell nicer. The sun didn't shine more brightly. All because Ashley wasn't there.

"Sophia," Marcus called from the front door of their home. "Glad to see you finally arrived." He leaned casually in the doorway. But he nearly vibrated with tension. "Do come in and join us," he said with a nod of his head.

Us. The Trusted Few had arrived already. Sophia took a deep breath for fortification and pushed past Marcus into the house. "Where is Grandmother?" Sophia asked.

"She stayed with Mother," he whispered out the side of his mouth.

Sophia tripped over her own toe. "She didn't return?"

"Apparently, she knew she wasn't returning when she left. There's a bit of a tale that you'll need to hear."

Sophia let Buncomb, the butler, take her pelisse. "I had to hear it twice before I believed a word of it."

Sophia nodded and stepped into the drawing room. Four gentlemen came to their feet and waited for her to curtsy to them. "Gentlemen," she said, slightly distracted by the fact that there were only four. "Where's Grandfather?" she asked.

Marcus's face fell. "It appears as though Grandfather is ill."

"Ill?"

"Gravely ill," Marcus said, his frown deepening, just as the furrows between his brows did.

"He was fine when we left. We should really send for Grandmother." She pressed a hand to her lips. "But we don't have Ronald."

Marcus looked around as though he could find him behind the furniture. "Where is Ronald?"

"The Duke of Robinsworth jerked him from the wind at the last moment."

The Trusted Few put their heads together and began to grumble almost silently, shooting heated glances in Sophia's direction.

Marcus leaned closer to her and whispered, "From what I can tell, all of this is Grandfather's doing."

"Where is he?"

Marcus nodded toward the back of the house, where Grandfather and Grandmother's quarters were.

"I'll go to him immediately," she said, starting in that direction.

"Don't be too startled by what you find, Soph," Marcus said, his voice softening. "It was a bit of a shock to me as well."

Sophia rushed down the corridor and knocked only momentarily before barging into the room when a maid opened the door. "Grandfather!" she cried when she saw him lying beneath the counterpane, his face gravely white.

"Is he dead?" she asked the maid.

"Not yet," her grandfather croaked from beneath the counterpane tucked around him. "I have a few things to set to rights before that happens."

Sophia dropped to sit beside him on the bed and took his hand in hers. "You were well when I left."

"I wasn't," he said. He shook as his body was wracked by a fit of coughing. She lifted a glass of water to his lips and waited while he settled. "That's why I put things in motion the way I did. I couldn't tell you about it. Or I'd ruin your mission."

"You put things in motion." What on earth did that mean?

"I think Grandfather has some things to explain," Marcus said from the doorway.

"I had some wrongs to right," Grandfather said. Then he was wracked by coughs again. He was deathly pale when he calmed.

"We should go and get Grandmother," Sophia urged Marcus.

"She'll be along shortly," Grandfather breathed. "If that duke of yours and that son-in-law of mine can figure out how to get by the fish." He chuckled lightly, which caused a new fit of coughing. "Let's hope they're smarter than they look." He settled against the linens and closed his eyes. "Let me rest for a moment, will you?" he groaned.

"Of course." She kissed his weathered old cheek and stood up.

She walked toward Marcus, who still hovered in the doorway. "What did he mean about getting past the fish?"

Marcus dropped an arm around her shoulders and guided her down the corridor. "I have a bit of a story to tell you, Soph," he began. He winced as though it was painful. "More than a bit, actually."

"When do you plan to get started?"

❧

Ashley stepped up to the doorway of Viscount Ramsdale's home and was rewarded by the door opening without him even having to knock. The butler did raise a brow, however, when the duke cursed beneath his breath. "Sod off, Ronald," he grunted as he lowered the burlap sack to rest beside his leg. The butler stepped back when the bag fidgeted at his feet.

Ashley reached into his pocket for a calling card and presented it to the butler. "If you don't go and find Ramsdale for me, I'm going to let it bite you," Ashley warned, when the man spent too much time staring at the bag. He ducked his head and motioned for Ashley to follow him into the foyer.

The butler disappeared for no longer than a moment, when Ramsdale himself rushed around the corner. "Please tell me my daughter decided not to go," he said, looking around Ashley as though he might have Sophia tucked in a pocket somewhere.

"I'm afraid not," Ashley grimaced. "She caught the wind first thing this morning."

"Where the devil did she catch the wind? I thought I'd at least get to see her off," Ramsdale groused.

The man must not have known that Sophia had spent the night with him. And Ashley wasn't certain it would be a good idea to inform him. A father on a rampage wasn't something he wanted to deal with at present. Just then, a flurry of yellow dashed around the corner and barreled directly into Ashley's side. He caught the slip of a girl and held her out from him. She looked very much like Sophia, and he could well imagine what Sophia looked like when she was younger. But she was the girl he'd met while waiting in the corridor all night for Sophia, her younger sister. She curtsied quickly.

"I'm so sorry, Your Grace," she said.

"What have I told you about running in the house?" her father warned, his tone not harsh at all.

"Don't run in the house. Don't fly in the house. Can I do anything in the house?" the girl quipped. A grin tugged at Ashley's lips.

"I hope you have a house full of daughters one day," Ramsdale said. The youngest Ramsdale scurried on down the corridor. "Follow me," the viscount muttered as he started toward the back of the house. Ashley bent to pick up the bag, which had grown strangely quiet. "What do you have there?" Ramsdale asked as Ashley lowered it to the Aubusson rug in his study.

"One very angry garden gnome," Ashley said. The viscount reached toward the bag. "It bites," Ashley warned.

"Quite right," the viscount said, bending to rub his ankle as he obviously remembered something. What

Ashley wouldn't give to know what it was. "It he alright in there? It looks awfully still."

Ashley kicked the side of the sack with the side of his boot. Ronald cursed. Prolifically. "Seems fine to me," Ashley said, settling into a chair.

"What can I do for you, Robinsworth?" Ramsdale said as he sat down and steepled his hands in front of him.

"My list is long and varied," Ashley said hesitantly.

"Start at the top, shall we?" Ramsdale was awfully calm. Almost too calm.

"He had inappropriate relations with Sophia," Ronald called through the burlap sack.

Ramsdale sat back and his eyebrows arched up nearly high enough to meet his hairline. "He had better be saying that to make me want to kill you. Because I will."

Ashley had no doubt of it. He opened his mouth to speak.

"She spent the night in his bed last night," Ronald called, his voice muffled by the bag. Ashley should have stuffed the gnome's mouth full of his cravat.

Ashley scrubbed at his face with his hand and kicked the side of the bag. Hard. "Shut it," he growled. "That's why I'm here, sir," he attempted.

"To admit that you took advantage of my daughter." Ramsdale choked out.

"To ask for your daughter's hand in marriage," Ashley rushed on.

"Put the cart before the horse, did you?" Ramsdale looked none too pleased. In fact, he looked murderous.

"She came to see me last night to retrieve Ronald."

Ramsdale didn't say a word.

"He was holding me hostage," the bag squawked.

"It's true. I was. I knew she would come for him," Ashley admitted. "I like to think she would have come anyway."

"I like to think she wouldn't," Ramsdale countered.

"I love her," Ashley admitted. "I told her that last night. So, you may as well know. And, with your blessing, I'd like to marry her."

"Now that you've defiled her, you think I should allow you to take her from me?" Ramsdale leapt to his feet and began to stalk across the room. "I've only just found her, man. Couldn't you have allowed me a few moments with her as my little girl?"

"With all due respect, it's not my fault you missed six-and-twenty years with her, Ramsdale."

His comment hung in the air like a bad stench. No one inhaled. No one exhaled. It was as though the world stopped.

Finally, Ramsdale's shoulders slumped. "You plan to make it right by her," he said.

"Of course," Ashley agreed.

"It wasn't a question, Robinsworth. You'll marry my daughter or you might just find yourself tossed from your own bloody tower." He glared at Ashley until Ashley couldn't stand it any longer.

A laugh built within him. He couldn't fight it. Finally, it burst from his chest. Of all the things people had said to him in the past, no one had ever threatened to kill him in the way his wife was murdered. And by doing so, Ramsdale had just bought his respect for life.

"If I don't make it right, I'll toss my own bloody self from my own sodding tower, by God."

Ramsdale nodded. "I'll hold you to it."

The bag squawked. "When the two of you are done having intercourse, I'd like to come out of the burlap."

"Ronald, is that you?" Ramsdale asked.

"Set me free and find out," the gnome taunted.

Ramsdale didn't move toward the bag. Instead, he muttered to himself, "I'd better get my wife."

That was probably a good idea. A low whistle emanated from the bag, and Ashley rolled his eyes at the sound of it. "You should be treading the boards, Ronald," Ashley muttered. "So much theatrics bottled up within such a small body."

"Small," the bag harrumphed. "I might be small in stature, but I'm mighty in will."

Suddenly, Lady Ramsdale burst into the room as though the hounds of hell were upon her heels. She skidded to a halt just in front of Ashley. "It took you long enough to show up."

Ashley tugged his watch fob from his pocket and glanced at it. It was barely morning yet. "Next time my lady leaves me for a make-believe land, I'll try to be more prompt when I arrive to bid you retrieve her."

Lady Ramsdale scoffed. "Retrieve her? If you are here to bid me to retrieve her, you are sorely mistaken, Your Grace. I have neither the magic nor the strength."

Ashley toed the burlap bag. "I have the magic and the strength," he said. "Well, I have directions," he corrected. Or at least he could. He hoped.

She raised one brow as she eyed the bag. "What's in the bag?"

"Hello, Lady Ramsdale," Ronald called from inside.

The good lady covered her mouth as a small shriek erupted. "Ronald!" she cried. She reached for the bag. But Ashley stepped between her and the object.

"Apologies, Lady Ramsdale, but his capture earns me a wish. But only if I free him." He quickly tugged the rope that tied the bag closed. It slumped forward as Ronald wiggled within. His head popped free of the bag, his hair standing straight up like a red flag. His face was the color of a tomato. Sweat stained his underarms and shimmered on his upper lip.

"Ronald," Lady Ramsdale said, her words coated with affection, just as much as her eyes shimmered with tears.

He bowed low before her. As low as a garden gnome could go, which was pretty low.

"Oh, don't stand on such ridiculous ceremony, Ronald. It has been a long time." She held out her hand to him and he pressed a lingering kiss to the back of her hand. She swiped a tear from her cheek.

The gnome adjusted his clothing and tried to smooth his hair down, but failed miserably. "Please forgive the state of my dress. It's not every day one is stuffed into a burlap sack and hauled across town." He turned to glare at Ashley. "Upside down." He snuffled. "With no air to breathe." He coughed into his fist. "Forced to perspire."

"I thought I'd never see you again," Lady Ramsdale said.

"Hoped is more like it," the viscount murmured. But his wife shot him a glance full of scorn. "Apologies," he muttered.

"I'll have my wish," Ashley said, enunciating each word clearly.

The gnome turned to him with a snarl on his lips. "I was hoping you'd say that," he said, a smile breaking across his face.

Lady Ramsdale held up one finger. "Be careful, Robinsworth. Gnomes are wily little beasts."

Ronald looked overjoyed at the thought of being called wily. "Thank you," he said, smiling up at her as though she hung the stars and the moon in the sky.

Ashley didn't know how to continue. "Would you like to give me a suggestion on how to word it?"

"Well, what are your goals?" she asked. She shot her husband a sly glance.

"I want Sophia."

"Seems to me you already had her," the gnome murmured, his hip hitched on a footstool as he appraised his fingernails much too closely. His mouth twisted with his stare.

"Why you little…" Ashley said, bounding to his feet and grasping for the gnome.

"He's goading you on purpose," a voice said from the doorway. Ashley turned to see Sophia's grand-mother standing in the entry. "He's hoping you'll waste your wish."

"That's not going to happen."

"So you say." She laughed as she stepped into the room. "What's your fondest desire, Your Grace? What do you want above all things?"

"I want to spend the rest of my life with Sophia." He didn't even have to think about that one.

"And what stands in your way?"

"She's in the land of the fae. And didn't leave a map for me to follow. Nor do I have an inkling of how to get to her." He exhaled heavily, feeling like bellows that had just been exhausted.

"Can you swim, Your Grace?" she asked, her brows coming together as she glared at him intently.

"You can wish for Ronald to lead you to the door," Ramsdale tossed out.

Ronald smirked. "Is that your wish?"

"No!" everyone in the room cried at once.

"Even if he gets to the door, he'll need magic to open it."

Everyone looked to Sophia's grandmother. "I need my magic to get me back through the portal. Much less the rest of you."

Ashley reached into his coat pocket and pulled forth several vials of shimmering dust. "How much magic will these buy for me?" he asked.

The room stilled. Sophia's grandmother held out one shaky hand. "Don't move, Your Grace," she said. She reached for the vials but he jerked his arms back. She hissed at him. "They are highly volatile. In other words, just waiting for the right time to explode when in the hands of the nonfae. It's a defense mechanism." She beckoned him forward. "Give them to me, so no one will be harmed."

He clutched them tighter in his palm, the vials slippery with sweat from his hands. "I think not," he finally said. He turned to Ronald. "My wish is for you to take all of us to the portal."

"The portal can only be opened at midnight," the gnome said.

"Then we shall all meet at midnight?" Ashley asked the room at large. He needed to collect Anne. And secure the wayward Claire. Finn could help with that.

"Where?" Sophia's mother asked.

Ashley looked from face to face but saw nothing.

"Portals are found in bodies of water. Such as the fish pond in His Grace's garden," the gnome said. He sauntered to the window and thrust it open. "See you at midnight," he called out as he fled through the opening. He was gone after a brief rustle in the bushes.

The portal was in his very own garden? How the devil could that be?

Thirty

ASHLEY APPROACHED HIS DAUGHTER ON QUIET FEET, content to look at her there in his garden as the sun played about her hair and she tilted her face up to the sunlight. She looked more content in that moment than he'd ever seen her. "I'm sorry I missed breakfast this morning, Anne," he said, breaking the silence. She looked over at him, a small pout on her face.

"Where were you?" She put her hands on her slim little hips and did the best imitation he'd ever seen of her mother. Yet a look of contentment still played about her face.

"I had to see Miss Thorne off this morning." He shrugged nonchalantly. "But I'm here now," he assured her. He rounded the corner of the path, and was surprised to see his mother and his grandmother there with Anne. He bowed to them both. The governess, who he knew to be Claire, Sophia's sister, was there as well. She dipped into a quick curtsy. "Good morning," he said. Drat it all. He'd hoped to have a moment alone with Anne.

"I had the strangest dreams last night," Anne said as she brought a flower to her nose.

"Not the terrifying kind, I hope," he remarked.

"Not at all. I dreamed happy dreams. About puppies romping in a field. With unicorns. And caterpillars that can talk."

"Nonsensical dreams," his mother exclaimed. She shot the governess a look. "You really shouldn't fill her head with such nonsense."

The governess looked up at Ashley with a wary gaze.

"On the contrary, I think all our heads should be filled with nonsensical things. It makes life more interesting," he said.

His grandmother harrumphed and raised her ear trumpet to her ear. "What did you say? You say your mother is lacking common sense?" She laughed. "I have said that since the day your father met her."

Ashley covered a chuckle in his fist. His mother raised her voice at his grandmother. "I have plenty of common sense," she called loudly.

"If you did, you wouldn't wear that awful shade of pink. It's much too young for you."

His mother jumped to her feet. "I am a young woman," she protested.

"And I'm the queen of England." His grandmother snorted.

Ashley addressed Anne, "So, you had brilliant dreams about all sorts of mythical creatures."

"They're not mythical," his daughter countered. "They're real."

"You can't let her go on believing such things, Ashley," his mother warned.

He gave his mother a glare that felled her mid-rant. "On the contrary, Mother, I believe it's healthy for the soul to believe in magic." He shot a glance at Claire, who avoided his gaze.

"What has gotten into you, Robin?" his mother sighed. "You used to be so focused. It's that Thorne girl, isn't it? I told you it was a bad idea for you to associate with her."

"Where did Miss Thorne go?" Anne said as she remembered his earlier comment about seeing her off.

He sighed heavily and said, "She had to return home. Duty called her back."

His grandmother bellowed much too loudly. "I do admire her beauty. I quite liked the chit."

So did Ashley. He didn't bother to correct his grandmother.

A footman approached from around the corner. He bowed low. "Beg your pardon, Your Grace," he said. "But Lord Phineas has requested entry to your garden. I wasn't certain if you wanted to allow him admittance." He waited patiently for a response.

Ashley waved a breezy hand at him. "Oh, yes. I invited him. Please do show him in." He turned to the group just as Finn joined them. He clapped Finn on the shoulder. "Finn and I had a long talk this morning." He noticed his grandmother straining to hear with the trumpet by her ear and raised his voice. "I need to get your opinion about something. All of you."

"Out with it, Robin," his mother said. "I have friends coming for tea in a few minutes."

"Heaven forefend I should interrupt your plans by telling you about my life," he grumbled. She flushed only a little when she heard him. He took a deep breath and plunged on. "I'd like to take Miss Sophia Thorne as my wife. Of course, I have to retrieve her and ask her for her hand first, but I hope she'll say yes."

He waited to see the reactions on their faces. His mother sputtered. "You cannot, Robin." But at the same time, Anne twirled and let out a most unladylike whoop of joy. His grandmother smiled broadly.

"An excellent decision, Robin. I may just have a great-grandson or two out of this one." She labored to her feet, pointed to her cheek, and said, "Give me a kiss and go retrieve your lady." He kissed her weathered old cheek fondly. "Give me one with the right parts and make me a happy old lady," she warned as she walked back toward the entrance. "Come along, Duchess," she said to his mother. "Stop your sputtering and let's go prepare for your tea."

"You cannot join us for tea," his mother warned. Of course, she was back to her own concerns quickly.

"I'll do just that if you don't come along now." Ashley's grandmother snapped her fingers, and with a huff, his mother followed her out of the garden. But then she turned back to Ashley.

"You know you do not have my approval." His mother raised her nose in the air.

"You know I do not need it, want it, or expect it," he responded. She turned in a flurry of skirts and followed his grandmother to the door. That left him with Anne, Finn, and Claire. He dropped onto a bench beside Anne. "What do you think of my marrying Miss Thorne?" he asked.

"I think it's positively brilliant," she beamed.

"With all due respect, Your Grace," Claire interjected, "what you propose simply cannot be done."

"I beg to differ."

He looked down at Anne and tweaked her nose. "I vote that we go and retrieve Miss Thorne at midnight, by way of the fishes." He looked up at Claire, whose mouth dropped open. Ashley pulled a single vial of shimmery dust from his coat pocket and passed it to Finn, who took it with reluctant fingers.

"It won't blow me to bits, will it?" he asked.

"I cannot be certain."

At the same time, Claire interjected. "It's highly volatile," she warned. "You should give it to me so it won't blow up." She held out her hand, which quivered just a little with what Ashley assumed was fear.

Finn tucked it into his own pocket. "If it blows off my dangly bits, I'll have you to blame," he warned. Her face colored profusely.

"Miss Thorne," Ashley started. "I'd like for you to go now with my brother, Finn."

She looked even more shocked by that than she had been by the dust.

"I'm not giving you a choice, Miss Thorne," he said. "Finn will keep you safe until my return."

"You plan to use me as leverage." Her eyes narrowed and her toe began to tap.

"Perhaps I just want to spend some time with you." Finn sucked absently at his teeth, a most annoying habit he had. "Don't worry, little fae one," he said. "I'll take great care of you." Finn looked a bit like a shark hunting for food.

"Where are we going?" She did not look amused. She looked worried. Very worried.

"Well, if I told you that, it would no longer be a secret," Finn said. "Come along and we won't have to argue. I'd hate for my temper to cause this thing to explode." He gestured to his pocket as he leaned closer to her. "My manly bits are at risk, you see."

She was not amused. She shot Ashley one imploring glance. "Your Grace," she cried. "You will regret this."

He had a feeling Finn would regret it more. But he needed a hostage from the land of the fae just in case things didn't go well when he got there. If he could get there at all.

⁓

Sophia sat with her face buried in her open palms, taking deep breaths and trying to still her skipping heart. She looked up from between her palms by spreading her fingertips. "Grandfather put all this in motion?" she asked Marcus.

"Evidently. He said he had some wrongs to right. He feels like this was the appropriate thing to do." Marcus paced from one side of the room to the other.

"No one has ever traveled to the land of the fae before who is not actually fae! What if Ashley is harmed? What if he brings Lady Anne with him and something goes wrong?" She brought her thumb to her mouth to nibble the nail.

"Either way, I don't see any good coming of it," Marcus grunted. He flopped down behind his desk, obviously overwrought from all the pacing. "You cannot have him in your life, Soph. You simply cannot. You have to understand and accept that."

A slow crawl of fear sneaked up her spine. Her body warmed with the heat of recognition. "What if I can?" she whispered.

"You can't," he finally snapped. Then he rubbed at his forehead in frustration. "I never should have left you alone on this mission. You have no idea how heavy my heart is with guilt right now."

"I completed the mission."

"And you broke every Unpardonable Error!" he cried. He jumped back to his feet and began his frantic pacing again. Then he stopped, leaned on his desk with the flat of his palm, and looked her in the eye. "You could be carrying his child."

Heat crept up her face and into her hair. She was probably as red as a beet.

"You know what it was like living without parents. Sure, we had Grandmother and Grandfather. But it's not the same." He turned from her and dropped into the chair again. "Do you want the same fate for your child?"

"I will never be separated from any children I bear. I will not allow it." She dropped her voice down to a whisper. "Why do you think that I left him?"

Marcus walked around the desk and cupped the top of her head in his hand. "Then don't get your hopes up. He's not coming to the land of the fae, no matter how much temptation Grandfather placed in his path."

"Grandfather didn't make him fall in love with me," she interjected. How dare Marcus discount

Ashley's feelings for her as being some of their Grandfather's machinations?

"You did that all on your own." He lightly tickled the top of her head with the tips of his fingers. "I do believe he loves you, Soph, but spend your time on more worthy endeavors. Enjoy the memories you made, and stop wishing for more than it can be."

He stopped at the door and called her name. When she turned to face him, he stood in the doorway holding on to the doorjamb with one hand. "For what it's worth, Grandfather only put the machinations in place to bring Mother home for a time. He didn't do anything to make the duke fall in love with you. That was all you, Soph." He clucked his tongue at her. "It's too bad he's not fae."

Thirty-One

A HUSH FELL OVER THE LAND OF THE FAE. THE BIRDS stopped chirping, the fireflies stopped chattering, and the spiders all slunk away into their hiding places. Sophia laid her quill on the desktop and looked around. Nothing seemed amiss. The walls weren't shaking. No one was screaming.

Marcus poked his head around the corner of the door. "Do you hear that?" he asked, his head cocked to the side as he listened intently.

Sophia came to her feet. "I don't hear anything." Something was wrong. Something was terribly wrong in the land of the fae. Buncomb and Margaret joined them in the corridor as they started for the front door. "Have you ever heard a quiet such as this, Buncomb?" Sophia asked.

"Never, my lady," he replied. His voice quivered and a shimmer of perspiration appeared on his upper lip.

There was always chatter in the land of the fae. There was always noise, from sounds of the outdoors to the sounds of the kitchen and every place in between. Now, not even the whisper of the caterpillars could be heard.

"Something is wrong," Marcus said, scratching his head. The house faeries came to greet them at the front door, as though they looked to the Thornes to protect them. Sophia had no idea what could be wrong. Suddenly, an urgent thump began at the other end of the corridor.

Sophia walked in the direction of the only noise in the land of the fae and found her grandfather, deathly pale and struggling with his cane. "Help me, Marcus," he said, his voice labored.

"Why are you out of bed?" Sophia cried as Buncomb and Marcus each slid under one of his arms and bore the weight of him.

"Things are afoot in the land of the fae, and I do not intend to miss them," he said. He pointed toward the door. "We must greet them."

Sophia mouthed to Marcus. *What is he talking about?*

But Marcus merely shrugged.

Perhaps Grandfather was just a bit mad with his illness.

"Bring a chair for me," he called, as Marcus and Buncomb carried him through the front door and out onto the walkway. A footman moved quickly to retrieve a chair and followed them out into the street. Sophia walked behind them and raised a fingernail to her lips to absently nibble as she looked up and down the street. People stood on their stoops looking cautiously toward the road.

"Grandfather," Sophia began. "Perhaps we should go back in the house."

"Perhaps you should let an old man have a moment

of peace," he groused as he dropped heavily into the chair. He mopped his brow with a handkerchief. "To the devil with getting old," he muttered to himself.

Suddenly, a fog broke at the end of the lane. The fog grew thicker until it became a colorful cloud, unlike anything Sophia had seen before. She stilled and watched as it spread.

"They've arrived," Grandfather called loudly. The Trusted Few appeared as though summoned.

"This is highly irregular," the oldest of the Trusted Few said. He started toward the mist.

But Grandfather held up a hand. He smiled broadly when his wife emerged from the mist. She stepped forward and dropped to a crouch at his feet.

"Are you unwell?" she whispered. But a smile hid behind her fear, Sophia could see.

"Let me enjoy the moment," he said. "Did you bring them?"

She laughed and nodded. "They brought me, actually."

The edge of a slipper protruded from the mist. Then it pulled back inside. "Who was that?" Sophia asked her grandmother.

"Just wait," she said. Her cheeks were rosy with anticipation.

The slipper appeared again, followed by a skirt-clad leg. Then Sophia's mother stepped through the portal. She brushed the mist away like puffs of smoke and stopped as she entered the land of the fae. She looked around, crossed her arms beneath her breasts, and just breathed. She looked from hill to dale, from the church to the cemetery, from the Assembly Hall to the rows of houses she could see in the middle of town.

"Welcome home," Grandfather said. He couldn't rise. He was simply too overcome by emotion.

Sophia's mother stopped and stared at him. "Papa?" she asked.

"Don't tell me you don't recognize me," he said with a self-deprecating chuckle.

"Of course, I recognize you," she said, as her eyes welled with tears. But then she looked back toward the mist. "What shall I do about the others?"

"What others?" Sophia asked as she stepped forward. Her heart leapt. "Do you mean Ronald?"

Ronald stepped up to stand beside her mother, his hand holding on to a slim arm. Lady Anne stepped through the portal and into the land of the fae. She looked around at her surroundings, taking them in quickly. The sun shone off her pretty blond hair, and she smiled broadly when she saw Sophia and ran toward her. Sophia swept the girl into her arms and spun in a circle with her.

Lady Anne pulled back and looked at her. She bent her head and whispered to Sophia, "My papa is in the mist. And your papa is in the mist." She covered a giggle. "And they don't have any clothes."

"No clothes," Sophia repeated.

"They traded their clothing for passage," Ronald explained.

"How gallant of them," the oldest of the Trusted Few said.

The mist began to thin. "We had better find something for them to wear before the mist dissipates completely." Sophia snapped her fingers at a serving maid, who ran toward the house.

Sophia started toward the mist. "Ashley?" she called. She was dying to see him, to put her arms around him.

"Sophie?" he returned, but it sounded like he was fathoms away.

"Walk toward my voice," she urged.

"I've been walking toward your voice since the day I met you," he said with a laugh. "But in this instance, it's better if I wait for some clothes."

"If you don't wait, I'll have to call him out," her father called back. "Can't have my little girl seeing him naked."

Ronald whistled a tune softly as he kicked a stone with the toe of his boot while looking askance at everyone.

"Shut it, Ronald," both men called from the fog.

"Wrap yourself in the fog," Sophia called.

"What?" they both called back at the same time.

"It's magical. It can be whatever you want it to be. So, grab it and wrap it about yourself."

❧

Suddenly, both men appeared from the mist, wrapped in fog from the waist down. "You do know how to make an appearance, don't you?" Sophia teased as she walked toward Ashley. He nodded quickly toward her father and made eye motions at her, as though beseeching her to greet her father first.

Following that cue, she went to her father and held out her hand. "Papa," she said, as she squeezed her hand in his. But he suddenly dragged her into his arms and hugged her quickly, then set her away from him. He looked down at his own naked chest.

"I believe we're a bit underdressed," he said.

"A wee bit," Sophia confirmed with a laugh. She turned to look at Ashley, but her father caught her chin and turned her back. "That's a bit too intimate for me." He held up both hands as though in surrender. "I'm willing to give on a lot of things, but this is not one of them."

Suddenly, Margaret appeared with clothing for them both, and held it out to Sophia and her mother so they could give them to the men. Sophia tossed a shirt to Ashley, winking at him as she did so. God, he loved her. And he couldn't wait to touch her. It had only been a day since he'd held her, but he felt like it was a lifetime.

He stepped back into the mist, donned trousers that were a bit too short, and pulled a shirt over his head. After he tucked it into his trousers quickly and stepped back out of the mist, he ran to Sophia and pulled her into his arms.

"How did you do it?" she whispered as she laid her head upon his chest and sighed heavily. She smelled like bluebells. Bluebells and comfort. He ran his hands down her back and wanted more than anything to kiss her, but they had an audience.

He shrugged. "A little bit of magic here and a little bit more there." He seemed to have a permanent grin affixed to his face. He couldn't stop smiling. But then several old men descended upon them. "The Trusted Few?" he murmured to her.

She nodded and lifted her head to look at him. Worry clouded her features.

"How does their ranking compare to that of a duke?" he asked.

"No comparison," she replied quietly. "They are the governing body of our world."

"Take them into custody," one of the old men snapped.

"That would be an unfortunate decision," Ashley said, using his strongest you-will-obey-me voice.

"You, sir, have entered our land without invitation," one of them blustered, his face reddening as he sputtered.

"Your Grace," Ashley said calmly.

"Beg your pardon?" another of them asked.

"Your Grace. That's my title and it's how you may refer to me."

"Your title means nothing here," Sophia warned.

"I beg to differ. My title has granted me leave my whole life. And you will pay me the respect I deserve." He stopped and inhaled heavily through his nose. "Or I shall inform everyone of my world about yours. And I'm certain you don't want more crossing the way I did."

"Impossible," one man snorted.

"Highly possible," Ashley countered. He approached the men slowly. "You see, you are unaware that I hold the high card. I have one of your kind, in faerie form, under lock and key in my world. I will not hesitate to expose her, along with the rest of you, should you not hear me out." He forced his tone to soften, though it was difficult. "You must grant me my say. That's all I ask."

The Trusted Few put their heads together and muttered incoherently. Finally, they motioned toward Ashley and Lord Ramsdale. "Follow, please," one of them said.

Ramsdale raised a brow at Ashley, and then the two of them fell into step behind the men. "Don't just stand there," the old man in the chair said. "You two help me up and take me with you. I wouldn't miss this for the world."

Ashley slid beneath one arm and Lord Ramsdale beneath the other. Lord Ramsdale turned toward his offspring. "Come along, son," he said. Mr. Thorne blanched, and then shook his head as though shaking off a feeling of discomfort, and fell into step with them.

"You're just going to leave us here?" Lady Ramsdale called.

"For now," Lord Ramsdale called. "We'll be back as soon as we're able."

"Ashley," Sophia called. He glanced quickly at her. "Be careful."

"I just came through a fish pond, played cards with a carp, slogged through smoke so thick I thought I'd have to saw my way out of it directly into *your* magical land, and you're telling me to be careful now?" He laughed out loud.

"Quite farcical, isn't it?" Sophia's father asked.

"Quite."

Thirty-Two

ASHLEY CRINGED AS THE LEADER OF THE TRUSTED FEW banged his gavel and called for order. The duke leaned closer to Lord Ramsdale and asked, "Fae court?"

"I have no idea," Ramsdale said with a shrug.

Ashley would have felt more in his element if he were wearing his own clothes. Or shoes. Or stockings. Or a waistcoat. He was sorely underdressed for the occasion. But he supposed it couldn't be helped.

Ashley looked over at Sophia's grandfather, who wore a look of resignation and warning. "Welcome to the land of the fae, gentlemen," he said with reverence.

Ashley dropped into a low bow. As did Lord Ramsdale. "We are happy to be here."

One of them harrumphed. "I'm certain you are. Thousands of years, and a human has never entered our land. I think they should be tossed in the gaol and left there to rot!"

Sophia's grandfather rolled his eyes and banged his gavel. "They're here on my invitation, gentlemen," he said. He coughed into his hand.

The Trusted Few looked shocked. "They can

be sent back immediately and their memories taken from them."

Ramsdale shot to his feet. "No one will take a single memory!" he bit out. "Not a single one. My wife went through years of torment because of your need for secrecy. I will not allow it. Not for a single moment longer."

One of the Trusted Few had the nerve to chuckle. Ramsdale rounded upon him. "Do not test me, old man," he warned. Ashley clasped Ramsdale on the shoulder and urged him to calm.

Ashley faced Sophia's grandfather. "You had a reason behind your summons, did you not, sir?" he asked.

"Summons," the Trusted Few sputtered.

Sophia's grandfather coughed into his handkerchief and waited a moment to catch his breath. Then he continued. "I am dying, I'm afraid."

Ramsdale made a noise in his throat but didn't say anything.

"But I had some wrongs I needed to right before I did. I got you here, gentlemen. Or at least I put it all in motion."

He sat up straighter in the chair.

"Pray continue," Ashley encouraged.

"My wife is a mission faerie, as was my daughter. When my daughter fell in love with Ramsdale, I gave no thought at all to the way things were done. I cut her from my life and let her move into yours, simply because those are the rules of the fae. It's the way we live. But it shall be the way we live no longer."

The Trusted Few complained amongst themselves.

"I allowed my own prejudices against the humans

to take my daughter from me. I let her choose. And she chose love. Looking back on it, I wouldn't have respected her had she chosen anything less." He chuckled lightly to himself. "When my granddaughter was presented with the same path, she chose to give up love for family."

He speared Ashley with a glance. "You love my granddaughter, almost as much as he loves my daughter. You fell in love with one of the fae, more's the pity. But that is not your fault." He stopped for a moment to catch his breath.

"It is my belief that with strict regulations, the fae and human worlds can mix. It's against the law of nature to take children from their parents. By doing so, I got to raise my grandchildren, but that's a travesty in itself."

Ramsdale looked enraptured.

"I raised three of them, but he didn't get the honor," Sophia's grandfather continued. "And he has three that I haven't even met and never will." Emotion choked his voice. "I will die without knowing my grand-children or their fates." He slammed his fist down on the tabletop, hitting it so hard that Ashley couldn't help but wince for him. "But the travesty is that he could have died without knowing his three children. Sophia, Marcus, and Claire could have been lost to him forever. And that, my good sirs, is a crime."

Ramsdale leaned toward him. "Who is Claire?"

Sophia's grandfather took a box from his pocket. "She is your third fae child."

Ramsdale's mouth fell open. "I have three children?"

His father-in-law slid the box toward him. Then he

opened his fist and blew some dust into the air. The Trusted Few looked at it incredulously, as though he'd be shackled in Bedlam within moments. But then he said, "May you share your pain with them all, so they can understand. Open the box."

Ashley had been there when Sophia opened her box of memories and remembered feeling like he was hit by a team of runaway horses when he'd felt her pain. He steeled himself as Ramsdale opened the box, but it wasn't enough. The memories swirled around the room like living beasts. They prowled and jumped and danced and fought with all the occupants of the room, and Ashley wanted to do nothing more than leave the chamber and run from the feeling. But he forced himself to experience the heartbreak that came with losing a child. A parent's desperation in knowing there's nothing he can do to prevent it. The aching sorrow of remembrance.

The Trusted Few felt it, too. One swiped at his eyes, as another clutched at his throat, choked by the feelings closing in upon them all. Finally, when Ashley worried he could take no more, the feelings dissipated. They settled like dirt after a broom throws it into the air, heavy and dirty.

"We should all be ashamed," one of the Trusted Few murmured.

The others were a little more reticent. But they slowly agreed. "How can we make it work? Our kind performs a service within the human world. If the fae strive to be part of that world, there can be recriminations."

"Ambassadors," Ashley muttered to Ramsdale.

The man appeared to have hope for the first time since they'd sat down. The ruddiness had left his cheeks, and he appeared to understand what was required of him. "Ambassadors."

Ashley shot to his feet. "We shall be ambassadors between your world and ours. We will come and go at will. But we will be the only ones who can, unless the Trusted Few approve of any additions to your world. We will ensure that no one of our world is apprised of your secrets, and by working together, we can preserve your anonymity and freedom." He took a deep breath and smiled. "We can work together."

Sophia's grandfather reached for the duke's hand. Ashley shook it in a firm grip. Then Sophia's grandfather got up and clasped Ramsdale in his arms. "I will leave it to the rest of you to work out the details." He called for some servants to take him back home. By the looks of him, he wasn't to be long of this world.

"Thank you, sir," Ashley said. Ramsdale bowed low before him. "Please know that I will care for your family as my own."

Sophia's grandfather beckoned the servants to stop. "I have watched you for years. You are a brilliant example of love, faith, and devotion. Teach that to my grandchildren and ensure that future fae do not suffer the same fate as my daughter. With this task, I entrust you. And my name is Lucius Gramerly. Be certain they remember me and this day."

"I promise. Good day, sir," Ramsdale said with a nod.

The servants carried the old man from the room, but he left with a light heart and a smile on his face.

"Let's decide how this will work, shall we,

gentlemen?" Ramsdale said, as he pulled up a chair and began to scratch a list on a piece of parchment.

❧

Sophia clutched her grandfather's hand in her own and willed him to grow stronger. If she could accomplish that by sheer will alone, she would. But it was not to be.

Her mother paced across the room, nibbling her fingernail as she muttered, "What on earth is taking them so long?"

Her grandfather didn't wake. Sophia feared he wouldn't. He was much too weak.

Suddenly, the door opened and Lord Ramsdale entered. Her mother looked anxiously at her father and waited for him to smile. "It looks as though we'll be staying in the land of the fae for a time."

Her jaw fell open. "How can that be?"

He nodded to the man in the bed. "Your father had a change of heart. He put all this in motion. He needed to lighten his heart and bring you back into the fold. And I get to come with you."

"What about the children?" she asked.

"They will come, too, if I can talk Marcus into taking over our affairs for a time. I need to talk to him and see if he's all right with it. He is my heir, after all."

"Your oldest son will be all right with that?" Sophia asked.

"Marcus is my oldest son. Allen will have to live with it." Ramsdale looked a bit worried about the prospects. But Sophia supposed it couldn't be avoided. "The other five will live with us here in the land of the fae, at least long enough to learn about the world you come from." He tugged at his wife's elbow. "Let's take a walk. I have much to tell you." She looked over at the bed, where her father lay so still.

"Go," Sophia encouraged. "I'll call you if he worsens."

Sophia's mother followed her husband into the corridor and closed the door behind them.

Sophia fell into Ashley's arms. He wrapped her tightly and stroked her hair.

"He's a wily old codger," Ashley finally said with a chuckle. "You have no idea how much it took for the man to pull this off. He planned for years, weighing his options, deciding the best way to proceed."

"What happened?" Sophia asked.

"Your father has replaced him as one of the Trusted Few," Ashley said. He shook his head in disbelief.

Ashley reached out to push her mouth closed. "I know," he crooned. "I didn't think it would work either. But we made them an offer they couldn't refuse."

She stepped back to look into his face. "What sort of offer?"

"They want to know more about our world. So they can protect their interests. So, I have promised to build a library and fill it with literature of the past, present, and future. I am also to be their liaison between the worlds. Kind of like a voice outside the fae. I'll represent them in Parliament, without anyone knowing it's in their interest, of course."

"Can you do that?"

"I can," he said with a shrug. "I won't compromise my principles for them. But I'll represent what is good and right if they need it. I can't see it happening often."

She laid her head upon his chest and took a deep

breath, feeling lighter than she had in a very long time. She took a deep breath. "I never expected it to all work out."

A sound arose from the bed. "It has to work out," her grandfather groaned. He fell into a fit of coughing, his body wracked so hard by it that Sophia feared he would expire on the spot. She rushed to his side.

"My lovely girl," he said, reaching a hand toward her. She pressed her face into his palm and a hot tear trailed down her cheek. She held his hand by her cheek until he slept, and then she tucked his hand beneath the counterpane.

"I fear it won't be long," Ashley warned.

"I know," she whispered back, as he gripped her shoulder in a strong grasp.

Thirty-Three

SOPHIA STEPPED FROM THE TUB AND WRAPPED A LENGTH of linen around her body. She glanced quickly at the clock on the mantel. Ashley would be expecting her at noon. She wrung the water from her hair. She would barely have time for her hair to dry, much less to have it piled atop her head in any kind of artful creation.

The door to her dressing room opened, and Margaret slipped quietly into the room. Sophia's mother walked in behind her. "We're here to help you get dressed," her mother said, her eyes shimmery with tears. She could have sworn Margaret blinked back a tear or two as well, but the maid turned away, cleared her throat, and reached for the wardrobe doorknob. She looked inside and turned back with a grimace. "Your green dress is the only thing fancy enough for the occasion," she said.

"Oh, wait." Her mother looked around the room and went to the door. She giggled lightly. "It was supposed to be delivered by now." She opened the door and stuck her head out. "I knew you wouldn't be able to stay away," she laughed as Sophia's grandmother walked into the room. She had a dress hung over her arm and a sly grin on her face. She looked at Lady Ramsdale and said, "You don't mind if she wears it, do you?"

A lone tear slipped down Sophia's mother's cheek, but she swiped it away and hopped onto the bed like an adolescent might. She stuck a pillow in her lap and rested her elbows upon it. "I can't wait to see it on you."

"What is it?" Sophia asked. She reached out to touch the material. It was as soft as the down of a newly hatched bird and as shiny as her magic dust. It sparkled and shone, rays of light bouncing off it like it was lined with prisms.

"It's my wedding dress," her grandmother said. "I thought you might like to wear it."

Sophia took the dress and held it up in front of her, and as she regarded herself in the looking glass, she could already imagine herself in it and the look on Ashley's face when he saw it.

"You can marry beneath the arbor in the church-yard. Where the sun can play upon it. It's well known that sunbeams bring good luck."

"That's an old wives' tale, Mother," Lady Ramsdale scolded. *Her mother* scolded. Would she ever get used to that? Perhaps with time. Her mother covered one side of her mouth with her hand, as though she had a secret to impart. But she spoke loudly. "It's also said that moonbeams are just as lucky."

"It's lucky just to be of the fae," Grandmother said a she cupped the side of Sophia's face. "I know you never felt that way before."

She never had. She'd concentrated on the loss, and not on the fortunate parts of her life. She'd concentrated on her missions and on the tasks set before her by the fae. But she'd never taken the time to actually enjoy her life. She planned to enjoy every moment with Ashley and Anne. Every single one.

"Help me to dress, Margaret?" Sophia asked, watching the woman closely.

"Yes, miss," the house faerie said quickly as Sophia took the dress from her grandmother and slipped behind the screen in the room. She turned back to her grandmother and her mother. "Would you mind leaving me alone with Margaret for a moment?" She made a nod toward the door.

Her mother looked wounded, but only for a second. "May I return when you're dressed?"

"Of course."

Sophia waited until they were gone and the door had closed softly behind them. Then she approached Margaret, waited until she turned to look at her, and then took her maid's hands in her own. Margaret looked everywhere but at her as Sophia tried to catch her gaze.

"Look at me," she finally said. Margaret looked at her fully. "You have been a friend to me my whole life." Margaret tried to pull back. But Sophia tightened her grip upon her maid's hands. "And even more than that, you have been a *mother* to me." A tear trickled down Margaret's cheek.

"You have a mother," Margaret said. She refused to look at Sophia as she sniffled.

"I do, and I am lucky to have her in my life now.

But you stood in her stead for such a long time. So, please allow me to say thank you for all you've done for me."

"I don't like passing you off to the hands of a human. I didn't like doing it with your mother. And I don't like it with you." She finally looked Sophia in the eye. "Where will you live? Here or there? Will you have children? Will you raise them to be fae or to be human? Will I ever see you again after you leave this world?" She was squeezing Sophia's hands even harder than Sophia squeezed hers.

"When I have children, I will want you to be with me. I cannot raise my children without you. Wherever I am, I hope you will be. With what Robinsworth has done here, we will be able to come and go at will, rather than at the whim of a few old men." Sophia laughed softly. "Times, they are changing."

"What if I don't like change?" The maid gave a watery chuckle.

"I don't think we have much choice at this point. Will you help me dress?"

⚜

Ashley waited beneath the arbor, so intent upon seeing her that he could not draw his eyes from the church courtyard entryway. "Hmm… Perhaps she changed her mind," one of the Trusted Few said.

"She had better not," Lord Ramsdale grunted. He stood beside Ashley beneath the arbor. A grub worm poked its head from the earth and chattered at them. "What the hell was that?" the viscount asked.

"No idea," Ashley muttered.

"He's offended by your frantic pacing," Ronald said. "He actually threatened bodily harm if you don't stop it."

"Bodily harm from a grub worm?" Ashley shot an incredulous look at the gnome.

Suddenly, the earth shook beneath his feet. Ashley held out his arms to the side to steady himself. "Don't tell me," the viscount muttered.

"Don't say I didn't warn you." The gnome whistled innocently.

No matter how long he stayed in the land of the fae, Ashley would never grow used to the magic, he feared. His daughter, on the other hand, was quiet enchanted by it all. "Are you certain Anne is all right with your wife?" She didn't know Lady Ramsdale, after all.

"My wife is enjoying every moment. And I'm certain Anne's fine. You can stop your worrying about it."

Just then, a sparkle from the entry to the church courtyard caught Ashley's eye. It was gone in a flash. Then it reappeared. Well, Sophia appeared. It was as though she appeared in bits and pieces, as shimmery as her magic. When the whole of her took shape, he looked at her and he couldn't believe his eyes. She was dressed in white and sparkled like a diamond, and holding hands with her was his daughter, Anne.

"Hi, Papa," Anne cried with a small wave. She was dressed in something the likes of which he'd never seen. It was tightly fitting, and the skirt hung only to her knees where it drifted in wavy, detached pieces of fabric. "They let me have a fae dress," she exclaimed. "Do I look beautiful?"

It was almost too hard for him to answer. To do so, he'd have to draw his gaze from Sophia. But he forced himself to look at his daughter and praise her appropriately. "Do you have a bit of fae in you, Anne?" he said as he crouched down on one knee.

"No wings," she whispered back.

"I don't have any either," he whispered.

"But I saw some. They're real."

"I know they're real," he affirmed. "I have seen them myself."

"Can I have some one day?" She cocked her pretty little head to the side.

He shrugged. "I believe anything may be possible in this land."

Just then, the birds began a song, a most melodious song, and Ashley wondered at the way they had lined up along the top of the fence posts. But then, a row of turtles joined them, each holding curved drumsticks, and they began a basic rhythm on their backs. They were joined by spiders that made four silken strings, each several feet in length. Upon these strings sat a handy little bug, which Ashley didn't even recognize. The bug began to pick at the strings, until he found a rhythm to match the rest of the symphony.

Sophia clapped loudly. Then she leaned close to him and whispered. "They haven't done this in years. This must mean that the balance is being restored. They're happy."

Ashley tucked a lock of hair behind her pointy ear. Would he ever get used to their differences? He supposed not. But life would never be boring. "Are you happy?" he asked softly.

"I'd be happier if I could marry you as myself," she said quietly. "But this will have to do."

"What do you mean?" he asked.

"I wish I could show my wings," she whispered for his ears alone.

"Why can't you?" he whispered back.

"Because they're the wrong color," she murmured, flushing as she remembered why the color change had taken place.

"I love you no matter their color. And I think you should be proud of them, because it was only by our actions that I arrived here. We're together. And we're making it legal."

Sophia appeared to mull it over. She drew her bottom lip between her teeth and worried it. If she did that much more, he would have to kiss it. She closed her eyes, and within seconds, her wings appeared. Her grandmother's antique dress was laden with fae magic, so her wings didn't disturb the beauty of the dress. They were the color of her skin. They flushed as much as she did. They weren't pink. Or red. Or any other telling hue. "I don't understand," she murmured, shaking her head.

Her mother stepped up beside her. "You love him." That was all she said. As though the answer could be found in those three little words.

"Was that fact ever in question?" Ashley asked, arching one playful brow at Sophia.

She nudged his shoulder with hers. "Never," she confirmed with a smile. She turned to her mother. "But I don't understand. What does love have to do with it?"

Her mother rolled her eyes. "The fae are an odd lot. They honor valor and deeds much more than ceremonies. For them, this ceremony isn't even necessary. They're only doing it because your father insisted upon it."

"I still don't understand."

"You did what lovers do. You committed yourselves to one another in the most basic way possible. You did it with forethought, and you did it despite the risk. It sealed the two of you together. Your wings are a reflection of what's in your heart." She looked longingly over her shoulder. "I wish I still had mine."

Ashley looked at Lord Ramsdale, who looked up at them with a grin. "You haven't given them to her yet," he said to Sophia's father.

Lord Ramsdale's face flushed. "I was waiting for the right time," he said. Then he reached into his pocket and held out a box. "Your father took these from you. And he wanted to be the one to return them to you. But with the way events transpired…" He let his voice trail off. It had been a fortnight since the old man's passing, and his death and the respect they owed him was the only reason Sophia and Ashley's wedding hadn't taken place sooner.

A tear trickled down Sophia's cheek. "You should open it," she whispered to her mother.

Sophia had come so close to losing her own wings. She was the only one who could even begin to sympathize. But Lady Ramsdale put the box in her pocket and patted it reverently. "I'll save them for later."

"Open it," Sophia protested.

"This is your day," Lady Ramsdale said. "And I'm

afraid they'll feel foreign to me. I'd like to open them in private."

Sophia nodded as though she understood.

Ashley looked down into Sophia's smiling face. "You plan to make an honest man of me today, don't you?" He shot a sly glance toward her father. "If you say no, I'm afraid he'll resort to fisticuffs."

"Let's get married, shall we?"

Thirty-Four

SOPHIA SQUEALED AS ASHLEY SCOOPED HER UP IN HIS arms. "Put me down," she cried.

"Not on your life," he growled low in her ear. "I have waited for deaths, bereavement, negotiations, settlements, a wedding, and a party afterward, and I plan to wait no longer." He kissed her soundly.

The door opened soundlessly at the little cottage by the river. "Magic?" he asked, raising his brows as he looked down at her.

She snorted. "More like a butler. Smythe, you can come out from behind the door!" she called. A cheeky, red-faced young man poked his head around the side of the door.

"Congratulations, Your Grace," he said with a bow and a grin.

"Someone in the land of the fae respects a title," Ashley mused. "I never would have expected it."

"I respect your title," Sophia said, as she tugged his cravat, bringing his head down to kiss her. When they were over the threshold, he lowered her feet slowly to the floor. She hadn't been alone with him for a fortnight.

A cough behind them reminded them they weren't alone now.

Ashley groaned in frustration. "Smythe, my fine fellow, I do hope I won't offend you when I tell you to get the hell out." He held Sophia close to him, as though he didn't want to let her go.

"Not a bit, Your Grace. I have left provisions for you."

Ashley looked around. "Where?"

Smythe's face colored. "In the bedchamber, Your Grace," he said, flushing even more.

"Perfect place," Ashley murmured against her lips. "Where is this bedchamber, Smythe?" he asked. He cupped the side of Sophia's face in his hand gently and tipped it up to his.

"Top of the stairs and to the right, Your Grace," the butler said. He looked everywhere but at them.

"Good-bye, Smythe," Sophia called to him. He made quickly for the door and was out it before Sophia could smother a laugh.

"You think this is amusing, do you?" Ashley asked as he spun her around and began to unfasten the back of her gown.

"Goodness, Ashley," she teased. "I thought you might have some finesse." She giggled. "Be careful with my gown," she warned. "It was my grandmother's."

"And you looked beautiful in it. But I bet you will look even better out of it." He laughed. Goodness, he was engaging when he laughed. It made her want to laugh along with him.

When he had her standing in nothing but her chemise, he picked her up in his arms again and started for the stairs. "I'll use some finesse the second time. Or the third time. Or the fourth."

Sophia threw her head back and laughed, swinging her feet in the air as he took the stairs two at a time. "Promises, promises," she teased.

"Whose house is this?" he asked absently as he walked into the bedchamber.

She shrugged as she watched him disrobe. "Grandfather's hunting lodge," she said. He tugged off his cravat with no care whatsoever. "Simmons will be angry at you if you destroy all your clothing."

"These aren't mine, remember? And Simmons will be overjoyed when he learns that he gets to purchase a brand-new wardrobe for me. And one for the fish as well!" Ashley flung clothing with abandon until he finally stood before her in nothing but his smalls. His gaze was predatory.

"I wish we had a pianoforte so you could play for me," she said, biting back a grin.

"A time like this and all you can think about is the pianoforte." He jerked her to him quickly, which made her laugh even more. "I'll play you like a pianoforte," he warned as he tilted his head, growled into the side of her neck, and scrubbed her with his bristly evening whiskers.

His hands began to ruche the fabric of her chemise in his fingers, lifting the hem of it higher and higher until he stopped at her hips. He kissed her, a kiss that could have touched her soul if she wasn't so nervous.

"Are you quite all right?" he asked, pulling back to look at her.

Sophia stepped onto her tiptoes and threaded her

hands around his neck and into his hair. "Quite all right, Your Grace. But I'm wondering how much longer you're going to play with my unmentionables." She tugged lightly at his hair. "Take it off me, already," she whispered against his lips.

With a low moan of contentment and a smile, he unthreaded her arms from around him, lifted the chemise over her head, and tossed it to the floor. Then he shoved his smalls down over his hips and stepped out of them. "Does that satisfy you, my duchess?" he asked. His hands crawled deliciously around to cup her bottom, and he yanked her against him.

"Do I look satisfied?" she asked playfully. His steely blue eyes darkened, the centers growing more prominent until his eyes were as dark as the shadowed room where they stood bathed in candlelight.

"You are the most beautiful woman I've ever seen," he crooned.

"Now you plan to wax poetic rather than take me to bed?" she asked.

He picked her up by her bottom, forcing her to wrap her legs around his waist, and he crossed to the bed. He fell onto it, landing on top of her with her legs wrapped around him. His hardness pressed against her heat and she rocked, trying to get closer to him.

"Do you know why I fell in love with you?" he asked, bending his head to take her nipple into his mouth.

"Goodness, Ashley," she warned. "Let me concentrate on one thing at a time, will you?"

He stopped and lifted his head. "Will you give me grief for the rest of my life?"

She tugged lightly at his hair, pulling him back

down to her breast. "Someone has to do it. Everyone else is afraid of the dangerous Duke of Robinsworth."

"And…" He raised his head. "That. Is. Why. I. Love. You." He punctuated his words with licks across her nipple.

"I'm not afraid of you."

He growled low in his throat. "I could eat you in one big bite. I do save those for the noninnocents, you know."

"So I have heard." He began to kiss a slow path down her stomach, making it clench in anticipation. "What are you doing?" she asked as his head descended farther and farther.

"Devouring you," he replied, his voice muffled against her skin.

"Ashley," she cried as he spread her thighs even wider and settled between them. His thumbs parted her, and he gazed down at her. "Don't," she protested, mortified at his perusal. She shoved at his shoulders.

But then he licked across the center of her. "I bet I can change your mind," he murmured as he slid two fingers inside her. It had been a fortnight since he'd taken her innocence, since he'd loved her so completely. But this was unlike anything they'd shared before. "Trust me," he said, his voice buried in the heat of her.

Ashley's tongue dipped, taking her to a place she'd never been. Her sheath clenched upon his fingers as he found that little ball of tension and began to worry it with his tongue. Sophia clutched the linens into her fists and lifted her legs more comfortably around his shoulders. "Ahh," she cried out as he sucked that little nub of pleasure into his mouth and worked his fingers inside her. "Don't stop!" she cried as sensation swelled within her.

He murmured something unintelligible from between her thighs.

Sophia arched to meet him, anxious to get to the peak. She threaded her fingers into his hair, pushing his head in a rhythm she liked. He drew deeper on her flesh and pierced her deeper with his fingers, scissoring his fingers and setting a rhythm better than any song he'd ever played for her. The crescendo swept over her, and she bucked against his hold as she quaked around his fingers. His mouth slowed only marginally, content to take everything she had.

His ministrations quieted, and she sagged against the linens, willing her breaths to slow. His beard stubble abraded her inner thigh as he wiped his mouth there, and then he climbed up her body. "Better than any pianoforte I ever played," he said as he settled between her thighs. He raised one knee up toward her chest and then probed at her center. "Mine," he said as he slid slowly inside her.

❧

Ashley slowly joined himself with her, inch by exquisite inch, and grunted when he was fully seated within her. Her cheeks were rosy with heat, and her body loose and languid from her climax. He would have to work to bring her another. But he was up for the challenge.

"Yours?" she asked playfully, her voice deepened by passion, sliding along his skin like silk.

"Mine," he grunted as he pulled out of her and pushed back inside, taking as much of her as he could. Her back arched and she tilted her hips, taking even more of him.

"Such prolific words from you," she teased, but her breath hitched as he adjusted her hip. God, he loved the noises she made.

"Did you want a soliloquy? I just gave you a song." He stopped moving for a moment and lowered her leg, allowing himself to lie atop her. "God help me, woman," he groaned. He wanted to spill himself already.

He rolled, pulling her atop him in the bed. She squealed playfully and stretched along his length. He was barely inside her now, and the silken hot wetness of her called to him. He kicked her legs apart with his own and tugged her knees forward until she straddled him.

He lifted, taking the tip of her breast into his mouth as he fitted her more snugly on his manhood. She surrounded him with heat. Now, as long as she didn't move, he wouldn't spend himself. But then she did. "Blast and damn," he grunted.

She stilled, looking down at him with a grin. "Is something wrong?" She squeezed her wetness upon him, tormenting him anew. She began to rock her hips ever so slightly.

He turned his head and thought about Finn. About a rack of lamb. About his garden. But all thoughts led him back to Sophie. He drew his gaze back to her, and she pushed up to sit atop him with her hands flat on his chest, her elbows locked.

"I find myself in a bit of a predicament," he squeaked. He cleared his throat. "I need but a moment. For you to be still." He grabbed her hips and held them, but her sheath milked at him, pulling him deeper and deeper into her body.

She smiled a siren's smile. "You poor thing," she crooned. Then a gasp left her throat as she raised herself slightly.

"Let me see your wings," he begged.

She stilled. "My wings?"

"Your wings," he said again, heedless of the panting sound of his own breath. "Let me have all of you this time."

She moved on him slightly. "I think you already have all of me. Or I have all of you." She laughed, which only exacerbated his need to finish.

"Let me see them. Let me touch them. Let them be part of us," he pleaded.

She stilled, thank heavens, and closed her eyes. She waited but a moment, and then her wings appeared. They were the color of her flushed skin, a dusky rose color, interlaced with a pearly color the same as the skin of her breasts. He reached out a hand to touch the silky little hairs that stood at attention on the rims of her wing. They glittered like diamonds, like a banked fire. "Don't touch," she said, jerking out of his grasp. "They're very sensitive," she reminded him.

He took her hips and pulled her firmly onto his manhood. "So is that," he warned.

She just grinned, and one wing arched toward him. "You can touch it, if you can be gentle," she whispered.

The edges of the bottoms of her wings tickled his

thighs, but it took his mind off his need to spend, at least.

He reached out one hand, only mildly annoyed to see his hand betray him as it quivering there in midair. When he touched the edge of her wing, she let out a hiss. Her mouth fell open. "I told you they're sensitive," she cried.

He moved his other hand to heat between her legs. "More sensitive than here?" he asked. He knew it was naughty, but he couldn't help it.

"Very much like there," she cried, as he caressed the outside of her wing, lightly stroking the length of it. "I thought I was done after the last one," she cried.

"You were wrong?" he asked with delight. She swatted at his chest rather playfully, but then she began to move upon him. "I'll never be done with you."

As he stroked those fine little edges of her delicate wings, she rose and fell on him, her head thrown back in abandon, her breath hitching with every down stroke. She ground herself upon his pelvis, rocking just where she needed.

As she got closer to her peak, he forced himself to wait. She rode him, rising and falling, and sparks began to fall around them, drifting like snowflakes floating to the ground. They filled the air around them. "What is that?" he was able to ask.

"Magic," she laughed. "We are magical." She ground her hips against him and squeezed, which took his mind off the sparks.

Ashley brought the tip of her wing to his mouth and tongued it gently.

"Ashley, I can't wait," she cried. Her movements

grew erratic, and he could tell she fought to maintain her perch upon him with her legs quivering, her arms shaking.

He took her hips in his hands and took over. She arched her back and cried out, then locked her arms and rode out her climax. The air filled with shooting sparks that shot across the room like stars as she came. Then he came with her, and as he soaked her walls, grunting with satisfaction as he screwed into her, the shower only got more heavenly.

She rode him until they both were spent. Then she collapsed onto his chest, sliding in the sweat between them. He brushed her hair to the side to look at her face as she placed a quick kiss to the patch of hair on his chest. "That was magic?" he managed to grunt.

"That was us," she affirmed with a nod, her cheek sliding in the sweat against his chest. She didn't seem to care. He could feel her smile against his skin. The sparks began to fade.

"Good God, woman. I never imagined."

"Neither did I," she said. He slipped out of her as she nestled into his side. Then her wing came up to cover them both like a soft, light counterpane. And she slept.

Epilogue

ASHLEY WRAPPED SOPHIA IN HER DRESSING GOWN, pulling it closed with a heavy sigh. "What's wrong?" she asked, tugging the lapels of his own gown and drawing him back to her.

"I quite like you naked," he said with a grin. He tugged her dressing gown back open quickly and pressed a kiss to the center of her chest. "I plan to keep you naked a lot." Then he closed her wrapper and stepped back from her. He sat down at a tiny table in their bedchamber and lifted a scone to his mouth. His appetite for her was only seconded by his appetite for sweets.

A quick knock sounded at their door. "Enter," he called absently as he opened his newspaper.

Sophia looked up to see Lady Anne as she entered the room. Holding tightly to her forefinger was their newest addition. "Margaret said it was all right to bring her to you," Anne said, somewhat reserved.

"It's always all right to bring her to me," Sophia said as she bent to pick up the youngest Trimble girl. She crawled atop the bed and beckoned Anne to join her. "What are your plans for today?"

But then, the sound of running feet in the corridor caught her attention. "Just when we thought it was safe to come out of the nursery," Anne groaned.

Through the door tumbled a dark-haired boy, their son and Ashley's heir. He was the spitting image of his father. He wore a billowing shirt and wielded a large stick he swung like a sword. Margaret followed him into the room. "Sorry, Your Grace. He got away from me."

"He seems to do that a lot," Ashley said, shooting his son a harsh glance. But the tot only squealed and wrapped his arms around his father's legs. Ashley picked him up and tossed him atop the bed with his sister. And his mother. Sophia rolled to the side, protecting her stomach from flailing legs as Anne tickled her little brother, making him squeal and roll around. "Careful," Ashley warned. The lad stilled. "Careful of the baby."

"Baby," the littlest Trimble repeated. She had no idea what she said, but she repeated nearly everything.

"It's better than that word she repeated of yours the other day," Anne teased. Anne laid her hand upon Sophia's belly. "Do you think this one will be a boy or a girl?" she asked reverently.

"Definitely a boy," Ashley said.

"Do you think this one will be magical?" Anne asked. She'd been somewhat relieved that the first two Trimble children weren't magical, from what Sophia could tell.

Ashley rubbed his hand down her hair. "All of our children are magical," he said as he bent and kissed her forehead.

"You know that's not what I meant," Anne said. She reached for the baby girl and passed her to Margaret. Then she picked up the lad and said, "Let's go and find some pirates to slay, shall we?"

He nodded enthusiastically and let Anne carry him from the room, with Margaret quickly pursuing them. Ashley rolled toward Sophia and opened her dressing gown. He pressed a kiss to the side of her huge belly. It rippled with a kick. He was always enamored of their children from the moment of their conception. It pleased her to no end. "Do you think this one will be fae?" he asked.

Somewhere deep inside, Sophia did want to have a child who was fae. She was quite happy with the three she already had, and they were magical in their own right, but having a little girl or boy with pointy ears and a penchant for good deeds would please her greatly. "Who can say?" she asked with a breezy wave.

Ashley crawled slowly up her body, parting her dressing gown with his teeth and baring her skin as he went. He plumped her breast in his hand and groaned, "I love it when you're like this."

She laughed and shoved ineffectually at his hand. "You must, because I seem to keep getting this way." With a gentle shove to his shoulder, she tossed him onto his back and crawled over him. She opened his robe as reverently as he'd opened hers. "I plan to use you well this day, my husband," she warned playfully.

"I am at your disposal," he said, laying his hands to the side as though in surrender.

As she crawled atop him, she scolded, "Whoever gave

you the name of the dangerous Duke of Robinsworth couldn't have been further from the truth."

He laughed. "I'll show you dangerous if you keep doing that." She kissed her way down his flat stomach. It clenched beneath her lips.

"Promises, promises," she breathed. But then she looked up suddenly. "Have you heard from Lord Phineas or Claire?"

"God, woman, at a time like this, you're thinking about Finn and Claire?" he groaned, yanking at his hair.

"I'm just curious to know how their mission is going."

"Just the thought of Finn and Claire on a mission terrifies me."

"Who knows? They might rub along together as well as we do."

"Somehow, I highly doubt that." He tipped her chin up to look into her eyes. "Get back to what you were doing," he scolded gently with a wicked smile.

So she did.

About the Author

As half of the Lydia Dare writing team, Tammy Falkner has cowritten ten books, including *A Certain Wolfish Charm* and *In the Heat of the Bite*. She's a huge fan of Regency England, and in her new series, she explores the theory that the fae can walk between the glittering world of the *ton* and their own land. Tammy lives on a farm in rural North Carolina with her husband and a house full of boys, a few dogs, and a cat or two. Visit her website: www.tammyfalkner.com.